ORLEANS

ORLE

G. P. PUTNAM'S SONS
AN IMPRINT OF PENGUIN GROUP (USA) INC.

EANS

SHERRI L. SMITH

G. P. PUTNAM'S SONS
A division of Penguin Young Readers Group.
Published by The Penguin Group.
Penguin Group (USA) Inc., 375 Hudson Street, New York, NY 10014, U.S.A.
Penguin Group (Canada), 90 Eglinton Avenue East, Suite 700, Toronto,
Ontario M4P 2Y3, Canada (a division of Pearson Penguin Canada Inc.).
Penguin Books Ltd, 80 Strand, London WC2R 0RL, England.
Penguin Ireland, 25 St. Stephen's Green, Dublin 2, Ireland
(a division of Penguin Books Ltd).
Penguin Group (Australia), 707 Collins Street, Melbourne, Victoria 3008, Australia
(a division of Pearson Australia Group Pty Ltd).
Penguin Books India Pvt Ltd, 11 Community Centre, Panchsheel Park,
New Delhi—110 017, India.
Penguin Group (NZ), 67 Apollo Drive, Rosedale, Auckland 0632, New Zealand
(a division of Pearson New Zealand Ltd).
Penguin Books South Africa, Rosebank Office Park, 181 Jan Smuts Avenue,
Parktown North 2193, South Africa.
Penguin China, B7 Jiaming Center, 27 East Third Ring Road North,
Chaoyang District, Beijing 100020, China.
Penguin Books Ltd, Registered Offices: 80 Strand, London WC2R 0RL, England.

Published simultaneously in Canada. Printed in the United States of America.
Design by Ryan Thomann. Text set in Sabon.
Water splash photo copyright © 2013 by Okea.
Water surface photo copyright © 2013 by Krystian Nawrocki.

Library of Congress Cataloging-in-Publication Data
Smith, Sherri L. Orleans / Sherri L. Smith. p. cm. Summary: "Set in a futuristic,
hostile Orleans landscape, Fen de la Guerre must deliver her tribe leader's baby over
the Wall into the Outer States before her blood becomes tainted with Delta Fever"—
Provided by publisher. [1. Science fiction. 2. Virus diseases—Fiction. 3. New Orleans
(La.)—Fiction.] I. Title. PZ7.S65932Or 2013 [Fic]—dc23 2012009634
ISBN 978-0-399-25294-5
1 3 5 7 9 10 8 6 4 2

BEFORE

EDMUND BROUSSARD MOUNTED THE STEPS TO the levee above the old Café Du Monde off of Jackson Square. The sky was pale and colorless above him, the grass a vibrant green at his feet as he faced the wide expanse of the rolling Mississippi River. Behind him, a handful of revelers on the ironwork balconies of the French Quarter could be heard drinking their Hurricanes and ignoring the voluntary evacuation order that had sent so many tourists home. The café was still serving their hot beignets and chicory coffee. A few persistent people strolled the green lawns of the square outside St. Louis Cathedral.

Edmund opened the black case he carried in his left hand and pulled out his trumpet. The yellow brass reflected the city back on itself in the flat afternoon light. He put the horn to his lips and defiantly blew "When the Saints Go Marching In" into the unnaturally still air. He was not leaving New Orleans, no matter what the weathermen said. He was not leaving his home. New Orleans would stand against any storm that came her way. The TV crews loved it, the image of a lone man facing nature, refusing to bend.

Hurricane Ivan turned east, barely brushing the city with rain as it ran its devastating course along the coast of Alabama. It returned to the mouth of the Mississippi and faltered there. New Orleans was spared. *Laissez les bons temps rouler.* The fabled city that care forgot danced on.

The next time, they were not so lucky.

August 29, 2005

HURRICANE KATRINA

Saffir-Simpson Category 3 at landfall

Casualties: 971; Survivors: 30,000

September 14, 2014

HURRICANE ISAIAH

Saffir-Simpson Category 4 at landfall

Casualties: 532; Survivors: 27,800

August 25, 2015

HURRICANE LORENZO

Saffir-Simpson Category 3 at landfall

Casualties: 1,432; Survivors: 22,345

June 30, 2016

HURRICANE OLGA

Saffir-Simpson Category 5 at landfall

Casualties: 2,022; Survivors: 20,323

July 27, 2017

HURRICANE LAURA

Saffir-Simpson Category 4 at landfall

Casualties: 1,371; Survivors: 18,952

July 29, 2017

HURRICANE PALOMA

Saffir-Simpson Category 5 at landfall

Casualties: estimated 3,500;

Survivors: estimated 15,452

October 20, 2019

HURRICANE JESUS

Category 6 at landfall,

based on new Saffir-Simpson Scale

Casualties: estimated 8,000;

Survivors: estimated below 10,000

AFTER THE STORM DEATHS CAME OTHER CASUAL-
ties: deaths by debris, cuts, tetanus, or loss of blood; suicide;
heart attacks caused by stress of loss, or stress of rebuilding,
or just as often from the lack of medicines used to treat common ailments. The list of no-longer-treatable diseases grew:
diabetes, asthma, cancer. Domestic violence rose, along with
murder.

Then came the Fever.

And the Quarantine.

Excerpt from the
DECLARATION OF QUARANTINE
*issued by FEMA and the Center for Disease Control,
September 20, 2020:*

𝕱𝖔𝖗 𝖙𝖍𝖊 𝖘𝖆𝖋𝖊𝖙𝖞 of the population at large, we deem it advisable to seal off all storm-affected areas of the Gulf Coast region. No citizens or personnel will be allowed to cross the border without blood testing for Delta Fever. This is an epidemic of proportions we have not witnessed since the Spanish Influenza of 1918. The Quarantine will be reevaluated as the disease runs its course and we make progress toward treatment and a cure. Until then, all borders will be sealed.

Excerpt from the
DECLARATION OF SEPARATION,
courtesy of the Smithsonian Collection,
March 11, 2025:

𝕿𝖍𝖊𝖗𝖊𝖋𝖔𝖗𝖊 it is with great regret and pain for our fellow citizens that the United States Senate has agreed to withdraw our governance of the affected states of Alabama, Florida, Georgia, Louisiana, and Texas. The shape of our great nation has been altered irrevocably by Nature, and now Man must follow suit in order to protect the inalienable rights of the majority, those being the right to Life, Liberty, and the Pursuit of Happiness, the foremost of those being Life.

Signed this day, the Eleventh of March, Two Thousand Twenty-Five, in the presence of witnesses,

The President of the United States of America

The Senate of the United States of America

The House of Representatives of the United States of America

The Governor of the former State of Alabama

The Governor of the former State of Florida

The Governor of the former State of Georgia

The Governor of the former State of Louisiana

The Governor of the former State of Texas

Part One

TRIBE

1

⚜ THERE BE SEAGULLS CATCHING THE BREEZE overhead. I sneeze and wipe my nose on the back of my bare brown arm.

"That's the batch of it, Miss de la Guerre. The two books, the formula, and the bottle, genuine glass." The smuggler McCallan point his boot at the things spread out on my blanket over the broken ground.

We be near the Market, where the old levee used to be, across from St. Louis Cathedral. What once been a green hill now be a beach dune made of debris—everything from washing machines to refrigerators and old cars been hauled and dumped here trying to shore up the levee. But the land gave way when the river rose, and the junk be left behind. Daddy used to say you could give a history of the place just by looking at those layers of trash.

Beneath us, on the river side of the hill, be a dusty gray beach of pulverized concrete, ground thin by storms. "The

13

fabled cement beaches of Orleans," McCallan call them. "Finer than the black volcanic sand of Hawaii, or the pink sugar sand of the old Caribbean." I don't know about that. Nothing left of Hawaii or the Caribbean since the water rose and the storms grew heated. It'd take a deep-sea diver just to find them. But Orleans still be here.

I snort at the blanket and give McCallan a hard look. "And the blood, old man? I done give you a good, solid downpay on it. What about that?"

McCallan's eyes crinkle like he be laughing at me. He should know better. Grinning like a fool only make me angry. "Sorry, sugar, they were out of both positive and negative at the banks. There's a blood supply shortage out there." He wave his gloved hand behind him, toward the wall and the Outer States. "I ain't risking my neck *and* smuggling to the Delta when I'm about to retire, now am I?"

I fold my arms. "We had a deal. I need that blood."

McCallan shake his head. "We could use more with your fire back home," he say. "I'll be missing you, Miss de la Guerre, that's for sure."

I'll be missing him, too, though I won't say it. McCallan an old guy, almost forty, but he smart. He been smuggling for more than ten years. He know who to bribe, where to breach the Wall, how to get over while the guard be changing, how to avoid the sniffer drones. I ain't the only one he doing trade with, neither. His regulars know his goods be clean and fresh. He don't sell dirty blood or fake medicine. Even after the government closed the Delta, he kept working—trading with the tribes. Delta Fever be harder to kill than a swamp fox. It be always changing, the way those little buggers switch back on they own trails. But if it stay confined to a blood type, if folks keep to theyselves by type of blood, then it slow down somehow. And that why folks like McCallan be necessary. Tribes ain't able to mix together long enough for real trade.

"I did my best, Miss Fen," he say and spread his fingers with a shrug.

I spit in the gravel and hold out my hand. "I want a refund."

McCallan sigh. "D'you want the stuff I got or no? I've come a long way and I'm not so sure anybody else is keen enough to buy these damn books off me. *Baby Naming* and *The Developing Years*. What are you up to, Fen? You're not knocked up now, are you?" he ask, eyeing my belly.

Shoot, skinny as I be, I sure as hell ain't pregnant. Lydia say I'd pass for a boy, if not for the braids she do for me, all wrapped in a topknot on my head to keep out of the way.

"Man, will you stop staring and just make good?" I say.

McCallan blush inside his encounter suit, one of the old kind with thick, mucus-looking skin that turn orangey-yellow when the heat rise in his cheeks. I'd be like to suffocate in something so thick, hot as I already be in my cutoff shorts and tank top. My hiking boots be bugging me they so sweaty, but he be wearing that whole suit like a murky second skin.

"Here, doll, take the books and the formula, the bottle." He bend down to the blanket and roll it up for me. "And here's your goods back." He hand me back the little bag of gold I gave as down payment. Took a week to scrounge it all up from the teeth of the dead inside the Dome, while I been pretending to pray with the Ursulines.

"I didn't even melt it down yet, in case you weren't pleased. Use it in the Market. Or better yet, find the O-Negs. They'll charge high, but there's blood to be bought and sold right here."

I shove the books into my pack and string the sack of gold around my neck to drop down my shirt. "We don't do that," I remind him.

My tribe be O-Positive, or OP. And our chieftain, Lydia, don't take kindly to the blood trade. O types don't be needing transfusions like ABs do. The Fever be in us, but it ain't eating O blood up from the inside like it do other types. So O types got to be extra careful of hunters and the farms where they be taking they kidnapped victims to drain them alive. O blood be the universal donor. If we give a drop, they be taking all of it. Lydia say that ain't right. Only ones worse off than us be O-Negs.

O-Negs don't got the Rh, or Rhesus factor, that O-Positives do. Daddy use to say O positive be like coffee and O neg be like water. You can add water to coffee and it still be coffee, but you add coffee to water and it ain't water no more. Everybody drink water, so O-Negs be used by everyone. Like the rhyme the nuns taught us about the Rules of Blood:

Types AB, B, and A
Need to stay away
From O and from each other,
Plus from minus, sister from brother.
O positive can feed

All positives in need,
But O neg is the one
For all tribes beneath the sun.

I feel McCallan's eyes on my arms as I pack up. He be looking at the shiny scars there along the insides of my arms, wrists to elbows and then some. Burn marks so thick, ain't nobody ever gonna get a needle in the easy way. Not everybody got scars like me. But then again, not everybody willing to die. Somebody want to take my blood, they got to go through the veins in my neck or thigh. They can only bleed me once and I be dead. But that better than being a blood slave.

McCallan shrug. "Best I could do," he say.

If I hadn't burnt myself up like that, I could give my *own* blood to Lydia. If she bleed too much while birthing and need it, I'd do it without being asked. But I can't or I be dead and she get no help from me after that.

So I nod. "Fair enough." Some choices, once you make them, they stay made. And I had my reasons.

"You know, there used to be music here all the time," McCallan say. He looking out across the city like he see someone he used to know and like. "Jazz and blues, zydeco. The kind of songs that made your heart sing."

It be my turn to shrug. "Not anymore," I tell him. Music be a surefire way to bring the hunters down on you, or any other kind of trouble you don't want.

With a final nod, I hitch up my shorts, raggedy edges

tickling at the tops of my thighs, and walk away. My old army pack be slung across my shoulders, and my work boots scatter little rocks as I pick my way down the trash heap, past the ruins of Café Du Monde, toward the bright blue tarps of the marketplace.

The Market be bubbling with people today. It hot for October, and folks be all about, trading and swapping this for that. There be food vendors selling fruits and vegetables, fish, and sometimes wild pig, or stewing it up in big pots over wood fires. I can smell the cooking and hear the clamor, but most of it be hidden by the roof tarps, bright blue in the afternoon sun. The Market be right at the edge of the Mississippi, with her back up against the Old French Quarter. The streets behind us belong to the A-Positives now, but the Market been here in one way or another since before Orleans been Orleans, and it be for everyone.

From the early days before the Wall, they been rotating security, this tribe one day, that tribe the next, keeping it fair and safe. Back when the Fever started, that the only way Os, As, Bs, and ABs could shop without catching they death from Fever. Shop on the day your tribe be guarding—if not your own tribe, then another of your type—and you be okay. Us O types, we can shop any day. Fever don't run through us quite so bad as it do the rest of them.

It be an AB day, and I see Harney and his boys messing with them AB girls like they got a chance. Harney be an OP like me, but that where the comparison end. He fifteen and brawny everywhere except the head. Them girls got tattoos, which mean they tribe with La Bête Sauvage. Only thing dumber than making trouble around one of La Bête's girls be making one pregnant. ABs and Os make A or B babies. That just giving La Bête more children for his tribe, and that ain't a good idea for us Os.

"Harney," I call him off. He come over reluctantly, long legs and arms shining with sweat in the sun. He only a year younger than me, but he listen when I call. That be the benefit of my experience. "Where Lydia at?" I ask.

He shrug and look around like he nervous or something. "You know. Where she ever at on Market Day?"

I swear under my breath. Lydia can't be messing with folks like that. "Get ready to go," I tell him. "I be right back."

I walk past the nods of ABs guarding the entrance to the market. These fools got tattoos, too, so you know they all La Bête's people. Most folks ain't dumb enough to risk blood poisoning or tetanus by sticking theyselves with a needle. But La Bête's tribe be big, strong, and crazy. At least today they here to keep the peace.

The market be big, a whole rabbits' warren of stalls, but I know where to go. Last one on the first row. Ain't nobody selling nothing nearby, not food, not clothing, not even rope to tie your tent to the trees. Nobody want to set up shop next to the nuns and they hospital tent. You could sell shovels, though, so the folks inside can dig they own graves.

The hospital be made of sheets of wood and rusted metal, like everything else in the Market, but it got a different roof.

Instead of blue plastic tarping, it made of clean white canvas. Don't know where the nuns be getting the stuff, but it let in the light so they can see.

The Ursuline Sisters been taking care of folks in Orleans since before the Civil War. Even before the city been part of the old United States, they been running that old girls' school out of the same building they shut theyselves up in today. They spend turns nursing them that's too far gone to be cared for by they own tribes, folks that be nothing but a burden with nowhere to go but in the ground.

I don't like this place. It smell like death. I stand outside a minute to take my last few good breaths, then I head inside to find the pregnant woman among the dying.

Inside the tent, row after row of straw pallets covered in bodies line the floor, some living, some not. Nuns and novices be drifting about like ghosts in them white shift dresses they wear. The nuns cover they heads with pieces of cloth, but the girls go bareheaded, young as can be. I'd worry about young ones like that out in the Market, out in the city, but they ain't my tribe, so I don't.

A man moan on the pallet next to me. Fool look like he been gored by a wild boar. Just a freesteader by the look of him, no tribe to help him with the hunt. Lady next to him look like she dying from tetanus, the way her jaw be all rigid and she missing a leg. She be wasting away, can't even open her mouth to eat. One of the nuns look up at me from the lady's side. I mouth *Lydia,* and she point me to the back of the tent.

My eyes follow her finger. Lord have mercy. The last row of the hospital, the one closest to the concrete hill beside the Market. That where the Fever victims go, the ones nobody can help. A black curtain hide it from view. I brace myself and make my way to the back.

"Shh," Lydia hush me when I push the curtain aside. She be sitting in that little room with the walls covered in blue tarps because they easy to throw out: Just roll up the bodies and carry them out back before lining the room again.

Not so many people dying of Fever these days, what with the Rules of Blood telling tribes to keep apart and stay healthy. The Fever ain't what it used to be. But sometimes there be an outlander, a smuggler from over the Wall, or a freesteader without a tribe, and he get sick and it be as bad as it been fifty years ago when they built the Wall in the first place.

Fever make you weak at first, tired and confused. That be the disease eating up your red blood cells. Then it make it so you can't sleep and you start seeing things. Crazy things. And skin that be black or brown or white all turn the same color— chalky yellow. That be your blood failing and your liver giving up. Bruises come up on the skin then, like something inside you trying to beat its way out. Then come cramps that knot a body up from the inside out, and the weird shifting walk of somebody whose joints ain't working right no more. Your lips crack, your mind go, and you start seeing more things that ain't there, knowing they be coming to get you. At the worst, when pain ain't doubling them over, folks with Fever be scream-ing nonsense and scrabbling with they hands, shoveling they mouths full of dirt. My daddy once told me they be looking for iron to replenish they blood. That be why some ABs drink blood when they ain't satisfied with just injecting it. Either way it goes in, it can cause more trouble, make you even crazier. And when you all used up and ain't got no more fight in you, you be like this boy in this dark little room.

Lydia be sitting next to this freesteader AB boy, reading a book. She crouch back on her heels even though her belly be eight months big and she should be sitting down for real. She want to show him pictures in the old mildewed thing she reading.

Lydia beautiful, even here in the low light of this death room. She in her own simple dress, made from homespun cotton, hair piled high in black braids on her head. She look like a queen. I be a scarecrow next to her.

She run a long-fingered hand across the boy's forehead, leaving a trail in his sweat. His skin must've been as brown as hers once, but it yellow now and graying from his own bad blood. His eyes be glazed over and his arms and legs don't bend the right way. He shudder like a puddle in a storm. She lean in to him and whisper the last line of the book. "'And it was still hot.'"

The boy smile an ugly smile, lips peeling back from his face in a grimace. He nod and I see him try to say the words back to her. Lydia press a finger to his cracked lips. "Rest, Ezekiel. Rest." The boy nod again and close his eyes. His chest be moving up and down. He ain't dead yet, but he will be soon.

"Fen, what is it?" she ask me, rising slow, one hand on her back, the other on her round belly.

"Time to go," I say. No use telling her she a fool for being here when she carrying a new life and her time be so close.

She don't argue. "Powwow's tonight," she say, and I nod. Lydia got peace talks on the table with the O-Negs tonight. Plenty enough to worry over with that. No need to add a dying boy at the Market. She push back the black curtain and wave one of the nuns over. The woman glide up and kneel by the boy.

"The City takes," the nun say, bowing her head.

"And God receives," Lydia reply. The nun will stay. Someone to hold the boy's hand when he do finally cross over. Lydia always make sure of things like that. Shepherd, that's what she be. It no wonder I follow her out of the hospital tent and back into the light of day.

"Leaving!" I sing out when Lydia and me reach the gates of the Market. We nod at the guards flanking the entrance, and I signal Harney and his boys. We walk past the row houses with they rusted bits of ironwork. We past the preserved streets now, and it ain't all picturesque like them old photographs at the library. The pavement be broken here, and I be glad I got me some new boots. That old smuggler be good for something, even if not for what I really need.

"You sure we ain't got to go to the library?" I ask Lydia. There be a jerry-rigged computer there, run on a foot pedal and who know what else. Electricity be rare in Orleans, so most folks do without. But somebody keep that computer running, and Lydia use it sometimes to send messages over the Wall. She use the old e-mail system left behind back when the Wall first went up. When I been real little, I got to send e-mails, too, at Father John's mission. But that a long time ago, when it looked like the Wall weren't gonna be there always, and folks on the other side still cared enough to sponsor kids in Orleans. Now there just be the one machine, and only chieftains use it, contacting smugglers and looking to set up trades. Maybe one day, the old computer be gone, too. Then Orleans be on its own for true.

"With the powwow and the baby, all my concerns are here, Fen," she tell me. "Orleans has got everything we need."

A skitter of stones behind me say the boys be running to catch up. Good. They got to learn. Ain't never a time to be fooling around at the Market. You in, you out. Just 'cause there be guards there don't mean a problem can't follow you home. Harney come jogging up all out of breath, but Erik and Matthias, they too young to know they should be tired from messing around in the sun all day. They skip ahead of us like a couple fool puppies. I grunt. See if I don't talk to them about that later. We OPs. We got to act dignified, for Lydia's sake.

"Let them be boys for a little while," Lydia say to me, laughing. "Once a week is all they ever get; don't let us be the ones that take it away."

"All right," I tell her. She the chieftain, so we do as she say. But if we don't break them of that foolishness, someone else will. And they'll keep on breaking them, too.

Even with they jumping and clowning, Harney and the boys keep pace with Lydia and me 'til we out of the Quarter, then out past the old cemeteries, St. Louis Number 1 and Number 2, and into the woods, where we separate like always. This time, I stay with Lydia. That baby got less than a month before it leave her belly. And I won't let her out my sight 'til it do.

2

✠ THE SKY BE GROWING DARK BY THE TIME WE get back. Around us, camp be swarming like a beehive with folks making last-minute preparations for the powwow. They funnel the smoke from the cook fires so you can't smell it so easy beyond the encampment, but up close my mouth be watering. They be fixing a feast for the O-Negs to show how good we OPs be living, how they could be living, too. My people risked they lives catching the wild boar they roasting, but it sure be worth a bite or two of that meat.

We pass by our storyteller, Cinnamon Jones, practicing his poems and songs on the edge of camp. He wave at me and smile wide at Lydia, then go back to walking his way through a pantomime.

Our camp be arranged in a circle, with cook fires in the center and houses on the outside. We ain't living in buildings like them ABs by the Market; we camouflaged. First glance, you see nothing but a bunch of fallen trees. Look closer and you see there be a few small huts and bigger hogans, cozy as fallen logs covered in vines. We use tent poles or young trees bent into arcs and hoops for frames, and cover them with green saw palmettos that ain't sharp enough yet to cut you with they serrated leaves. The hogans be like low tunnels, tall enough to stand in the middle, with sleeping mats on the sides. On cold nights, most everybody sleep in the hogans. On a night like tonight, when it still a bit warm, most folks stay in simple tents and lean-tos instead, and the hogans only shelter them that needs protecting, like pregnant women and the injured. Hogans take time to build and, being OP, we ain't always able to stay in one place that long. With the blood hunters other tribes be sending out, a body got to keep on the move fairly regular or risk being trapped in they own home.

"Eh la bas!" my friend Caroline calls to me from across the way. She and her husband, Theo, got a big house, long as a shrimp boat and then some, to house all they kids. She mother to five of her own and two of Theo's. Little Selene be sleeping in her mama's arms. She ain't got the O positive blood, so she'll be moving on to her new tribe when she a bit older. But for now, Caroline rock her youngest and smile at me. Lydia stop to play with the baby and I wait. We at camp now and I ain't got to be on guard duty, but I ain't gonna relax 'til the powwow be done.

"Big night tonight," Lydia tell Caroline, passing Selene back to her mama. "Maybe we'll have time to play with both our little ones when there's a lasting peace."

Caroline smile and say she hope so, and I walk Lydia all

the way to her hogan, checking to see it be clear before I leave her safe inside.

My hut be right next to Lydia's like it been at every camp since I joined her four years ago. Used to be we shared a hogan. Well, Lydia got tired of me sleeping in the dirt outside her door and made me come inside. I been like a dog then in more ways than one. I been wild, for sure. It took a kind hand and lots of patience to bring me back again. Now I got my own place, not so big or well-made as some, but quick to put up, easy to leave behind. I don't use tent poles like others do—can't rely on always finding a full set of aluminum that ain't rusted through, and I ain't gonna be risking my life to save them if we got to move real quick.

The ground between our huts be starting to wear clear of grass, like the floors inside the houses. It slap loud beneath my boots. We been getting too comfortable here. Soon it gonna be time to move on.

I duck into my hut, drop my pack, and look around to check it ain't been messed with while I been gone. I scan my low bed on the right, made of sacks stuffed with cotton and straw, next to a crate I found at the edge of the swamp one day and turned into a cubby for my books. The books be all wrapped in plastic to keep them dry when it rain. I keep a kerosene lamp to read by at night, covered on three sides so the light don't give the camp away. I squat down and look at the cubby. I got too much crammed inside it to be hiding Lydia's gifts there, too.

I stand up again and stretch long and hard. My bed be

looking real good to me now, especially with that smell of rain on the way, but I got things to do. No matter how early the sun set in October, there still be business to take care of. I look at my backpack on the floor. I got two packs: One I keep ready in case of emergency; it got food, a blanket, a knife, and a change of clothes inside. The other I used today be my everyday pack. It a good pack, waterproof canvas with easy straps. I tie it up tight and step outside to find a place to hide it. I'll get it tomorrow, give Lydia her presents after the powwow. Like a celebration, if things go well. If not, maybe they make her smile anyway.

Just west of camp, I find a good tree. Easy to climb, but not so easy that every nosy kid in camp be shinnying up in the branches. Trees be where you keep things you don't want animals to get at. Sure, in camp we got places to store food and all. But how you gonna keep something secret if you put it in the storehouse with everything else? So I climb my tree with a bit of rope and tie my pack high enough so I can see it, but nobody else will unless they know where to look. Then I go get Lydia ready for the powwow.

"There she is," Lydia say when I come through the door. She sound like she be laughing at me, but I be the one laughing, looking at her on the ground, belly all big and round as a kettle, trying to reach something under the bed.

"Just in time to help me," she say. "You always know when I need you." Lydia rise up and smile all the more. She ain't got but an inch or so on me height wise, but she clever with her braids, keep them on top her head to make her taller. It work, too, with those high cheeks and slanted eyes, she be looking regal, like a real leader. Maybe one day I'll tell Lydia our tribe too big to carry on like this and she make me a leader like her. We'll have two tribes together, side by side, and help each other like she always going on about, 'cause we a big family, but we be safer if we split up. Smaller tribes be easier to move, easier to run.

"What you doing down there?" I ask, shaking my head.

"I think my brush rolled under there. Just trying to reach for it."

Lydia and her hairbrushes. You'd think they be made of gold, the way she treat them, but they been her mama's at one point, I guess, so they mean something to her.

"Back away from there," I say, and when she move, I pick up her bed and slide it out. It ain't nothing but a frame of bamboo and a woven mattress, but it nicer than mine, with wild cotton stuffing on top of straw to keep it soft and firm at the same time. The brush be as far away as it could get, back against the wall. I dust it off for her. Nothing but a plastic hairbrush made to look like wood faded brown with a swirl at the end that say *Goody*. A family name, maybe. I seen it before. She even pulled it through my own rough hair once or twice. Lydia be happy when I hand it back to her.

"Now, enough of this foolishness." She tuck the brush away in a box on her table. I can see she keep all her precious things inside—ballpoint pens and inkwells, clean paper. Lydia be a scholar, more than most folks here. I ain't seen supplies like that outside the Professors' and the Ursuline

Sisters' places. But that what I like about Lydia. She do the improbable and she make it special.

"I'm ready," she say at last. She straighten her dress and touch her hair one last time. She look every bit the chieftain. Outside, I hear a commotion in the camp. The O-Negs be arriving.

3

O-NEG DAVIS. HE BEAUTIFUL. EYES LIKE AGATE or river rock, greeny-gray and copper, too. Hair in thick, long dreads, all milky brown, like a lion mane. Hard to take my eyes off him, but I do so I can see what else he brought with him. Ten O-Negs, all decked out for the powwow. They move soft and quick, following Uncle Romulus through our compound, but not so stealthy as they'd be out in the woods. Davis be they chieftain, so he at the front. There be a woman beside him, acting like she own him and the rest of the world, too. Natasha. Lydia done told me about her. Important in the tribe, she older than some, so must be wily. From where I be looking, she seem soft to me, decked out in the same ceremonial vest as Davis—alligator leather and pheasant feathers—over wide homespun pants. She got black and blue beaded bands on her wrist that match Davis, showing they related somehow. The armbands and feathers look regal on Brother Davis, natural even, like he part animal. But not on Natasha. She lean, true enough, but her people be carrying bows (Rom's got, they arrows 'til the powwow be over), while her own hands be empty. They the hands of a fat woman, someone being cared for by others. And she probably think she deserve it.

"Welcome to our place of rest," Lydia say, clear and strong in her beautiful voice. She could talk the trees into walking if she wanted.

"Greetings, Lydia Moray of the O-Positives," Davis announce. His voice just as fine as the rest of him, not too deep but not too high, neither. Those gray-green eyes flicker over our group—Lydia, me on her right, Uncle Romulus on her left—so he know we got Lydia's back, and her ear. Caroline and some of the others fall in behind us. The rest of our tribe be waiting around the cook fires for the feast to begin. "Thank you for inviting us into your place of rest."

Lydia nod and say some more formal greetings. She introduce us by our skills, and we learn the O-Negs' in return. "This is Fen de la Guerre, known for her fierceness, and Uncle Romulus, known for his wise council." In the Outer States, I hear folks be shaking hands when they meet. Not in Orleans. Somebody get a hold of you with one hand, they could have a knife in the other. So we learn about each other instead. Davis say Natasha be the clever one, but he ain't got no fierce one on his side, like Lydia got me. Maybe Davis fierce enough on his own.

Introductions done, Lydia relax and lead O-Neg Davis to our cook fire as she offer food and rest to his people as our guests. The real talk, about uniting our tribes, won't start 'til after the meal.

I stay close to Lydia, arms crossed so I look relaxed, but I can still reach the knife in my belt fast if need be. Lydia be the dreamer, but I be the fighter. She got a good dream, too, bringing together not just the Os, but all the tribes. Not for us all to live in one camp—the Fever be what's preventing that. But she say maybe we can live in peace. No more blood hunting. Freesteader and tribe living in the city without fear. It a big dream, a crazy one, I think. But Lydia done saved me. Maybe she can save the rest of Orleans, too.

Lydia offer the O-Negs a spot to sit beside her on rugs and cushions made of homespun cloth stuffed with feathers. Davis drop down in front of the fire, cross-legged and easy. Natasha take a moment to decide if the seating be to her liking before she join him. I kneel behind Lydia, ready to stand if need be. Caroline and some of the girls bring around a big wood plank piled high with roast pig and mirliton squash stewed with shrimp from the Market, boiled crawfish and slow-roasted wild sweet potatoes. Lydia serve up the food in bowls for the O-Negs and hand them out herself. It be tradition for the head of a household to serve guests. She continue dishing up the bowls 'til the whole tribe been served. Lydia will eat last.

Not every night be a feast like this. The rich smell of pork fat and sweet smell of stew make my mouth water, but I'll eat when Lydia do.

The air be growing cooler as the evening settles in, but the fire be warm and friendly. It make me proud to see our tribe so strong. I hope the O-Negs see it, too. They don't got to join us, but they should think twice before crossing us, too.

Our storyteller, Cinnamon Jones, stand up now on the far side of the fire. "In the early days, before the sky got so angry at the sea and went to war, there was a piece of land between them, and they called her New Orleans. She was a beautiful place, a city that sparkled like diamonds, sang like songbirds, and danced a two-step to stop men's hearts."

He sway his hips as he speak, and though he a bean-pole of a man, the way he wear his robes, made special for times like this, you'd think he the most beautiful woman in the world. The grace of a dancer, Lydia call it. And he can pitch his voice to sound like girl, woman, baby, or man. His daddy name him for the color of his skin, ruddy brown and smooth, and it stick because his stories be like cinnamon, too—sweet, savory, and rare. Uncle Romulus say when he been a kid, folks came running when they smelled cinnamon in the kitchen 'cause it meant something sweet baking in the oven, like it Christmastime. Well, Cinnamon Jones be in the kitchen tonight, and Lydia be hoping he spin a tale sweet enough to make them O-Negs take a bite.

"And the people," he say. "Lord, the people. They was black, and white, and yellow, and brown, and pink as a lobster sometimes, too, but they was beautiful. Because they could dance like the city, and sing like the city, and love like the city was loved by the sky and the sea. It was the *people* who made the city of New Orleans."

The rest of the camp be sitting around the cook fire, tamped down now so the flames don't give us away, just enough light and heat to make it cozy. The O-Negs look satisfied, O-Neg Davis leaning back on a log like he own the place. Natasha sitting next to him, looking even more like a lioness. They be family, all right. I can see it in they lines, the way they both be draping so lazylike in front of someone else's fire. Brave fools, I think. And that mess run in the family.

"Did you eat yet?" Lydia ask me quietly. I shake my head and she hand me a bowl. She take the last bowl for herself before Caroline take the serving board away. The leftover wild boar and sweet potato will fry up into cakes for breakfast. Lydia eat slow, and I know she be studying Davis as much as she be listening to Cinnamon's story.

I bolt down my food, push my bowl away, and whisper into Lydia's ear. "Got to check on them boys around the perimeter, make sure they be working like they should." Lydia nod and squeeze my hand when I rise. She look real tired tonight. That baby be weighing down on her something awful. If we ain't lucky, she be giving birth before we move camp again. But there be no profit in worrying like that now, so I squeeze her hand back and head to the edge of the light.

Cinnamon's story be reaching the point where the sky and the sea can't live without New Orleans being they own, so they start to fight over her, sending they daughters and they sons to wreak havoc. I be too far away to hear him naming the storms that tore the city down, but I know the names: Rita, Katrina, Isaiah, Lorenzo, all the way up to Jesus, or Hayseus, like Cinnamon say. And that be the end of New Orleans. She love that last storm so much, she run off with him and leave only Orleans behind.

The woods be dark and deep tonight. I smell pine needles, fresh after yesterday's storm, musty and sharp at the same time. The air be cooler here, away from people and the fire. I look behind me and be glad to see we built this place right. Ain't no fire seen from here, the way we shaped the hogans, wove them tight, blocked the view. It been Romulus who taught us to build camp in a spiral so there be rows enough to block the light, but it be my daddy who show me how to dig a fire hole deep enough to cover real quick. Uncle Rom be surviving in a group, but Daddy show me how to survive on my own.

I reach the edge of the clearing and wait for my eyes to adjust. To my right I hear an owl screech. I hoot soft and the owl don't answer, but some of our boys do, off to the left.

Then the wind pick up from another direction and I hear something else. Rustling from deep in the woods. I hoot again. This time there be no response. Whoever it be, it ain't our boys.

Then I see torches. Headed toward camp.

"Allez! Allez!" I scream the alarm, warn everyone to flee. I pull my knife and run back to camp. To Lydia.

4

✤ WHEN I GET TO CAMP, EVERYTHING BURNING, like the sky be on fire. But I run into it. I got to find Lydia.

The smell tell me they be blood hunters, come to harvest our camp. But they ain't just taking, they killing, too. It don't make sense. I keep running, looking for Lydia.

A shadow move in the light and I see the crazed eyes of an AB in front of me. ABs got it bad when it come to Delta Fever. It kill off all they good blood, so they need more. Now they trying to take it from us. This one rise up in front of me, six feet tall and wiry like the green trees we use for tent poles. He grin real wide and I smell blood on his breath, see scars on his arms in the firelight, thick like mine, but made from needles, tubes, reeds. He got a sling in one hand, loaded with a rock, but I be too close for that, so he pull a short, ugly club out his waistband and swing at me.

ABs need what blood they got, so they use blunt instruments, no blades or arrows—nothing that cuts a body, 'less it be for one of they transfusions. But I can dodge a club. And throw a knife. My cuts heal.

My knife catch him in the gut and he go down. I take the AB's club, wipe the knife on his pant leg, and keep going.

Lydia ain't at the fire, but I see Uncle Rom done gave the O-Negs they arrows back. I hear them split the wind like giant mosquitoes and I flinch. In the light of the fire, I see my people go down, hit by clubs and bolos—rocks tied to rope that wrap around they legs and drop them to the ground to be taken by drug-fueled ABs. Peyote, cannabis, scavenged drugs from before the Wall—the ABs shoot, swallow, and smoke anything to forget the pain of living with, but not dying from, the Fever. Lydia been trying to stop all that, but that ain't nothing but a fool's dream now.

I dump nearby buckets of sand on the fire to give the hunters less to see by. We OPs know our camp, we can run it just as well in the dark. But the ABs been busy. Our hogans be on fire, burning thick with smoke as the green leaves catch light. It hard to see much without burning my eyes.

I got to find Lydia. I swing the club at shadows I don't recognize and move on.

She not in her tent. Not in the talking circle. I run to the latrine. Not there, either. Everyone be running and running. Children brush past me, getting snatched up by strangers and parents alike. My vision gone narrow as I hunt for Lydia.

I finally find her, crouched like a possum, behind the scrap heap where we collect things for trade on Market Day. She look beyond me when I say her name. Proud, beautiful Lydia. She so tall and calm most days. But not now. I take her arm and she shake her head, moaning. I look down and see why: She squatting in water. Her own baby water. She been betrayed by that baby. It coming right now, whether she ready or not.

"No," I tell her. "You got to walk." But she don't move. "Stay there, then," I whisper. I run back to my hut and it be burning. I duck inside anyway to grab my emergency pack— but it already on fire. Instead, I grab the sheet off my cot. At least it still in one piece. Then I hear voices. I freeze, even though the fire be rising around me. I hear a woman cry out for O-Neg Davis, and I think it must be Natasha.

Suddenly the leaves of my hut flare up. The voices move away. I slip out and 'round to the salvage bin, trying not to look at what be happening to our homes. I got Lydia to care for, and her baby, too.

I come around the salvage heap and thank the Ursulines' God Lydia still there. She be moaning again, but now the fire be roaring so loud, you can't tell. "Low and quick," I hiss at her and grab her hand. She pull back, but I pull harder. We stumble forward and now she be moving with me as I steer her left and right, around the groups of men, none of them our own. We lucky they ain't got hounds. Hounds can sniff out blood, round folks up by type. Small blessing, but I'll take it.

Lydia groan and fall to the ground. I do my best to hook my arms around her and drag her to the brush. It slow going, and seem like we gonna be caught, but they ain't coming for us, and I wonder if this hunt be for the O-Negatives. It don't matter to me as long as the Devil ain't come for the two of us today.

· · ·

"It gonna be all right," I say to Lydia. I been pulling her along, wrapped in the sheet I thought I'd be using for the baby. But there ain't gonna be no baby if we ain't safe. "It gonna be all right," I say again. Lydia nod, her forehead beaded with sweat, and I worry again about them dogs. O-Neg hunt or not, they'd be after us. Because now there be blood on the sheet coming from between Lydia's legs. We still not safe enough. I slide her through the woods 'til we get to a protected place. Protected as can be in these thin trees, with a little pond of water and enough moonlight to see by.

I lay her out on the cleanest part of the sheet, and she look so weak lying there. She don't even be moaning and crying anymore, just calm, like she asleep. "Fen." She try to sit up, eyes wide. "Are we there yet?" she ask.

"We here. We at the hospital. We gonna have your baby now," I tell her. She smile at me. Ain't been a real hospital in the Delta since before I been born. They all been turned into crypts or tribe houses, and the Ursulines' tent be more like a morgue than a place where babies be born. Not everybody live in the open like us OPs. We a big enough tribe to care for ourselves, watch our own backs.

Used to be, anyway.

"I'm going to push now," Lydia say suddenly, and she grip my hand like she gonna break it. She take in a sharp breath and push down.

"Okay, okay, breathe easy," I tell her, and wish I had a blanket or something to pillow her head with. Instead, I make sure there be no rocks under her head or back. She lie there with no complaint and the contractions hit again. When they come a third time, I let go of her hand and go down to see where the baby be at. Lydia bleeding real bad, and I can't help but listen for dogs. It too soon for all that blood. All that OP blood.

She reach for me again and I take her hand. I won't need both hands 'til the baby start to show. I count with her and sing when I remember a song, and tell her them stories she used to be telling me when I been little and scared.

"Once upon a time, there was a magical place called New Orleans . . . There you go. Breathe, two, three, wait. Push. There was magic in the water, magic in the trees, and magic in the people. Two, three, there, I see a head!"

I forget the story 'cause the baby's head seem so big. It look like a melon pushing out, or a full moon, pale blue in the moonlight and bald. I let go of Lydia's hand.

"Keep talking," Lydia whisper. "Please."

"Um . . . but most magical of all was a woman named Jeanne Marie. Jeanne Marie was—"

"Clever as a clock and pretty as a sunset," Lydia say. She be smiling, and I smile, too. That always been my favorite part, describing Jeanne Marie.

"She was smart as a whip and pretty as a new moon," I say. Lydia chuckle, then groan and push again. I hear a gushing sound and the baby come free in my hands, like a storm surge, but the water be mixed with blood and Lydia's life be tied to the other end, gushing out.

"Wait, Lydia, wait," I beg, and wipe the baby's mouth clean, and suck its little nose clear. I hold it up to her so she can see it, but Lydia be looking at me.

"The City takes, Fen," she say. "I can't stay here. It's too much. Too much to change." She look around at the swamp and the ring of trees that hold out the rest of Orleans. "You're a fighter. You'll survive. Promise me you will look after my baby. Give him a better life than this. Teach him to be strong."

"But—"

"Promise me. *Promise.*" She grip my arm so hard, I almost drop the baby, all slick and wet with Lydia's blood.

I cry out with pain. "I promise." She let go, and I hold out the baby and say, "But Lydia, she a girl. A baby girl."

Lydia look and her eyes light up like the midday sun. "A girl. I was so sure it was a boy."

And then she dead. Like that. Eyes dull and staring. The baby, cold in the October night, start to cry like she know she at her mama's funeral. I stare at Lydia and feel like that baby crying for her mama. Only I had something this baby never will. I had Lydia.

I wrap Baby Girl up in the edge of the sheet and cut a section of cloth and the umbilical cord with my cleanest knife. I swaddle her the best I can in her mama's shroud and take off my shirt to make a sling to carry her. My skin be covered in goose bumps, but I been naked in these woods before. Only a matter of time before what happen once happen again.

I close Lydia's eyes, roll her up in the sheet, and sit down beside her, waiting for the sun to rise.

5

✦ THE SMELL OF GASOLINE FILLED THE AIR, sharp and noxious over the deeper stink of diesel fuel. Daniel unplugged the rental truck from the fueling station's bank of electric chargers. Across from the kiosk of dark green outlets, eighteen-wheelers and cargo trucks idled, waiting to refuel at the fossil tanks. A few old jalopies waited behind the trucks, families crammed in ancient cars, moving east, west, wherever they had heard things were better. Freeways throughout the country were filled with cars like these, broken down on the side of the road, families huddled under blankets, waiting for help that was slow to come. What was so wrong with their homes that they traveled north so many years after the hurricanes had blown away?

Overhead, black clouds threatened more than the current sprinkling of rain. Daniel hurried, dropping the cord to reel itself back into the charger stand. He clambered back into the cab of his pickup just as the rain began in earnest. He turned on his headlights and checked the tarp over the truck bed through his rear window. Everything was secure. Turning back around, he caught sight of himself in the mirror. He looked young, like a teenager, instead of his twenty-four years. He looked like his little brother, Charlie. He ran a hand through his dark hair, wiping back the dampness on his forehead that he knew was more than just rain.

"Pull it together, Danny." He tore his eyes from the mirror. Daniel tried to remember the boy his brother Charlie had been before the Delta Fever set in. The happy kid with a snaggletooth and a love of banana-flavored candy, comic books, and, surprisingly, movies about horses. Danny and Charlie. A nine-year age difference, yet somehow they'd still always been a team. Daniel had been off at school when the Fever swept through Charlie's class. They never traced the route of the disease. But it didn't matter how it had arrived, just that it was there.

Daniel had returned home to find his little brother in quarantine, sealed in a white room at a hospital, where he scratched at the floor with bloodied fingers, his scarecrow-thin shoulders shaking, unable to stand. Daniel had asked if he could bring him anything, candy, comics. Charlie had barely been able to speak, but he'd asked for one thing: dirt. He was so hungry and it was the only thing that sounded good anymore.

Daniel knew Charlie hadn't been hungry for dirt, but for the minerals it could provide, minerals being stripped from his own blood by the Fever. Anemia had ravaged him and iron was only a temporary solution. Daniel had given blood, there had been transfusions, but it would never be enough.

Charlie had died before his eleventh birthday. And Daniel immediately went to work on a cure. How many other Charlies had died since? The Fever seemed unstoppable, but so was he.

He changed his thesis to target Delta Fever specifically. After graduating with multiple degrees, he went to work for the military. They had the best laboratories and access to viral cultures of Delta Fever. Daniel started adapting methods used for cancer therapies at the turn of the century. Retargeted viruses, they were called. A way of invading a disease and altering it so that it attacked itself, or alerted the body to fight back before it could take hold.

It was careful work, retargeting a virus, but he had done it. Daniel had bioengineered a new virus with one purpose— to attack Delta Fever in the bloodstream. It was a subtle invasion that attached a new protein to the infected cells. Like pulling a fire alarm, this new protein signaled the body to attack the infection with everything it had.

At least, that had been the plan.

What actually happened was something much more dangerous. Daniel's cure for Delta Fever had created an even deadlier strain of the disease. Charlie had taken over a week to die. Daniel's virus would have killed him in less than twenty-four hours. It was worse than a laboratory mistake. It was a weapon, a time bomb that only killed Delta Fever carriers, which now included every inhabitant of the Delta Coast.

The United States economy was suffering. If the Delta could be recovered, stripped of Delta Fever and harvested for its natural resources—timber, oil, shipping lanes, and more . . . If the military knew about Daniel's virus, they might very well use it. Genocide in the name of money. And it would be his fault.

His first instinct had been to destroy it, to run his samples through a steam autoclave, a machine designed to cook viruses and bacteria until they were dead. Or he could have drowned the whole batch in bleach. But he hadn't done it. Daniel had looked at those six tiny vials, each no bigger than his little finger, and seen years of effort, money, time, and determination. And something else: a key. One that could unlock the doorway to a cure. As dangerous as this step was, it was also necessary. Now Daniel was on his way to break through the quarantine, into Orleans.

A line of military trucks barred the entrance onto the freeway, an olive drab caravan of canvas-covered stake beds and flatbeds bearing heavy equipment. Daniel joined a long line of waiting vehicles. Work at the Wall was never done, he had heard. The military employed more and more civilians each year to keep back the swamp, shore up the barricades.

The final truck passed, and at last the line of civilian cars crawled forward, merging onto the four-lane highway. Daniel's truck came up to speed and the dashboard chimed as it slipped into autodrive. Daniel pulled his foot off the gas and relaxed. He had a long drive ahead of him in one direction. South.

• • •

PEARLINGTON, MISSISSIPPI. The interstate sign loomed over-head, clearly visible in Daniel's headlights now that the rain had stopped. According to the map, this was the last stop for gas and food before the Wall. The best place, a sign on the side of the road said, to turn around. Once upon a time, the country had gone on for almost another hundred miles, but now the Southernmost tip of the United States of America was here in Pearlington. Orleans was forty miles away by the old interstate. It was hidden by the Wall, which acted as both dike and quarantine for this tiny town. Pearlington had been all but erased from the map from storm damage until the Wall was built, forming a break against storm surge and high winds. Then the people rebuilt and stayed, for reasons Daniel could not fathom.

To Daniel's right lay the Louisiana Delta Region Military Base, the entire state claimed by eminent domain for use by the military. It had been a staging area for rescue and relief operations until twenty years ago. Now, its main purpose was to protect the Wall. Daniel eyed the long, high fence that marked the state line. In the distance, the lights of watch-towers flashed intermittently across the night sky. Then the road turned away. Daniel followed the new freeway left as it dwindled into a two-lane road that stopped in the heart of Pearlington.

The scent of mildew rose up as he drove on. There were houses, a few with porch lights on. Dogs raced along fences as he passed. The street was well lit, and there were clear signs pointing to a cluster of motels along one side of the road.

Then the road stopped. Just stopped. And the smell of mildew grew stronger. Big concrete blockades had been dragged across the street, shored up with sandbags and detritus. Past that, the town continued on, but it was a ghostly reflection of Pearlington. Houses, like the ones he had passed, stood or staggered here, leaning, sagging on their foundations, faded to browns and greens as algae grew up the sides and black mildew devoured the rooftops. A fence had been built here, as well, and it marked the line of demarcation. A half mile south, Daniel knew, was the Wall.

He stared into the darkness at the dead side of town and wondered how people could live so close to their own ghosts. Then he backed up, drove to the nicest-looking of the three motels, and checked in.

"Tourist? Or you got family at the base?" the woman behind the desk asked when he signed the register with a fake name. "We offer a discount to military families visiting loved ones."

Daniel smiled sheepishly. "No. I'm here for the hunting," he said. "I hear there's boar in these wood like we don't get back home in Virginia."

The woman snorted. "Got that right. My Herb caught a big old sow out by the fence there some ways east of here. Ate like kings for a week, the whole town did. Course, he's dead now." She nodded toward a photograph on the wall behind her, of a solidly built man in hunting gear.

"Sorry to hear it," Daniel said with a nod. "He'd have been a great guide."

The woman squinted at him. "The best." She sighed. "The

Fever took him. Some of the kids, too. Damned smugglers bring out more than gold and silver when they go digging around over there." She scowled. "But that was a long time ago." She reached beneath the counter and pulled out a key. "Lucky number seven. Sleep well, mister, but don't sleep too long. Boar hunting's best at night, or just before dawn."

Daniel smiled. "Thanks for the tip."

The woman nodded and pointed at a bowl of small candy bars on the counter. "Help yourself," she said.

Daniel grabbed a handful of the black-and-orange themed wrappers. He'd forgotten. It was almost Halloween.

"Don't be shy," the woman said. "Ain't nobody else here to eat them."

Daniel blushed and took a few more. "Thank you. Good night."

He drove his truck around to the far end of the motel and parked directly in front of his room. He stood for a moment with his arms out at his sides, letting the chill night air wipe away the humidity and sweat, then he hauled his gear from the truck bed and went inside.

The room had seen better days, but it was clean. Daniel spread out his equipment on the faded floral bedspread and double- then triple-checked it. It took a lot more than determination to get into Orleans these days. An old smuggler had told him as much when he interviewed him last spring about the rate of Fever deaths among smugglers. The encounter suit, standard hazmat gear for any smuggler breaching the quarantine, he had bought online, and he spent three solid weeks upgrading it. He had never planned on venturing into

Orleans, at least not without military approval and support. But then he had created the DF virus. So close to a cure, but something was missing, something he couldn't get in laboratories or catalogs in the United States. He needed to go to the source.

The suit maintained a vague human shape as it lay across the bed, limp as a deep-sea diver's wet suit. Beside it sat his datalink, a black wrist computer no bigger than his forearm that fit like a cuff. Self-contained, with no satellite capabilities, it was more of an e-book than a full Web-access computer, linked to a receiver embedded in the bone behind his left ear. Such hardwired data ports and tech shunts were a necessity in the halls of higher learning, and had found a following among gamers, too. The datalink could present information on the goggles of Daniel's encounter suit, or speak to him in whisper mode. Daniel need only think a question, prefaced with the key word *inquiry,* and the datalink would collate the data and respond like the old GPS systems in vintage cars, but in a voice only he could hear. Daniel had chosen a woman's voice for the program. It helped him separate his own thoughts from the machine's responses.

Of course, if he had upgraded it to do the "link" part of its name and access the Internet, he'd be in the brig quicker than he could blink. Satellite links were traceable, a huge liability for an illegal mission like his. And so his datalink was nothing more than a vast library and a small, if capable, computer. He had spent countless hours downloading every iota of information he could about Orleans, including census data and maps from before the storms. Most of the latter might be obsolete now, fifty years out of date, but it was his only guidebook through the Delta.

The jetskip was his biggest prize. Purchased off the black market, there was little use for them recreationally these days, when so few could afford real recreation. And this was of a more industrial grade, the kind used by the military, coastal construction companies, and smugglers. Looking for all the world like a glorified window fan, the jetskip was made out of a lightweight fiberglass shaped into a cone, with handles around the rim of the wider end and a turbine set inside. As it spun, water was pulled through the fan, propelling the skip and its rider through the water. He'd used them before, in research trips to Vietnam. The lab required a training session for every technician before they did any fieldwork.

It was good to get out of the lab and into the field again. Orleans. That mysterious, abandoned city. It was legendary in the rest of the United States, like Shangri-La or Avalon. And Daniel was going to be one of the few civilians of his generation to see it. With the exception of a handful of scientists at the Institute of Post-Separation Studies, no one did research over the Wall anymore. The Institute's people had made the ultimate sacrifice for their research—they remained in the city after the quarantine, and could never leave. As far as Daniel knew, there had been no communication with the Institute in his lifetime. But it might still exist. If he could find the Institute, or remnants of their work, he might also find answers. The kind that could lead to a real cure.

A few hours before dawn, he reloaded his truck and drove

east down a dirt road and onto matted grass. He angled south until he was screened by a cluster of twisted old crape myrtle trees. He cut the engine, grabbed the jetskip and a large duffel, and headed for the fence.

It took some doing, climbing the fence with a towline tied to his waist. Once over the other side, he used the rope to pull his gear over the top. First his waterproof duffel bag, with the encounter suit and his payload inside. Then the jetskip, dangling from the end of the rope like a fish strung through its gills. Shrugging the duffel bag onto his shoulder, he hoisted the skip in his other hand and dashed into the dark. In a matter of minutes, the Wall was before him.

It was huge, at least twice as tall as he was, and gleamed pale in the moonlight. He crouched down against the rough cement blocks, filled with steel rebars and concrete. He scanned the top of the Wall for the telltale blinking lights of the little remote-controlled sniffer drone hovercrafts—named sniffers for the biofilters that helped them detect Delta Fever carriers—but he saw nothing. It was time to suit up.

The encounter suit was essentially a hazmat membrane, a thick wet suit–style coverall that encased the wearer like a second skin, albeit a thick one. The suit was the translucent yellowish color of an umbilical cord and acted like a placenta, protecting the wearer. Like an umbilical cord, it also processed bodily waste, sweat, and other secretions into pouches, breaking solids into fluids, and distilled fluids into drinking water. Putting it on was like trying to climb inside an uninflated party balloon. It took close to half an hour of struggling to peel the last of it securely around his fingers, where the skin was thinnest to allow for dexterity, and then up and around his face.

Even though he had practiced wearing the suit, the moment the seal tightened around his throat, Daniel panicked. He started hyperventilating in sharp, quick breaths, too rapid for the suit to process soon after activation. Unable to draw in enough oxygen to support himself, Daniel blacked out.

Daniel came to with a jolt. He tried to sit up too quickly, and the rubbery tightness of the suit snapped him back. His heart was racing again, but his breathing was regular. As it warmed, the suit would become more malleable. Stiffness would not be a problem by the time he got over the Wall. In the meantime, it felt like his skin was numb, as if his entire body had fallen asleep from lack of circulation. That, he knew, meant it was working. The suit regulated body temperature, compensating for the air outside, making him feel as though he were floating in a bath the exact same temperature as his skin. A necessity, Daniel knew, for the humid days and frigid nights of Orleans in late autumn. After a moment of adjustment, Daniel rose to his knees and began to don the rest of his gear.

"Dress as a leper." That had been the old smuggler's advice. It would disguise his hazmat skin and have the added effect of keeping away what locals there were. Fever carriers were particularly susceptible to blood and skin diseases. "Lepers are anathema in Orleans," the old man had said. Daniel pulled on a pair of brown canvas cargo pants, a long-sleeved shirt, and sturdy black boots to protect from the dangerous debris known to still cause tetanus and death to the unwary swamp traveler. Wherever his "skin" was exposed, he wrapped himself in long windings of gauze, doctored with food dyes and Vaseline to resemble bandages over weeping sores. His face was hidden behind a long black scarf, his hands and ankles wrapped like an ancient mummy. The dun-colored overcoat with several sealable pockets remained inside his duffel bag. He would pull it on, and the accompanying wide-brimmed hat, once he was over the Wall. For now he needed mobility. And a little bit of luck.

A dull sun was beginning to stain the eastern sky. Daniel moved toward the growing light at a trot, hoping the smuggler had told him the truth. "The Wall gets shorter as you go along it to the east," he'd said. "Short enough to climb onto eventually. Then you double back west until you hit water."

Daniel looked up. He raised a hand. The top of the Wall was just inches from his fingertips, but the sun was rising. He dropped the jetskip and slung the duffel bag across his body lengthwise, the strap firm against his chest. Retying the jetskip's towline around his waist, he took a minute, pumped his legs, and jumped. His fingers grazed the top of the wall, then held. He scrambled for a few horrible seconds, boots kicking and scuffling for purchase. And then he was pulling himself up and over, across the wide surface atop the Wall and down again, towing his equipment behind him. He landed hard, gasped, and flexed his legs. He was fine. He was alive.

Most importantly, he was over the Wall.

Part Two

FREESTEADER

6

❧ *I BE AT THE COTTAGE IN THE WOODS. THE SUN be shining, and Mommy be sitting in the chair outside, reading from one of her books. Daddy be in the shed behind the house, stacking wood for the fire. I sit at Mommy's feet and read a book of my own, a big one with pictures about the Flood and the Ark. I ask Mommy if the Flood was Hurricane Jesus, and she say no, and I ask if it was Lorenzo, and she say it was long ago, before that. And I think that must mean Katrina, and she laugh when I say it and kiss me on the head. And I laugh, too, though I don't know why.*

I wake up when an owl fly overhead, wings beating like a sheet in the wind, clapping over my eardrums. My knife already be in my hand. Sun be coming soon if the night birds flying home. Stupid to let myself shut my eyes. That as good as asking to be killed around here.

I look down. It got cold in the night, and the baby be quiet against me. For a moment I think she dead, like Lydia. But she stir and I know she alive and be hungry soon. Food and shelter be high on the list, then I got to look after Lydia.

I see there been some prowling in the night, tracks in the dirt from foxes and the like. In the early light I walk the clearing and find a good tree. It take some work, but the stream that feed the little pond got the right kind of bank, soft clay that dry up hard. Wrapped in the sheet, Lydia gone stiff, which only help me now. I untie the baby from my chest and set her down in a soft protected spot. Then I put her mother inside the tree. That the best I can do before this baby start wailing, so I tie her back on and race through the woods to find my hiding tree. There be food up in that tree for the baby, formula and bottled water. Lydia's funeral gonna have to wait.

I got to figure out what come next.

Only so many places to run to when you ain't got a tribe. Maybe I find another group of OPs somewhere, but Lydia's tribe been one of the biggest and strongest. If they ain't safe, nobody be. It ain't easy finding a new tribe, neither. Everyone take babies glad enough. If you live with folks your whole life, you ain't so likely to turn against them. But if they take in someone older, even if they only seven or eight, they ain't got an idea what kind of egg they got—chicken or snake. So even if you ain't turning against them, *they* might turn against *you*, just to be sure.

Lydia say she want Baby Girl to have a *better* life. Can't see how a tribe gonna give her that. Ain't no such thing as a better life in Orleans. Not really. Only chance this baby got be in the Outer States. So I gotta get her there.

It ain't gonna be easy—sniffer drones at the Wall would smell the Fever in my blood. But there be Father John. He a good man runs a mission across the city from here. When I been real little, he like family to me, like tribe. He used to trade supplies with my family. Ran a school out the old store where he set up his church. Not so nice as the Ursulines' place, but he tried. Daddy used to say Father John be a servant of the people. Used to reach out to folks over the Wall, find sponsors to help put shoes on kids' feet and the like. I had my parents back then, but I had a sponsor family, too, before the bad times come. I be needing that sort of help now.

So, we gonna go to Father John. Baby Girl brand-new. Cleanest blood there is. She ain't got the Fever in her yet, and won't if I be careful, don't give her Orleans water, or cuts to taint her blood.

Seven days before the Fever take hold in a newborn. It be a dangerous time. Hunters love to get they hands on an untainted baby. Babies don't know how to hide, how to stay quiet. They bring hunters down on they whole tribe if folks ain't careful. Father John a long way off. More than a day from here. I got to take it in stages, then. That mean finding safe places to stay the night. And the safest place on the way be Mr. Go.

Mr. Go knew my mama and daddy, back when they still at the Institute with the Professors. Back when Orleans ain't seem so bad. I been looking for Mr. Go the first time I found myself alone and naked in these woods. By then, I started to learn what the nuns say. The city take. Don't know if God receive, though.

Hunters took my parents. Almost took me, too, but Daddy knew what they do to little girls like me on blood farms, so he say run, and I ran. Into the swamps, 'til the dogs don't be chasing me no more. And I kept going, but it got dark and I got lost and I ain't find my way for days. Maybe 'cause I been so little, I don't know, but the forest weren't the same without my parents showing me the way.

I been making my way to Mr. Go, but other folks found me first. To get to Mr. Go, you got to pass through some bad territory. If you see little children, you best head the other way. Back then, I been a kid myself. Didn't seem dangerous, little kids all together, full bellies and smiling faces. I learned my lesson. I ain't looking to learn it again. So I be careful this time.

Mr. Go brought me to Lydia and gave me a home. Halfway to Father John, he be the best place to rest. I feel so tired just thinking it, even though I know I dozed in the night. I want so bad to be there, safe and sound. But nothing more useless than a wish in Orleans. It don't watch your back or feed you, that for sure. Only I can do that.

Baby Girl and I close enough to camp now that I can see it still smoldering. Nothing left standing anymore. Lucky for me, the fire ain't gone as far as my hiding tree. I look up and there it be, my pack in the branches, tied tight against any hungry birds. I untie the baby and she start up crying when I lay her on the ground. It be okay, though. This place a graveyard now. Nobody here but ghosts. I shinny up the tree to the lowest branch, find my tie line, and cut it. The pack drop from the tree like old fruit, and I be glad I put the baby out of reach of the fall.

I scoop up Baby Girl and tie her back to my chest. She snuggle close. In summer, Orleans be steaming like a pot of stew, but it close to winter now. Never mind the heat at mid-day, it still be getting cold. Together, we crouch down over the sack and I see what I came for: that glass baby bottle from McCallan, wrapped in a sack to keep from breaking, and two cans of powdered baby formula that took me over a month of scavenging to trade for at the Market. We got all kinds of canned stuff in the Delta, left in warehouses and big food stores after the storms. Some be hidden underwater, and the best divers get it, the ones can hold they breath the longest. But diving in a sunken store be worse than a cargo ship, 'cause they ain't meant to be underwater and a beam of metal be just as heavy today as it been fifty years ago.

Sometimes the water pull back and a grocery store be lying there like bones on the beach. Can scavengers, the little Japanese women from the Market, they go into the small places and pull cans out, clean 'em off, and if they ain't dam-aged, it be safe enough to eat. The Delta got all kinds of things, Lydia say, enough to last a hundred years if the cans hold up that long.

I got the formula as a gift, 'cause she been so busy saving the world and everything, ain't always gonna have time to be breast-feeding the baby. I'd have been Lydia's nanny when she needed, bottle-feeding the baby when we in powwow or whatever. Long as Lydia needed me, I'd do what I could.

I look at the tiny baby in the shirt tied 'cross my chest. She don't look a thing like Lydia, all purple and blotched and tight in the face. She ain't beautiful or strong or nothing.

Maybe she take after her daddy, whoever he be, but to me, she not worth the life of our chief.

Still, I made a promise.

There be bottles of water in the sack. Only three, but that still be something. I read the can and mix it up in the baby bottle, put on a nipple, and stick it in the baby's mouth. She don't like it at first, and I know it be cold, but not much I can do for that. After a minute she still ain't taking it, so I put the bottle in my waistband and stuff the rest of the formula and water in my pack. The day be wasting. If she don't mind not eating now, I don't, neither. My back gonna be hot and sweaty by the time I get her mama buried. If I keep the bottle against me, maybe later it be warm enough for her to drink.

I put Baby Girl down one more time and rip three holes in the seams of the sack the glass bottle been wrapped in. I pull it over my head. It fit me like a tank top now, rough and prickly, but it give me a bit of warmth. I tie the baby back on against me, pull my backpack over my shoulders, and take a last look around before heading back to Lydia's waiting grave.

By the time we reach the stream, the baby be fussing, so I give her the bottle again and watch while she take it. She got a strong pull on the nipple, which be good. Books I been reading say that important. She know how to feed. She hungry, too. She take the whole bottle and a little more besides. I tuck the rest of the second bottle away in my waistband, burp the baby, and settle her on the ground between the roots of the tree.

64

With one of my knives, I cut clay from the edge of the stream, making rough bricks of it. I carry them back to the tree by the armful. It take half the day, but there be enough to seal Lydia inside the tree. I don't say any special words or sing. If we had a tribe, they'd be doing all that. But there be no going back when the hunters come down on you.

I don't look at Lydia's face when I put in the final brick of clay. I smooth it over with my fingers and press the clay into place, then carve into it with the knife, an *X* in place of a cross. In the top crook of the *X*, I put the number one. To the left I scratch an *F*, to the right a plus sign. At the bottom, an *O*. *One Female O Positive*. The only marker most of us get in Orleans. Don't matter that she once been a chieftain of a tribe. That she had a baby, or that she been the only person truly good to me. She dead now. That be what counts.

There be folks who should know about it. Mr. Go, maybe the Ursulines so they ain't expecting her at the hospital tent no more. But that gonna have to wait. For now, I got a baby to care for, and a promise to keep.

Lydia's baby been staying quiet through all of it, but she be rustling now, fixing to cry, no doubt. I rinse my hands in the stream and scoop her back into my arms. When she settle down, I head deeper into Orleans.

This still be a crescent city. It still curve with its arms wrapped around the river. I be walking west, where most of the people be. I don't want people now, but I'm gonna need more food, and shelter. On my own, I'd be at Mr. Go's by now. But taking time for Lydia and walking with a baby in my arms make it slower going than usual. Dry land ain't always dry here, and I can't be dragging this child through Delta water. We pass canals what used to be roads and swamp what used to be dirt. We skirt the swamps and it take time. At this rate, we ain't getting to Mr. Go's 'til midday tomorrow, especially with night coming on. So we stuck, unsheltered and unfed.

I search the trees and brush as we travel, looking for fruit, for anything I can eat. Stupid, Fen. I should have taken some mirliton off Lydia's vines at the back of camp. But I ain't going back now.

I hear something in the distance; sound like someone walking through the brush. It ain't fast, so I know it ain't dogs, but it mean somebody out there. I hear him talking, though he far away. Birds be silent right now and a voice can carry. I drop down low and find a fallen log to slide under, pray the baby don't cry. But she look up at me and I see it coming.

I reach back behind me, under the pack, and pull out the second bottle in my waistband. It ain't hot, like I been hoping, but it warm enough and the baby be waving her fist at me, so I stick the nipple in her mouth and she take it.

The leaves be thick here, and this old tree gave up its life only to turn into a foxhole, soft and quiet, covered with fungus and bright green moss. I hold on to Baby Girl and curl up deeper. It be a hidden place, as good as any. Be safer up in a living tree, but not with the baby. Can't climb with her on my chest, and it ain't safe slinging her across my back in this makeshift thing.

Overhead, I see the outline of a boat stuck in the trees, like a bird resting on a branch. Look to be a shrimping boat; still got the nets spread like moth wings in the leaves—I shake my head just looking at it.

It dangerous, the storm fall that still be hanging in the high branches, tossed there by them killing winds. Sometimes the branches give way, and before you know it, there be a boat falling on your head, or a piece of house, or a hunk of car if you in a neighborhood where they ain't all gone to rust. I hear the first few drops of rain spatter down on the leaves around us. The wind be picking up now with the shower. Above me, I hear that boat creaking and it give me the shivers. Plenty of people killed by trash in the trees, but it give me an idea.

The baby finish her bottle. I rub her back 'til she burp up some milk, and I wipe it with the edge of my sackcloth. The moss be thick, so I take some and tuck it in around her bottom beneath her swaddling. It gonna have to do 'til I find more cotton to wrap her in a diaper.

She seem happy enough with the moss, and she fall asleep fast.

Once she quiet, I move out.

Three things be sacred in Orleans, and a girl with a baby alone in the woods ain't one of 'em. Places of the dead, like the potters' fields and the Dome, be one. Only the Ursulines or tribal counsels be going there, but I don't like the idea of being surrounded by dead people right now. The second place be the Market. But the Market ain't safe for me tonight, with my own tribe attacked and the ABs on guard duty. I ain't going there 'til I know my situation better. That leave me with: church.

Churches, temples, whatever still be standing that used to have a god—for some reason, folks be respecting that well enough. Orleans proper, over by the Market and Uptown, had more churches than the woods have trees at some point or other. There be enough still that a body can find some rest in the middle of the city. But where we at be swamp and thicket, foxholes and sinking mud.

I pick my way through dry land knowing that, sooner or later, there got to be a stilt house in these woods. Hanging in the branches like storm fall, they built to last, easy to rebuild, and stay high above the flood line. Some be hunting blinds kept by tribes for sighting boar and deer. I'd take one of them, too, if it be empty, but you always risk someone finding you. Better if you find a church.

I almost pass it before I know it be there. Built on the legs of four close-grown trees, with a rope ladder tied to the side of the largest trunk. I look up and the rain splash my face as it fall, soft and light, through the trees. Clouds be purpling to deep blue now, but I can make it out, a square cypress hut wedged into the trunks, like a hunting blind, but with a tiny cross atop the roof to show you this be a house of God.

I jump up and tug the rope ladder free from where it be looped to a stub of branch. It unravel into two ropes knotted to cross ropes every couple of feet to help with climbing. This'd be easier without a baby strapped to my chest, but a lot of things be easier without that. At least it don't be like hugging a tree trunk. I hop onto the swinging ladder and let it bounce itself out. It be awkward, leaning so the rope don't rub against the baby, but I do it. Then I shinny, slower than I'd like, all the way up to the trapdoor in the floor of the church.

7

DANIEL DRAGGED HIS JETSKIP OUT OF THE water. It was late afternoon now, the sun nothing but a pale pearl behind a sheet of gray sky. He dragged the skip through the soft mud of the bog, leaving a trail in the mossy grass that pooled with dark brown water swirled with bright yellow-green foam. In the distance he could just make out the silhouette of a building.

Daniel released a breath he hadn't known he'd been holding. So far, the old smuggler had not let him down. The gap in the Wall had been where he said it would be. The jetskip had done its job, too, pulling him through the bayou that formed a moat on the Orleans side of the wall. On land, however, the skip was too heavy to carry, but Daniel wasn't worried. If he hid it well enough in the woods, there was no reason to believe it wouldn't be safe. Orleans was all but deserted these days, from what he had heard.

A few minutes later, heading southeast, he could see more

than just the bulky shadow of the building through the trees. It was odd—one moment, he was thick in the bayou, the next, on a street in the middle of town. He marched through the skinny trees and came out on the edge of a crumbling parking lot. Civilization, he thought, or what passed for it these days.

He switched the definition on his goggles, refocusing on the shape blotting out the rain clouds overhead. The building looked like some sort of storage facility or megastore, with three walls still standing and a chestnut oak growing through the shattered roof. Tide lines marked the brick sides of the building like stone strata in a canyon, showing where the floodwaters rose and left their mark, higher each time, and now streaked with mold so virulent, it left black and green marks like rings around a dirty bathtub. He tromped forward to investigate.

It had been some sort of warehouse after all, with two cavernous rooms inside. The metal doors on the front of the building were still standing, but twisted to the side. The wall itself had tumbled in, a pile of large, dusky bricks, made deeper red by an earlier rain shower. Daniel looked around. The building fronted on a wide street, maybe a highway once, that ran level to the buildings. The pavement was shattered with cracks. Rich mud oozed out between the floes of asphalt, like dark blood on ashen skin.

Daniel went into the room with the tree growing inside. The roof was gone, but otherwise, the space itself was intact. The tree was young by oak standards, but still large enough to take up a good ten feet of the room between its sprawling roots. Daniel scanned the room, but found no sign that any-one had been here in a long time. There was a nook in the tree roots that was large enough to hide the jetskip.

Daniel dropped his duffel and returned to the woods where the skip lay waiting. He took care to carry rather than drag it to the warehouse. His footprints in the carpet of moldering leaves made him nervous enough. A deep groove leading up to the doorway would have raised curiosity in the idlest of passersby, or predators. The city might be dead, but that didn't mean the woods were.

The last census was taken nearly fifteen years ago, and best estimates put the surviving population in the Delta region at eight thousand, approximately sixty-five hundred in or near the environs of the former city of New Orleans. And that was a generous estimate, given the easy transmission of Delta Fever, the hundreds of other hazards in the damaged city, and the lack of proper medical care. Blood transfusions, a common treatment for the Fever, were notoriously danger-ous in the field, where blood could not be spun clean in cen-trifuges and separated from the plasma. A field transfusion could result in death from fatty deposits, liver damage, and even heart attacks. Daniel doubted the census guesstimates had factored in all of the ways a person could die. Even so, eight thousand people—that was less than a full football sta-dium, less than the student body of his university, and he had avoided hanging out with most of them rather easily. Navi-gating the empty streets of Orleans should be simple enough.

The *New* in *New Orleans* had been dropped after the

second chain of storms, when the Fever was at its worst. It had been before Daniel's time, but he wouldn't be surprised to learn it was a publicity ploy or a media joke. There had been attempts to re-create New Orleans in the surviving South. Somewhere near Charleston, a private island was sold to the government with plans to relocate the more historical structures, and many of the city's people. But Hurricane Lorenzo had dispensed with those plans. The first ground-breaking had been interrupted by a hurricane warning late enough in the season to take people by surprise, and the government had pulled its funding. Daniel knew this because the island, now simply known as Folly Island, had been one of the places he and his team were allowed to collect environmental samples. Not quite the same flora as you would find in the Delta, and certainly not the same mix of toxins in the water, but as close as one could get outside of the quarantine zone. It was like a theme park version of the real place, Daniel thought.

He accessed the datalink strapped to his wrist.

INQUIRY: Entered city at coordinates 56 SW 32 NE. Draw map to Institute of Post-Separation Studies from here.
RESPONSE: Feeding coordinates now. Instructions on screen.

Daniel tweaked his goggles again. A red line appeared on the green overlay of the city. The map was hopelessly out of date, but the main features would be the same. Especially for a landmark that important. *Assuming it was still there,* a cynical voice said inside his head.

The Institute of Post-Separation Studies had been established shortly before the Wall went up. Staffed with scientists willing to dedicate their lives to the cause, the goal of the Institute was to study the closed environment of Orleans—socially and medically. He knew the official charter was to study intergroup relations after the residents were divided into groups by blood type. They had an interdisciplinary goal of understanding social bias and hate crimes—if people divided along medical lines, would race or gender matter?

In the early days, data flowed freely from the Institute to data banks at universities across the States. But by the time Daniel was in school, the information had all but dried up. He was convinced the Institute still existed, in records if not in people. His goal was to mine their data and solve the riddle of Delta Fever.

Daniel's excitement flared up again. He dragged some vines over the jetskip and shouldered his duffel, relocating its dangerous payload to an inner pocket of his coat for safekeeping. It was risky, traveling with the vials of his fatal virus, even secured as they were in their casing. But it would have been riskier to leave the vials behind where a supervisor or routine inspection might stumble across them, with the virus still in its weaponizable state. With luck, the Institute would have the equipment he needed to continue working. If not, at least the vials would be safe.

Patting the pockets of the weatherproof oilcloth coat he wore over his suit, he found another length of dirty linen gauze and wrapped it around his neck like a scarf. Feeling more like a dime-store mummy than a local with a skin disease, Daniel headed out into the gray afternoon.

8

⚜ THIS CHURCH AIN'T SEEN GOD IN A LONG TIME. It be dark as pitch in here and don't smell too clean, neither, but there be a fire in a grate to the side of the altar, and it nice and warm inside. Especially to me, without a proper shirt. I pull myself up and look around. The branches below done a good job of hiding this place. The floor be gritty with dirt, and the walls be dark from wood smoke. There be six rows of benches, a pulpit with space in front of it. There be a door in the far wall, so there be at least one other room. No priest, no priestesses. Might not even be a church anymore with no one here tending it.

Then my eyes adjust and I see there be a few people sitting on the benches. The front row even got real pews, probably taken from some drowned church. They been painted up and stuck in a place of honor right against the altar. There be no service right now, so I take a minute to check out who be here with me. We safe enough, it being a church, but you still got to keep your eyes open when you decide to leave.

In the second row on the right there be a big guy, muscle and fat from what I'm seeing. And he got tattoos, which mean he either AB or a blood hunter. I don't like the thought of being in here with him, but if he here, it most likely because he reformed. Blood hunters don't go to church. Too much temptation inside, and even they respect that one law. Nobody ever been taken from a church. Not to say they don't get jumped at the door, though.

Behind him a few rows be a nervous little man muttering to himself. He got a bald spot on top his head and patchy hair growing 'round the sides. He tugging at it like he don't even realize what he doing. Freesteader, I guess. Nobody with nerves like that be in a tribe worth its salt. He be in his church best, dress shirt rubbed thin with wear, and what used to be a decent pair of pants. I wonder where he camping down these days. Maybe that why he so nervous—'cause, like me, this be it.

What worry me most be the person on the other side, in the second to last row of the pews. Man or woman, I can't tell, but they be shaking and sweating worse than the freesteader. Whoever it be, in the light I can see two things: First, he used to be a smuggler—still got parts of the encounter suit he wore rolled down around his neck like a scarf, afraid to take it off, but knowing he might as well; and second, he got the blood Fever. This smuggler be white, whiter than you see in Orleans anymore, with yellow-blond hair stuck to his forehead with sweat. It remind me of Lydia kneeling at that boy's bedside the other day.

Yesterday.

It take the wind out of me, thinking how much be changed in so little time. How much lost. And I been worrying she'd catch her death in the hospital tent. Show what I know. Childbirth been killing women long before the world ever heard of Delta Fever or blood hunting or Orleans. Lydia didn't have the baby the right way, in a bed with a healer or somebody watching who knew what to do. Just me, and I ain't enough.

It be warmer in here than that little fire grate can explain, and I know I come to the right place, 'cause that mean there be a kitchen back behind the altar somewhere.

It started with the missionaries that came after the first storms. I guess there always been a tradition of church folks feeding the hungry. Even now, when the churches be in trees and religion be as mixed up as the people, there still be food coming out at the end of each service. I settle in to a back pew and tuck Baby Girl in my arms just as nice as can be. Maybe we both can rest up awhile, get some food in our bellies, and then be on our way. We in God's house, so we gonna let him provide.

Soon as I think it, the curtain behind the altar open up and two kids come out, skinny and tall. They look enough alike to be brother and sister. The boy stand behind the altar, pale long-sleeve shirt buttoned to his chin, arms too long for the sleeves. His pants be too short for his legs, too, like he grew three inches just before he walk into the room. The girl be wearing a dress the same pale color as his shirt. Homespun, dyed with salmon berries. It look like a pillowcase on her, hanging on a drying line. She come stand by the front pew holding a big silver-painted tray. The boy raise his hands to the ceiling.

"Welcome, brothers and sisters, to the House of the Rising Son. I am Brother William, and this is Sister Henrietta. Join us, won't you, in prayer?"

He got a soft voice, like a bale of cotton, serious for his age. Something change people's voices when they find God—soft and gentle, or loud and fiery, there ain't no in between. I been hoping for a fiery preacher to keep me awake. But with the heat and this boy talking, it gonna be hard for sure.

Before he get to preaching, the girl, Sister Henrietta, walk up the aisle, passing the plate for donations. I sit up and dig through my bag for a bottle of water, glad I got two left for Baby Girl. When Sister Henrietta reach me and hold out the plate, I put it in next to the freesteader's dried fish and the pheasant the blood hunter already donated. The smuggler too far gone to be giving up anything but the ghost, and soon. Still, it gonna be a good dinner tonight, if the plate be any sign.

The trapdoor bang open across from me and I jump at the sound. A man with one leg climb through, and I wonder how he managed the rope ladder, even with them big arms. He drop a smoked ham hock on the collection plate, and that be it, five people and a tidy heap of food. They gonna give us some, save the rest for later, but that pheasant ain't keeping like the hocks and the fish, so we doing all right.

The girl smile at the man, all soft and sweet, and let him

pass. He move himself up to them front pews and prop up his legless thigh. I tuck into my corner and watch the whole room. Sister Henrietta slip behind the curtain with her platter of food, and I work harder than usual to keep my eyes open, waiting for the word of the Lord.

"Thank you, Sister," Brother William say in that drowsy-making voice of his. "And many thanks to and blessings upon you, sisters and brothers. For it is a blessing that each and every one of us is alive and drawing in the blessed air tonight. Did not the Lord say that Heaven is like unto a grain of mustard seed, grown into a tree in which the birds of the air made nests in its branches? So, too, do we nest amongst the arms of cypress trees and know that we are closer to Heaven."

I listen for a while just to have something to do that ain't dwelling on what happened to Lydia, but it hard to pay attention when they just be preaching the same mess you hear in any church up and down the Delta. "Be kind to each other. Do unto others as you would have them do unto you." With some mess about Job and Noah thrown in for good measure. It don't go on as long as some of them Catholic masses the Ursulines hold, though, I'll give them that.

Soon it's over and Brother William announce the meal being prepared and we all welcome to stay. He and Sister Henrietta work they way down the aisle, shaking hands and talking to the handful of lost souls they got. I start to think of a story for when they get to me.

It come soon enough, especially since they both avoid the smuggler, who still be sweating up a storm in his half-worn suit. Sister Henrietta smile all big and tender when she see Baby Girl in my arms.

"Blessings, sister, and to your little one. Welcome to the House of the Rising Son," she say, hands clasped in front of her like she be praying with every word. They drop down on the bench beside me and I feel trapped. But they just two little church people—nothing I can't handle.

"Sister, you seem tired," Brother William say. "You are welcome to rest in our House as long as you require. Indeed, if you are in need of a Home, you are welcome to join ours. Sister Henrietta here is quite smitten with young ones, and you would be most welcome, along with your babe."

"Never let it be said there was no room at the inn," Henrietta say with a chuckle that I don't like, but seem harmless enough.

"Thanks, but we just stopping for the night. Got people to meet come morning."

Brother William nod and rise from the pew. Henrietta be a bit slower to accept. "Are you a freesteader?" she ask me.

I raise an eyebrow. "Do I look it?" I sound sharper than I should. These people be feeding me and I don't got to bite they heads off just for asking obvious questions. Then I see her eyes drop down to my arms. She ain't looking at Baby Girl; she looking at my scars. I tilt my chin up and dare her to say something. She pull her eyes away and clear her throat.

"My apologies, Sister . . . ?" She wait for my name, but I don't give it. What can I say? It hard to be nice sometimes.

"I only ask because we offer care for the little ones, as Brother William implied. I am the nursery attendant. Several of the freesteaders in the area rely on our services with their children. If you find that you are in need . . . Well, please think of us as your friends."

I smile then, and it ain't a nice smile. Anybody in the Delta say they your friend, you best be watching your back when they come 'round.

"How nice," I say. "Thanks for your offer, but my chief wouldn't be too happy with me if I be leaving my baby with strangers. That what the tribe be for."

Henrietta sigh and stand up, her pillowcase dress swaying with the movement. "Certainly. Tribe is life," she say like she heard it before. Probably lots of folks come in for a nap and got to put up with her pushy form of friendship. She ain't never had a tribe of her own, or she'd know what it be about.

"Tribe is life," I agree, and nod. She walk away, and I be left alone waiting for dinner. She got me thinking, though. In Orleans, you either a tribe, a religion, a hunter, or a freesteader. Better a tribe than a religion, but freesteader be as good as free-deader, so you choose second best sometimes. Leastways 'til you figure something else out. And I got to keep reminding myself that I ain't tribe no more. Least not for the time being. That make me a freesteader 'til I get to Father John. Or maybe a member of the House of the Rising Son.

I look down at Baby Girl in my arms. She look peaceful. Probably because it so warm in here. "What do you think?" I ask her. Ain't like she gonna answer, though. She wiggle at the sound of my voice, and I wonder what her mama'd think of me leaving her here. "These folks used to handling babies," I tell her. Maybe I stay on a little while to make sure it all right, then I make my own way. Lydia want a better life for her daughter. I look around the dim little church. It ain't paradise, but it be safe above the ground, protected as a church. No blood hunters burning her out of here in the middle of the night.

"Maybe," I finally say. Not decided, but maybe.

The curtains open at the front of the room again and I sit up straight. The smell of food waft from the back room, and Brother William come out with a big old steaming pot of stew. Sister Henrietta follow, passing bowls around, and they singing some hymn or other about the Lord being a shepherd or something. My mouth be watering.

Everyone be tucking into they bowls, and I ain't no different. Henrietta give me a large ladleful from the pot, and I pick that bowl right up and start eating. Bits of pheasant and salt meat, potatoes and yams, mixed up in thick brown gravy. It be just about the best thing I ever ate, seeing as how I been going all day on empty. When I be done, I'll ask them to heat a bottle for Baby Girl. We doing all right for our first night on our own.

I scrape the bottom of the bowl, belly full and eyelids drooping. I shouldn't have eaten so fast. I set the bowl aside and put my arms around the baby in her sling. But my arms don't want to be holding her, they so heavy. I let her rest in my lap and my head jerk back trying to stay upright, I be so dead tired. Around the room, everybody else doing the same thing, nodding off over they empty bowls. I hear a clatter as some spoon hit the ground, and I realize something ain't right.

Then I smell it. Incense. They been burning it in the cooking fire, and I ain't noticed over the smell of food. But it ain't just perfume like they be burning in some churches. This be something stronger, and it ain't good.

Damn. I shake my head and pick up Baby Girl, but I ain't got no strength left. I look at my empty stew bowl. They done drugged us all. But why?

Fighting the incense and the poison in the food, I force myself to keep my arms around Baby Girl. Around me, folks be swaying in the pews and I hear a drum being played. *Tat-ta-tat-tat-tat.*

A jolt of fear go through me as I recognize the rhythm and the smell of them burning herbs. I know whose house this be, and it ain't God or the Rising Son. This be one of Mama Gentille's places.

Mama Gentille's name means *kind,* but her name be the only place you'll find it. Hers be the kindness of the gator to the rabbit, the snake to the bird. Before Lydia took me in, I been one of Mama's girls. And I got the scars to prove it.

9

✤ *I AIN'T CRYING. NO, I AIN'T CRYING. NINE BE*
too old for that.

Daddy say run and I run. Day turn to night and my boots
be crashing through the weeds and moss, splashing through
the swamp. I hit concrete, sand, and gravel and keep running
'til I don't hear the dogs no more, or my mama screaming, or
Daddy crying. I run 'til I know I be lost. Daddy say run, but
he also say where to get help, and I be a long way from it.

I be so tired. I find a place under a fallen tree to hide,
shaking like a rabbit. "Fen, Fen, Fen, Fen." I sing my name to
myself nice and quiet, like Mama sometimes sing it. I got to
find Mr. Go. I stay quiet. Maybe Mama and Daddy come find
me, if I be still and good. They always do, they always do.

Then I remember them dogs and the hunters, with they
chains and ropes and things, and I know Mama and Daddy
ain't coming for me. That's when I start to cry.

I wake up. A little boy, old as me, be peeking at me. It dark, but he holding up a burning torch that light him up. I don't leave my spot beneath the tree, but I watch him.

He be wearing a man's T-shirt that look almost like a dress on him, except he got pants on, too. He could be a ghost, except I don't think ghosts got skin that black-brown, and they don't giggle like he be giggling. The whites of his eyes flash in the torchlight as he look at me, and then he turn and disappear into the woods.

I don't move. I close my eyes, but I still want to see, so I open them again, and he be back, giggling and holding hands with a girl, this one older, but dressed almost the same. She got a rope belt around her big shirt, though, and it look more proper somehow. She put a bowl on the ground and then they leave together, the boy looking over his shoulder at me. I don't leave the bushes. I don't touch that bowl.

Next morning, when the mist be steaming off the ground like will-o'-the-wisps, the girl come back, only now she got a man's coat on. It hang off her like she a scarecrow. She sit down in front of the bowl and mix it, and I see there been a spoon in the bowl the whole time. After a minute, she shrug and eat it herself. By the look on her face, it just as good cold, and I'm wishing my daddy had said it be okay to eat from a stranger's hand, so I don't be left with nothing but growling to fill my belly.

The next night, she leave me another bowl. This time, the girl take a spoonful while I be watching, then she wipe the spoon off carefully and leave it behind, so I know it ain't poisoned or nothing.

"Wait," I say when she start to walk away. The girl turn around and scan the bushes for me.

I come out and ask, "Where's the little boy?"

The girl shrug. "He got work to do."

"What about you?" I ask, sidling up to her.

She smile. "You be my work tonight and every night 'til I get you to come out."

"Well, I'm here," I say, and try not to look so cold and small, but I know I be just that, and she know it, too.

"Yep," she say. I sit down. She follow, crossing her legs Indian style.

"Eat," I say, and she take another spoonful of food. Fish stew tonight. I see the shrimp in it, pink and white, and the tiny black veins in a piece of catfish. She wipe the spoon off and set the bowl down. I pick it up and, after sniffing it, I take a bite.

My stomach clench like it gonna turn on me. My mouth water, and for a second I don't know if I gonna be sick or it just saliva. I glare at the girl, but she smile back.

"It ain't poisoned," she tell me. "You just hungry."

"I know," I lie. I been hungry before, but never so hungry that food make me sick. Mama and Daddy never let it get that bad. I swallow hard so I don't start crying about them.

The girl take another bite and I follow suit. Together we finish the bowl, and I know I be keeping it all down.

"You alone out here?" the girl ask.

"No," I lie again.

"Me neither," she say. "I mean, before, yeah. But now, I never am."

I give her a suspicious look.

"All because of Mama Gentille. She take care of all the little kids, and when we grown, we take care of her. It ain't hard. And soon I'ma be grown enough to start paying back all the good she done me. That why Alfie be gone today. Alfie can only do little things, like pick berries. Tonight he snapping beans back at the house. But I get to come out here and talk to you. You want to come with me? You should be with us kids, and Mama Gentille."

It sound nice—a house, other kids, snap beans and berries. "Are you a tribe?" I ask her.

The girl shake her head. "No, silly. Mama don't believe in tribes. She say God made us all for something, and she take care of us all just alike."

"And you ain't get sick being together like that?"

The girl shrug. "Sometimes. But we tend to each other."

I grunt, thinking about it. "You freesteaders?" I ask. I crouch on the ground and watch a beetle making his way across the dirt, a leaf on his back. What he doing with that leaf? I wonder. Daddy'd know. Mama, too. But I guess I never will.

"No, silly, we ain't freesteaders, neither. We Mama's kids. That's all. We a family."

Family. Something move sideways in my chest, and all of a sudden I start to cry. I can't make it stop and don't want to.

Like, if I try to hold it in this time, I like to drown. I cry and cry so hard, I can't see the little beetle no more or the stew bowl or the spoon or the forest. The girl don't say a thing 'til I be done. And then she say, "My name be Alice. You want to come with me?"

And I go.

Mama Gentille's house be big—an old mansion that been a plantation long ago, according to Alice. I meet Alfie again and we share one of the old rooms on the ground floor. The top floors be too shaky to sleep in, 'cause they might fall down when you ain't awake, and then where would you be? In the kitchen, Alice say, and I think that's so funny, I actually laugh for the first time in a long time, and it feel all right.

Alice tell me that me and Alfie are still little kids, so we do little jobs. We snap beans and peel potatoes for the evening meal, and we pick berries when they ripe. No farming at the house, just finding what we can. Sometimes, Alfie and me even go to the bayou and catch crab.

It ain't so bad, and I don't see nobody even looking like a blood hunter or a bad thing for days and days and days.

Then Mama Gentille come home.

It be a big deal in the house. Everyone running this way and that to get ready for her being home. Me and Alfie catch twice as many shrimp and crab, and we help make 'em up nice, too. Then Alice surprise us with new shirts to wear, and they almost the right size for us. We wash our faces in the basins with fresh water the other kids brought up from the stream, and we all be lined up like sunflowers in a garden across the old front porch when Mama Gentille's little wagon pull up, towed along by a mule with long gray ears.

"Mes enfants! Mes enfants!" she shout when she step off her wagon. Mama Gentille be big and round and jolly like Santa Claus, only her skin be the color of old wood, and she be dressed in purple and red, with lips and nails to match. She got a face like the moon and she be beaming at all of us. Some of the little ones can't wait and run down the steps to hug her. The older ones follow more properly and offer to carry her bags. Me and Alfie, we wait like we been told to. I be new here and not ready to be hugging on some stranger.

"And who do we have here?" Mama ask when she finally see me standing at the top of the stairs. Her arms be full with stray cats and babies and presents and a shoulder bag like to burst with good things—carrots, greens, radishes poking out the sides.

Alice be the one who answer. "Mama, this be Fen. She one of us now, if you'll have her."

I study my feet and feel my lip tremble. What if she kick me out, just when I be feeling so good about being here? What if I got to find Mr. Go on my own after all?

Mama Gentille be silent for so long, I can't stand it, and finally I have to look up. She look stern, frowning at me, and I see she ain't as old as all that. Maybe old as my mama, maybe older, but not like Mr. Go. He be the oldest man alive. Mama Gentille got nothing on that.

I look away again. If she don't like me, it be all over. And nothing people hate more than a kid that look at them too long. I been told that by the Ursulines, and I believe them today.

"Of course she can stay!" Mama shout, and everybody cheer except for me, because it take me a while to understand what she say. And then I be cheering, too, and Alfie be hugging me, and I feel like I'ma be all right 'cause I found myself a home.

That night, I feel somebody grab me before I hear anything, then the breath, hot and heavy in my ear. I open my eyes, dead asleep to dead terrified in an instant. The room too dark to see anything, then too bright as a candle come 'round. White gleam in front of me, and then it re-form into a shape I recognize. Mama Gentille.

"Hello, bébé. Sorry to wake you, chère. Just checking in on my little ones, and you been whimpering in your sleep."

"Oh," I say, and my voice sound like a tiny thread. I pull my arm away, but she hold on tight. Then her grip turn gentle, and we both stare at the inside of my wrist, my arms smooth and brown in the candle glow. Mama run a hand down my arm.

"There there, petite. So many babies come to me with nightmares, but they go away in time." She pat my hand and I pull my arm back under the covers. "You've not had it so bad as the rest," she say, nodding at my arms. "You speak like a little lady, and your skin be smooth." My tummy start to hurt, because she be right. I forgot to talk tribe like Mama and Daddy say to do. Now she know I ain't like the other kids, and I start to be afraid.

"*Some come to me so scarred with holes, they look like lightning struck them. Abused, abused,*" she murmur like she singing a lullaby. *I wish she would go away.*

"*Ah, well, there ain't nothing to be done about that, eh, Fen? Tomorrow be a new day, as they say.*" She stand up with a heavy creak of the floorboards and drag her chair back toward the door. How did I sleep through that? *I wonder. I will never sleep so deep again.*

"*Close your eyes,* petite fille. *There will be no nightmares in the morning. Good night.*"

Against Mama's advice, I can't sleep the rest of the night. I hear singing outside my window, and when I look, I see the big kids in a circle, dancing around Mama Gentille. She shaking and jumping like she got spiders on her back. It scare me good. She seem nice on the outside, but I still feel her fingers on my arms.

I'ma be more careful tomorrow. Tomorrow, I'ma blend in.

A few days later, Mama got a visitor, a man in a black hat. I see him coming up the drive from the dorm room where Alfie and I be making beds.

"Who that?" I ask Alfie. He run to look out the window, then turn away.

"That be the man," he tell me. "He come for the big kids sometimes."

"What do you mean, come for them?"

Alfie shrugs. "I don't know, 'cause I don't never talk to none of them that he come for, but he an important man, Mama say, and he ask for the big kids sometimes."

"Do he hire them to work?" I ask, making sure I speak like Alfie.

Alfie shrug. "I guess. Like I say, I never asked."

We finish the beds and head to the kitchen to start chopping vegetables for the soup and I forget all about the man in the black hat. Only later, when we be beating rugs on the front porch and he pass us, do I remember. He pause at the top step, considering me and Alfie as we shout and pound the rugs and pretend to be pirates in battle. He smile at Alfie, tip his hat at me, and continue down the drive, a satchel in his hand. The man in the hat got eyes black as night.

"Mama Gentille be interested in you," Alice tell me one day. I be brushing her hair and trying to braid it nice for a change. She almost a full-on woman now, and I want her to look her best.

I grunt and say nothing. Alice continue, "I can tell because she ask about you."

"She do?" I say. I stop brushing long enough to smooth a lock of hair and split it into three pieces. But it still too frizzy, so I pick up the brush and go at it again.

"Sure, she say, 'How my Fen doing? How that girl coming along? Staying out of trouble?' and all that kind of thing."

I shrug. "That be nice, I guess."

"You guess? You guess! It be nice, Fen! Nicer than I ever got. When they moved me in with the big girls, I found out they keep a chair under the door at night to keep the boys out. You know that? Mama'd never let that happen to you."

I blush. "Why would a boy want to be in my room at

night, anyway? I got plenty of boys with me: Alfie, and Roger, and the twins."

Alice shake her head and my braiding work come undone. "That not what I mean. She ain't wanting you to be used up on one of the boys here. She got something special in mind for you."

My mouth go dry. "Special? Like what?"

Alice shrug, and I know she got a secret. "I don't know, Fen, but when it happens, don't mess it up, okay? Promise me. Promise!"

I mumble okay, but keep my fingers crossed behind my back.

At the end of the week, the man in the black hat come back.

"He asked for you, Fen," Mama Gentille say, laying a new dress—a real dress!—on the bed for me. This be a new bed, in a bedroom all by itself in one of the outbuildings back behind the house. I never been here before. I thought they be empty and haunted, but this room be real nice, with wood panels that glow in the firelight and a fireplace so big, you could roast three rabbits in it.

"That's a big honor," Mama explain.

"What he want from me?" I ask.

She touch my cheek and it feel like a caterpillar crawling up my skin. "What only you've got to give, chère. You ain't never been touched by a needle before."

"Have too! I even know my blood type. I'm an O—" Mama shut me up with a quick slap before I finish.

"Girl, you listen to me. Your arms be smooth and free of

needles. That all that man need to know. Now, maybe your parents pricked you in the leg when you was a baby, maybe they took it from your arm once, but so long ago that the holes ain't showing. And that's what this gentleman want. A virgin, untouched by needle or knife. So you be that for him. You young enough, and Lord knows you inexperienced enough to pull it off, but say a word about knowing your type and he'll know you been pierced, and I will throw you out into the swamps myself."

She pause for a minute, breathing heavy like she run a race and lost. Then she mop her forehead with a handkerchief from her sleeve and smile. "Now, put on this dress, ma petite. You'll look so grown-up in it. I want to see before the gentleman comes. Can you do that for Mama?"

I don't answer, but I do as she say. I put on the dress and she approve, and she set me on the bed just so, hands in my lap, legs crossed at the ankle. The dress be long and white, more like a nightgown than a dress, but that be what the gentleman want, she say, so I don't complain.

Not even when she leave me.

Not even when there be a knock at the door and he come in with his big black hat and deep black eyes.

He put a satchel down on the little table by the fireplace and take off his hat and smile at nobody. Then he take off his coat, undo his suspenders, and take off his shirt to show he nothing but a mass of scars, dark and darker, shiny and pink some of them, all across his arms and chest. His back been whipped to mounds of tissue, but he don't act like it matter.

Then he turn to me and smile again. The firelight dance in

his eyes. "Good evening," he say, and his voice be deep and rumbling.

"Good evening," I say back.

"What is your name, dear?"

"Fen," I say. My voice sound as small as I feel.

"Fen, how old are you?"

"Ten next month," I tell him proudly.

"Ten next month," he repeat, and chuckle.

And then he at the bed, and he be spreading my legs, and I clamp them shut but he force them wide and run his hands along my knees and thighs and over the insides of my arms.

"Clean," he say to himself. "Clean, like she said."

He let me go and stand up, slipping his suspenders back onto his bare shoulders. "Well, it looks like I'll owe Mama Gentille a little extra tomorrow," he say with a grin. His teeth be white as the moon. "Lie down, little girl."

I can't move, so he slide me up the bed and press me down onto it. Then he open his satchel, remove four leather belts, and use them to strap my wrists and ankles to the bed. I don't fight. I don't know how.

He rip the white dress down the middle and slide it off me. I pull my body in as much as I can, but that ain't much.

He run his hands over my body, and at least they warm.

When he enter me, it be through the skin. First a swift wipe of a cold cotton pad, then a needle, sharp and hot, into the biggest vein of my right arm. I cry out, but don't dare move 'less the needle tear me even more. He be sweating as he pierce my arm, the soft mound of vein inside my right elbow. He stroke my legs as the blood flows out my body into the waiting bags. So red, like rubies in the firelight. He take from me 'til I faint. When I wake up, he do it again.

The next morning, I be told I done well. Alfie give me apple juice but don't ask any questions. Alice take one look at the bandages on my arm and turn away. Mama Gentille take care of me. She soothe my forehead, kiss it, tell me I be the gentleman's favorite, that I be her favorite, and I fall asleep again.

The next night, Mama Gentille let me join the big kids when they dance with her 'round the fire.

She call it religion, say she call down spirits that make you feel so good, like you been lifted up to heaven. The kids say Mama a priestess. That how she keep us safe from hunters and trouble from the tribes. I don't know what it all mean, but if it mean I can get away from the gentleman and his needles, I do it.

I dance, and I don't know if I get lifted up or not. I don't know if I go to heaven. But the stuff she burning make me light-headed, and when the sun come up, I go to sleep for a long, long time.

I do not go back to my duties. I wait two weeks for the gentleman to return. When he do, he take my blood again, from the other side.

"What he do with it?" I ask Mama.

She shake her head. "Drink it? Sell it? I don't know, and I don't care. It be his to do with as he pleases. Bought and paid for. Now, drink this, it will keep your blood thick and strong."

•••

One day, Alice come to me. "I got a secret," she say. "The gentleman like you so much, he done bought you in full."

"I ain't for sale," I say, but it a lie. I been sold and he has me.

We don't leave the cottage for a month. "Like a honeymoon," Mama Gentille say. On the last day of the month, when the man be out and the stew pot be left untended, I wrap my arms around it and hold them there 'til they burned near to the bone. They find me lying on the hearth, bloody and burnt.

The gentleman want his money back. Mama Gentille see it different, though. She say she proud of me. Impressed. She nurse me back to health, tell me it been a test, a trial. I been a good strong girl and I passed it. She sing me to sleep every night, smiling. Only to sell me to the gentleman one last time.

He take me to the cottage when I be out of my mind with fever from the burns. My arms be healing, but they scarred thick for good. He tie me to the bed again, and when he pierce me, it ain't with a needle, but his own hot flesh. When he done, he untie me and shake his head. My legs still be smooth, he say, but it be too easy to kill me, taking blood that way. I ain't worth the trouble when there be a houseful of kids to choose from. When he leave, he don't shut the door.

Mama Gentille don't come for me. The man don't want me. I guess she don't, neither. If this been a test, I guess I failed.

My body be sore, and my arms itch from the burns, but I finally dress myself and go outside. I see Alfie on the back *porch, beating rugs, but he don't see me. Nobody try to stop me, so I walk on away from the house into the bayou.* My name is Fen de la Guerre, *I tell myself.* I am an O-Positive. *I'ma find a tribe, or let the swamp take me. But one thing for sure, I ain't never gonna cry again.*

10

⚜ MAMA GENTILLE.

The church house feel like it shifting beneath me and I come back to myself. Baby Girl wake up and start wailing, but she right to cry. These children be older than Alfie and Alice, but they still belong to Mama. Stupid of me not to see it, but I done swum into a crab trap. Baby Girl and I both as good as dead.

Brother William and Sister Henrietta be at the front of the church now, swaying to the music William be making from a little skin drum. There ain't nothing between me and the exit, but I ain't a fool. If I shinny down that rope right now, guaranteed Mama's people be waiting for me at the bottom. This supposed to be sacred ground, but it a spiderweb. Brother William and Sister Henrietta just be a front, honey to draw the flies.

A woman's voice, deep and strong, come pouring out the back room. I remember that voice in my dreams and it just about stop my heart. The curtain to the kitchen swing open and out come Mama Gentille.

Mama be big as a house, fat and squat, but somehow she feel tall, like she filling the room. That be her mojo rolling off her, her power, rising like heat from a fire off her coffee-brown skin. For the life of me, I can't see how she got here. No way did she come up that rope ladder, 'less she slithered up it like the snake she be.

She look around the room with eyes all painted peacock colors, lips red as blood. Then she see me and she stop singing. She smile wide. Seeing her again set the scars on my arms to itching. I remember what I told myself back then: never let her take nothing from me again.

But here we at.

Mama be wearing one of her crazy muumuus, pieced together from all kinds of fabric. She got on a hat that look like a turban, with feathers and things wrapped up in it. She look ridiculous, like some messed-up bird done fell from the sky. But she ain't nothing to laugh at.

"Fen!" she say in a big voice. She draw out my short little name so it seem like to snap in two. I freeze with Baby Girl in my arms. "Fen de la Guerre," Mama purr and hold a hand out to me. I don't take it. Her eyes drop down to the baby I be holding and she smile.

"Oh, now, Fen, *chère,* don't be like that," she purr in that awful sweet voice. "Mama Gentille be so glad to see you. Her favorite little girl, Fen de la Guerre. How long has it been, child?"

Six years and then some, but I ain't never gonna tell her

that. Not long enough be the real answer. I glare back at her, swallow hard, and stand my ground.

"What you doing in a church, Mama Gentille? You ain't no Christian."

She shrug and reach out to pat my cheek with her fat hand. My skin crawl.

"God a business, just like any other. And occasionally there be blessings, you know? Miracles. Like you being here. And your baby. You came back to Mama Gentille, *ma chère*. After so much time, did you miss your Mama?"

I ignore her question. Mama saved my life, just to throw it away again. Now she got her sights on Baby Girl.

I got to play this right if we gettin' out of here okay. What I need be time to think. "Ain't no miracle," I tell her. I drop my arm, let the sling take the baby's weight. I be reaching for my knife.

"Fen, girl, what you doing? This a house of the Lord," Mama say. I see her face go hard when she look at my burnt-up arms, and she cluck her tongue. I turn my arm out at the elbow, let her see how she ain't never gonna get another pint from me again. The wounds done healed and kept me safe from other needles, but safe be a relative thing.

Her face go sour, but then she laugh. "You was strong, girl. Strong like your Mama Gentille. I thought you was something special, 'til you let that man use you like that. Let him take away your power. Now look at you, underfed with some bastard whelp in your arms. Fen, Fen, Fen. You could have been mambo after me." She shake her head and turn away.

This be the woman behind the freesteader nursery? I know what she doing to them kids. I spit to get the bile outta my throat. It land on the bare wood planks with a smack. Mama Gentille recoil in disgust.

"You lose your manners," she drawl, and cut me a look that once upon a time I'da tried hard to dodge.

"I ain't never been your girl, Mama Gentille," I tell her. "I just been your slave."

Mama Gentille smile and use her wide shoe to smear my spit on the floor. "Now, Fen, we talked about this. There ain't no slaves in Orleans. Only them as know they place, and them what's got to be told." She say the last word with emphasis, and it take a lot to keep me standing right there, two feet from her, instead of trying to run.

"Now." She clap her hands. "Sit down. The second service be about to begin." She return to the pulpit, and Brother William bring out a big chair woven from dried vines. She settle herself and start singing.

One thing about Mama Gentille, she ain't no Christian woman, but she something, all right. She talk to spirits the way them Ursulines pray to they crucified god, but Mama's spirits, or loas, help her get her way like I ain't never seen other gods do. Mama be a true priestess, a mambo.

I look around and everyone be swaying in they seats, all except the smuggler. Slowly, slowly, the drums start to rise and Mama take off her turban, letting her hair swing down. Her hair be long and black like she got Indian blood in her, it so shiny and thick. Brother William take that button-up shirt off and I can see his ribs and the needle marks on his arms. He and Henrietta spread out and Mama Gentille start to say something, but my ears be full of the sound of my own heartbeat now. I know what she be doing even before Henrietta jerk to the center of the circle. Mama worship something between spirits and gods. She can bring them loas down from the air into a body. I seen it when I been with her. I ain't never wanted to see it again.

Henrietta come out to the center of they raggedy circle and sweep her arms down to the floor, then up to the sky. She be moaning when she do it, and it got a rhythm, the same rhythm coming from the drums, from the swaying, from Mama Gentille. I be scared now like I ain't been in years.

Mama take blood from children for selling and trading. She use folks up gentlelike, for years, 'til they run dry. Then she give them to her loas. Them loas climb up and ride a body the way some folks ride a horse or donkey. They climb inside and take over, use a body to walk the earth. Henrietta about to be ridden by a god.

I can't move. Incense be thick in the room now, and I be caught up in the trance like everybody else. It hard not to watch, like seeing a snake in front of you about to strike. Behind her pulpit, Mama Gentille smile, big and wide. She rise up and sway her hips left and right. She the mambo in this house and she be in charge of everything, and everyone.

Mama Gentille run her ring-covered fingers down her plump brown arms, shaking her hips as she dance. It give me a shiver to see it. For all the folks she done bled, nobody ever done bled Mama. She say that why she such a powerful mambo now. When I burnt my own arms, she seen it as a sign of power. She think I been something special. A daughter, or an heir. But then she gave me to the gentleman, I guess to see what I would do. I didn't fight him, though. He used me up and I ran away.

I shake my head to clear it, and look around. I ain't a little kid no more. I learned how to fight. Across the floor, Henrietta be stalking around, proud as a peacock. She strut past Mama Gentille, who reach beneath the altar and pull out a bowl of stew. She call to Henrietta's loa, "Ibo Lele," and hand him a bowl of stew. Henrietta smile wide, so wide her face almost split in two. I guess Ibo Lele be pleased.

This a bad night for being here, with the spirits swinging low to earth this close to All Saints' Day. I feel myself moving forward, drawn to the circle, drawn by the drugs in the food and the incense in the air. By the power. I try to fight it, but even Mama Gentille going under, pulled down by her own spell.

Mama's head jerk up, her eyes roll back in her head, and she boom in a voice like thunder. I try to run, but my eyes be closing. My legs feel heavy unless they moving to the beat, my body weighed down unless I be dancing. So easy to let go, to let the spirit ride me. When the loas come up over you, it take you out of yourself, out of Orleans for a little while, and it feel so good. I ain't felt good in a long time. I want to lay this baby on the floor and let the spirit take me. That be all I gotta do. Just let Lydia's baby go.

11

⚜ THE RAIN WAS COMING DOWN SOFT AND warm. The smell of heated pavement rose up, wet and mineral, from the broken road. Daniel kept his eyes on the ground. The humidity fogged his face mask and the rain dotted his vision with tiny magnifying droplets, giving him a sense of vertigo. Evening was falling fast. He adjusted his goggles for lower light, his breath heaving like a bellows in his ears. The Superdome was ahead of him, where Poydras Street was partially blocked by a wall of debris. According to the datalink, he needed to go west of the Dome, into Uptown. But the Superdome was an icon of old New Orleans—the defining silhouette of the city's skyline, the sports stadium that had housed thousands of football games and concerts in its heyday. Now that he was here, he couldn't help but take a look.

A causeway of broken concrete had been laid out like a dam, a crossing for the earliest funeral parades. At LaSalle

Street, the young river that was the far end of Poydras became a pond. He could see the dull grayish sheen of the water up ahead as he came down the road. And then he saw the memorials, like faces of the dead peering up out of the water—masques made for Mardi Gras of years past sunken beneath the surface as if pulled under by mermaids or undines.

The Drowned Dead, names painted lovingly along the cheeks and brows on the masques, slowly deteriorated beneath the muck. It accounted for the milky quality of the water leaking from the pond into the river stream. Daniel had mistaken it for silt of some sort, minor pollution. But it was the face paint and the decorations of these memorial masques, washed away by the gentle lapping of the dammed pond.

Thirty thousand people had huddled inside the Superdome after the first of the big storms. Katrina turned the Dome into a refugee camp. Lorenzo turned it into a morgue. Jesus turned it into a tomb.

INQUIRY: Number of dead buried in the Dome?
RESPONSE: The New Orleans Superdome can seat up to seventy-two thousand people. Number of dead unknown.

The street was wide and exposed. Daniel was grateful that the sun had set, leaving a dim twilight through the fading rain. He had no desire to run into any of the locals. He reached the causeway, the peaked tumble of rocks and debris that blocked the flow of water and lead across Poydras to the ramps of the Dome. Daniel looked at the footing, the tiny slides where the rocks were unevenly stacked. Marking his path, he hauled himself up to the crest. The path was surprisingly even on top. For a moment, he could picture the long line of mourners two-stepping beside the shrouded bodies.

Wide enough for a parade, he thought.

The Dome loomed above him like a poached egg in a cup. The top was shattered, tapped by a giant spoon. He picked his way across the bridge to where the old wheelchair ramps led up to one of the double-wide entrances.

"It weren't no parade," the smuggler had told him when Daniel first commented on it, six months ago in that small bayfront divers' bar on the Chesapeake. "They started piling bodies to keep down the rot. The Dome had generators and air-conditioning back then, so they ran it high like a refrigerator and kept bringing them in."

"It wasn't done second line, like New Orleans used to do?" Daniel had asked. He had seen footage of the funerals, tearful black-draped crowds on the way up the slope, cheerful dancing mourners on the way back. It was this second line of partiers, often strangers joining the dance, that gave the marches their name. They carried feathered umbrellas and were led by jazz bands. One news story had shown a photograph of a woman, mascara running with tears as they carried her husband and child into the Dome. The headline had read RESILIENT—THE SOUTH WILL RISE AGAIN. The woman was quoted as saying Jesus had risen on the third day, and for New Orleans, the third day was coming.

"Hell, no," the smuggler had cursed. "That was a show

for the reporters, something the mayor and the governor fixed up. By the end of it, there weren't no coffins or nothing, just bodies, wrapped in a sheet if they had it, and when the bodies got too high, they sealed the doors and built a ramp around the building like this." He waved his hand in the air in a zigzag motion.

Daniel saw the ramp now, a pebbled sort of beige concrete that rose in a graceful series of slopes up the side of the Dome.

"You see, they couldn't use the door anymore," the smuggler had explained. "Bodies. All the way to the top, bodies."

No one held burials here today. "They just dump 'em in the swamps now," the smuggler had said. "Let the river take 'em." Practical, Daniel thought. He thought of the funeral he held for his brother, Charlie. No parades or bright music there. Few flowers, fewer people. After burying so many Fever victims, funerals had become smaller. More affordable.

What am I doing here? Daniel asked himself. But he knew the answer. Daniel was here to save the world. So no one else would have to lose their little brother to this disease. But such ambitions needed support, research, evidence. And then there was also morbid curiosity. Orleans was a necropolis, a city of the dead. He wanted to see it for what it was.

He had gone no more than a quarter of the way around the Dome when it drifted toward him, above the hum of the wind, from somewhere inside the Dome. Singing. Girls' voices, or maybe young boys. High and sweet, like a Christmas choir. Daniel froze. Was it possible that his encounter suit had already been compromised? That he'd contracted Delta Fever? That he was hallucinating and this venture into

Orleans would be the death of him? Then he saw the lights up ahead, so small they might have been fireflies or a sprinkle of powder on a length of black velvet.

The Dome was as wide as a city block, and while the sidewalks had once been broad to accommodate the crowds of concertgoers and sports fans, they were now broken and shadowed, treacherous to cross. Daniel dialed his goggles up and hugged the bulging side of the Dome.

Just at the edge of the building's curve were a pair of double doors. A flare of little lights, bright green dots, danced along his vision, and he adjusted his goggles again. The battered doors had been pulled apart, rust settled into the scratches. They were standing wide open, and a line of people was flowing inside. They couldn't see him, he was sure. But the candles they held, tall white columns clutched in both hands before them, and their few torches flared in his night-vision goggles. He blinked, dazzled. Women. Wearing simple gowns of white cloth, veils of the same material draped over their hair like brides, like ghosts. And in their wake, a line of young girls carrying flowers.

Daniel's heart leapt in his chest. His mind staggered, wrestling with what he was seeing. In the heart of a dead, diseased city, here was a group of women and little girls. They bore no weapons, only flowers and candles. They were defenseless, vulnerable. And yet they survived.

A second thought occurred to him. These women and girls had to be Delta Fever carriers, every last one of them. You could not live in Orleans without contracting some form of the disease. And here he was, with a weapon in his bag that could kill them all. Daniel began to sweat beneath the skin of his encounter suit. He'd thought the entire city was a tomb, but Orleans was clearly very much alive.

INQUIRY: Are there nuns in Orleans?

Daniel shook his head. The question sounded wild, even to him. But the datalink did not judge.

RESPONSE: Historically, there were several orders of nuns within the city limits of New Orleans. Most famously, the Ursuline Sisters, overseers of the Ursuline Academy, the oldest Catholic school in the United States. When the Holy See pulled its resources out of the Gulf Coast, the Ursulines were the only sisterhood that remained. Their motto: *Serviam,* I will serve. Current status of the Ursulines is unknown.

Daniel took a deep breath. *Serviam.* That is what he was doing here, too. But he couldn't let himself be seen, even by a group of nuns who clearly had more bravery than the rest of the Roman Catholic Church combined. He looked at his chronometer. He had been in the heart of the city for almost four hours. Daniel steadied himself and leaned back against the rough, pebbled wall of the Superdome. He would wait for the nuns to leave.

As the evening moved toward midnight, he heard the nuns leaving the building. When the last candle disappeared into the night, he knew he should leave, too. But he couldn't simply walk away. Where common sense left off, curiosity stepped in. As a scientist, it was the fuel that drove him.

Daniel retraced the nuns' path, back to the entrance of the Dome. The doors had been shut, but they hadn't sealed closed, thanks to the crowbars that had originally pried them open. He turned up his night vision, peeled back the door with a loud scrape on the pavement, and entered.

The night-vision goggles were not enough. Even they needed a light source to draw from, no matter how slight. Daniel pulled a glow stick from his pocket, adjusted his vision, and snapped it on, flooding the corridor with a sickly green light. He found an archway leading into the stadium down a flight of wide stairs, and his footsteps echoed hollowly. As he entered the stadium proper, he gasped.

A cool smattering of starlight filtered in ever so faintly from the gash in the ceiling of the Dome, but what it illuminated was no lye pit, no holocaustic vision of piled corpses. He turned in a slow circle, noting every row, every seat in his range of vision. Occupied. By bones.

Tens of thousands of seats, row upon row, and on each plastic chair, a carefully stacked set of bones, with the skull on top. A second skull rested before bones on the floor beneath every seat. Flowers had been placed at the base of each skeleton, a cross painted on the forehead of each skull, like a marking of ash at the start of Lent. The Ursuline Sisters had turned the Superdome into a catacomb.

Daniel sat down heavily on the stairs and hung his head. He did not dare walk down the aisles for fear of disturbing the bones. The flowers were fading where he sat, but he imagined somewhere they were fresh. How long must it have taken? You could not replace a hundred forty thousand flowers in a single night.

Below, in the green sweep of the field, more bones were piled. Daniel shivered inside his encounter suit. He felt like a grave robber in an ancient pyramid and wondered briefly if there were curses laid on this place, too. He laughed to himself. The sound echoed loudly around him, then faded as the enormous stadium swallowed the noise.

He patted his coat pocket with the vials inside, his own Pandora's box. How many more Orleanians could it kill? Daniel's body ached as the enormity of his journey overcame him. It was too much. He turned and remounted the stairs, going back the way he had come.

Where were the lye vats, he wondered, that had allowed the nuns to strip those drowned and fevered corpses into gleaming white piles of bone? He scraped the door shut and made his way across the broken pavement to Poydras Street. Despite his night vision, he lost his footing and splashed into the little pond where the masques for the dead lay submerged. Cursing silently, he hurried on, hoping he hadn't been heard. The city rose and fell around him, scorched brick, shattered plaster, and gleaming shards of ancient broken glass.

He hurried into the shadows of a nearby building, an ancient parking structure, its levels collapsing one on the other, a layer of algae and thick black mildew blooming across the face of it. Behind him, the street was empty. He scurried on, hauling his bag behind him, terror rising in him like he'd never felt before. For all the risks he took in the lab, handling virulent strains of Fever, Daniel had never been afraid. But this was not a laboratory, or even a civilized city. It was more alien than any place he'd ever been. He would return to the building with the tree in its center, take his jetskip, and go home.

He fled.

Half an hour later, Daniel could see the ruined building that held his jetskip in the distance. He would sleep, just long enough to handle the trip back across the Wall. Then he would go. He took a deep breath to steady himself and picked his way out into the broken lane.

"Run, run, run, fast as you can," a voice said softly behind him.

Daniel froze, and they were on him. Leper or no leper, they grabbed him, dragged him down. Not innocent young girls with flowers, not nuns in veils and white dresses. These were men. Large, scarred men, draped in coats over thick canvas overalls.

Broken teeth gleamed in the moonlight, half hidden by rough beards and twisted leers. Chains wrapped around Daniel's gloved wrists, snagging his datalink, pinching him even through the encounter suit. He yelled in fear, praying that the ragged leper disguise would do its work and save him. But it did not.

12

⚜ MY KNEES BEND AND I BE ALMOST TO THE ground when Baby Girl start to scream. It sound like the Devil himself be screaming. A spike of fear shoot through me like lightning through a dry tree. This be Lydia's baby. She ain't mine to give away.

I stand up and pull Baby Girl closer to me, bouncing her as I come awake, her screams clearing my head. She ain't gonna die here. Ain't gonna be one of Mama's babies, sold for blood and sex and magic, any more than I am. So close to the circle now we almost in it, I can see they all be gone, carried away on whatever Mama's religion done to them. Even Mama be gone, rattling in her throat like to beat a storm down, smiling up at the sky.

When I duck under her arms, nobody try to stop me. Then we in the kitchen of the church, not more than a little room with a chimney hole over the cookstove, open to the night sky. And a door in the back. I open it real slow.

A rope bridge lead from the tree house to a nearby tree and switch back three times to the ground. That be how Mama Gentille made it up here. I tug at the bridge, tied to hooks in the doorway. Easy up, easy down. They can cut it loose if need be, and tie it up again. I go back to the kitchen and find a knife, still smeared with sweet potato and bits of pheasant meat. I don't bother to wipe it off, just stick it through my belt behind my back, where Baby Girl can't reach it. Then I tie her on tight and grip both sides of the bridge as I make my way to the ground.

Nobody waiting for us here. If there a guard, he at the rope ladder 'neath the tree. It be true dark now, and I know we be hard to see. If we keep quiet, maybe we get past them. The swaying of the bridge sound natural, like a cradle in the breeze. Then I be off the bridge with dirt under my feet instead of air. It feel good to be on solid ground again, even if the night be cold enough to bite after the warmth of the church.

We lucky to be alive, I know. I don't take it for granted. I walk a ways from the church, 'til I know no one will hear me, and then I run.

It be past midnight when I stop to find another hidey-hole, a foxhole like the one I avoided earlier in favor of the church. I won't make that mistake again. Mr. Go's place be better, but I'm like to fall down tired if I keep going.

Baby Girl stop crying, my running done took her breath away. But she still ain't been fed. Now that I stop running, she catching her breath, maybe to start up hollering again.

Quick as I can, I mix another bottle to keep her happy, and it work. She drink and I burp her. She close her eyes. I draw my legs in under the side of the fallen tree, drag some leaves and moss in around us. That'll make a good diaper for her in the morning. But not now. I be too tired.

I watch her for a while, and then my eyes close, too.

I be at the cottage again, hidden in the woods. Lovely, dark and deep, like that poem Daddy used to read. I got a vine in my hands and I be skipping it the way Mama say they used to skip rope. She got me singing a song she taught me about a mama chewing tobacco. It make me laugh, and she laugh with me. Mama got a young voice when she laugh, but her eyes, they old. She use them when she look at Daddy, and he look at her the same way, and I wonder why. But now I know why.

I wake up. Nightfall come thick in the woods. Farther out there be starlight and the sky be almost white it so heavy with stars. I wish we be lying out beneath the stars now. I'd see if I could remember they names. But I be here in the dark with a crying baby what woke me. It ain't safe to have a child crying in the dark when there be more than animals about.

So I mix her another bottle of formula fast as I can, and I spill some of it 'cause I be moving too fast. It cold, but she take it anyhow. We both cold, too, and I can't stop shivering. We might die out here, Lydia's baby and me. I could make it on my own. I wouldn't be so stupid if I didn't have this baby. This little screaming baby that don't know how alone she really be. 'Til I get this baby out of Orleans, we be freesteaders. And freesteaders don't stay free for long.

Like I called bad luck down on me, I hear a rustle in the woods, and another, and it be fast and low and I know they be dogs this time, real blood hounds, like the ones missing last night. Now they back to claim what be theirs. I stay in my foxhole, so scared I almost pee myself. My hands be shivering all over when I take away the baby's bottle and put it in my waistband, ready to run.

Lord, oh Lord, help me. I crouch there in a sweat, baby crushed against my chest.

"No point in running when the dogs come," Daddy told me. "They'll only eat you alive."

Last time I ran, I didn't get eaten. But that 'cause they been too busy eating someone else.

I look down at Baby Girl, snuggled up against me. I want to run so bad, but she so tiny. Too tiny to hold the dogs off me for long. Then I close my eyes and feel hot all over, I'm so ashamed. Lydia ask me to look after her. I ain't gonna throw her away.

The dogs almost here, men, too. I climb out of our foxhole so they don't let the hounds drag me out. I sit on the fallen log, and when the dogs come I stand up, waiting. They snarl and snap, but they know not to bite. Blood hounds don't attack prey 'less it run from them too far. Blood hunters don't waste blood.

Baby Girl done eating and now she asleep up against me without a care in the world. I silently tell Lydia I've given her a few more seconds of life. Best I can do. A man step out from behind a tree, and there be three more with him, in long oilskin coats and low-brimmed hats. The first man, a big man, he got himself a whip and a length of chain. He grin at me around a chicory cigar, and I wrinkle my nose at the bitter stench of it. That make him grin even wider.

"What have we here?" he ask his friends. "An O-Positive, if the dogs are right. That was an OP howl, weren't it, Vancey?"

Vancey, a skinny fellow with skin that look yellow even in the blue moonlight, nod and grin with teeth the same shade as his skin. "That right, Orvis. We'll test 'er at camp to be sure."

"And a brat, too." He shoo the dogs away and clasp the chains to my wrists where they be cradling Lydia's baby. He peel my hands away and look into the sling. "A new one. Fresh blood. Maybe not even the Delta taint. We can sell that for twice the price."

"Three times," Vancey say, excited.

My mind be racing. Baby Girl ain't got to worry about growing up in Orleans no more. They gonna keep her alive for two weeks, just to drain her dry.

I don't cry about it. I don't scream. I don't fight them, neither. Lydia told me to care for her baby, and look at me now. Good as dead, and sooner if I fight. So when they pull that chain, I walk after them. I follow and I stay quiet when they tie me to two others they found. In the dark, it be hard to see, but one of them a freesteader, sure as can be. He got a look, like he still surprised it finally happened to him. The other I don't recognize. He wrapped all up in rags and look like a leper, like what the Ursuline Sisters tend to in the Quarter by the Market. I stay as far from that one as the chains will let me.

Maybe we be dead in an hour, maybe in a week or two, but as long as I be healthy and upright, I can survive.

I have to.

13

WE WALK OR GET DRAGGED THROUGH THE woods, dogs nipping at our heels if we stumble. Jesus help me, Jesus. My mouth be sour, but I pray anyway, like the Ursulines. Suddenly, I smell wood smoke and cooking meat and my mouth be watering even though I don't want it to, and there be another smell beneath the charred wood. Baby Girl wrinkle her nose, even in her sleep, and I know she smell it, too.

Blood. Sweet and hot, rotting and cold. Lots of it. I fall to my knees and vomit nothing but water. The hunters curse at me, but it still a minute before I move. I shake and shudder. Then I get up and they march me into the blood farm.

The camp look like Hell. All Saints' Day be starting early at the blood farm. They be cooking up a storm, a whole row of cook fires at one end of the camp. Fire after fire, and them cooks be the Devil's handmaidens, stirring pots full of souls. Uncle Romulus told me stories when I been younger. How the Devil live in these woods and he out hunting for people. Daddy tell me, too, but he say the Devil ain't real. He say the Devil a man just like everybody else. But I don't know for sure. Standing here seeing them faces, pale in the yellow light, maybe they ain't all human. I know we ain't human to them.

It look like a real farm here—buildings made of wood, likely cypress. Most other wood don't stand up to the weather here, and these look like they been here a long time. I know I be right when we pass a sign, half broken and lying in the weeds, that say, HENNESEY DAIRY FARM—DRINK MILK, IT'S GOOD FOR YOU!

The stench get worse as we get closer, but you'd think the hunters can't smell it, they so pleased with theyselves. They be grinning as they pull us through the gates. We pass them cook fires so close, I see the meat roasting—rabbit and pheasant on spits, pots on the boil full of crawfish and shrimp. Enough food for a hundred people at least. More than our camp, even on a feast day. I wonder what they be celebrating, but I keep my mouth shut. The leper be the one who ask.

"What's the occasion?"

I glance at him in spite of myself. He got a funny accent, flat like standing water. He not from the Delta. Not from Orleans, anyway. Maybe they sound like that down in Florida, or out Texas way.

"The occasion?" the tall hunter ask, the one they been calling Orvis. "Shoot, we throwin' a party for you!" He do a little dance then, like them beggars at the Market, and I'd laugh if I didn't want him dead.

A woman come out from behind the cook fires, a big old spoon in one hand and a chalkboard in the other.

"Orvis, you late again."

"Sure am, Maylene. Saving the best for last."

Maylene look like she heard this from him before. She snort and push some blond hair out her face. She be bleaching it for sure. Her skin be too dark for blond hair.

"What you bring me, a leper?" she say, scowling. "A leper and two skinny kids too small to fill a drip bag."

"Aw, Maylene. Use your imagination. Once you fatten 'em up, who knows how much sauce they'll pump. And I got you something special, since you so special to me," Orvis say. He yank me forward with a pull on the chain.

"Look at that, wrapped up neat as a present." Maylene come closer and squint at me like she need glasses. I stare her down, but she ain't looking at me no more.

"Girl, how old that baby?"

I don't say nothing. Why make it easy? They gonna test her blood, anyway.

She snort at me and shake her head. "What's with this one? She on drugs? Ain't you look at her?" She yank one of my arms away from the baby and hold it up in the firelight. "Scorched all up and down. No good for blood, lessen you wanna take it from the throat and be done with her."

I swallow hard and pull my arm back.

Maylene shrug and turn to Orvis. "Stable 'em and feed 'em. Bring the boy to the workhouse. We'll build him up mucking the latrines. Have 'em test the girl for drugs, then stick her in the brothel. Take the baby to the nursery. We'll handle 'em from there."

Brothel. My flesh crawl and my stomach clench tight. Once be more than enough for me. I feel the bile rise in my mouth again but I hold it down. Ain't gonna do me no good. I just have to see what I got to deal with when I get there.

Orvis tug at the chains and unlock the boy, but they still be cuffs around his wrists. The skinny hunter, Vancey, lead him away. That boy don't look at me when he go, but I hope he able to escape somehow.

"Where do you want the leper?" Orvis ask.

Maylene shrug again. "He ain't contagious long as you don't kiss him. Put him in with the girl, lot seventeen. We're full up this morning. You took too long."

Orvis nod and reach for Lydia's baby, and suddenly, something snap in me. I be so cold and tired and scared, I can't stop it. I start to scream.

"What's a matter with her?" Orvis ask.

Maylene wave her hands and walk away.

Baby Girl start wailing, too, 'cause I be holding her too tight. She be the last bit of life I got left to me. Tomorrow we both be bleeding or dead. I know it, and maybe she sense it, too. We be screeching like owls. The hunter haul off and slap me 'cross the face.

I stop screaming then, but tears be coming as much from pain as from fear. He reach out and start to tug the baby from me, but then he stop.

"Christ, this bitch is pouring milk all over the place," he

say. I know my shirt be wet from Baby Girl's formula, but I let him think it.

Orvis look at me, then Maylene, but she already gone back to her pots and fires. "Feed your damn baby," he say to me in disgust. "We'll take her later."

I clutch Baby Girl to me like she my lifeline and nod. He march me, the baby, and the leper toward one of the little barns, a dirty white block with a shingle roof and a number painted on the side: 17.

14

✤ *"THE FIRST RULE OF ESCAPE: ASSESS YOUR situation."*

Daddy be pacing the floor of the cottage like it a classroom. I ain't been to the nuns' school since I been tiny small, but now I listen to Daddy. He a good teacher and he be teaching me how to survive.

"Look around you, Fen, know your situation. Then identify your assets. Anything that can help you escape."

I be looking to escape, to get outside in the sunshine to play, but Daddy say this ain't a game. This be serious. It be serious all the time, and I don't like it, so I say so. Daddy get real close and bend down and look me in the face, and his eyes so big and dark, I can see my whole head in them. He say, "Baby Girl, this is life or death we are talking here. I know those are big ideas for a little thing like you, but that's what we are up against." He pull me into a close hug then, so tight, it like to break my arms, and I hug him back just to get him to loosen his grip. I don't know why, but for some reason, I start to cry.

Baby Girl be crying again, bringing me back to myself. She screaming in my arms, and I know I been hurting her. I tell myself to let her go, to relax my fingers from digging into her through the swaddling. It take a long minute or two, but I finally let her breathe and lay her down on the floor.

My chest be so cold from her not being there that I start to shiver again. A song come to mind, one my mama used to sing me to sleep. I sing it now to calm Baby Girl, and maybe myself, too. We got to both keep it together if we getting out of here alive.

I look around. We in a white room, maybe twelve feet by fifteen, maybe less. There be small windows in the shorter walls, set high and covered with wire instead of glass. The sky be turning gray through them windows. If I strain, it enough light to see by. Sunrise not too far away. There be one wooden door in a long wall, with a lock I seen on the outside and metal bars across. There be hay in the room, spread on the floor for sleeping. I be in one corner, on the floor with the baby. They took my pack, but I still have a bottle wrapped in my waistband. The leper be leaning his back up against the far wall, looking like he already dead. May as well be, with the disease in his blood. Hunters'll kill him the minute the fire's hot enough.

Baby Girl stop crying. I turn my back so the leper think I be breast-feeding her. I give her the bottle and try to concentrate.

The first rule of escape: Assess your situation.

We in a room; but a room within a room, like a closet almost. They walked us through the main building when they brought us in here. It be like a hospital out there, beds set up three in a row, with silver stands next to each one. They be running the generators here night and day to keep that equipment running.

A locked room in a building on a blood farm. And it close to morning. The hunters go out at night, so soon they be going to bed and nothing but a few folks be awake, the blood workers running they tests and sorting they catch. Technicians. Maybe we can get by them. And the dogs. Dogs got to sleep, too. And they be locking them up for sure, so they won't go harassing the captives.

The second rule of escape: Assess your assets.

I got two legs and two arms that work, so that be something. They took the chains off when they threw us in here. I got a half-empty bottle of baby formula. I got a shirt tied into a sling, and a baby. I got some hay, and that about it. Not a lot to go on.

Then a cough come from the other side of the room and I remember I got one other thing. I got the leper.

His coughing make me cringe, and I think maybe I can use him like a weapon. But he got to want to help me. If he know they going to burn him up, he'll help. He got to know.

"Eh," I say. "*Eh la bas.*" Don't know if he speak the patois or no, but he look up at me and his rags be coming off his face, and in the pale gray dawn I see what I ain't seen by firelight. Now I know why his voice sound so flat. He not a leper. He a smuggler.

I hiss at him. "Hey," I call, quiet in case they be listening at the door. He ain't been coughing 'cause he sick, but 'cause he been crying. His rags slide off his face and I see he ain't got a nose showing because he in an encounter suit, filtering his voice and the air he breathing. I seen it with McCallan.

McCallan. That old bastard supposed to bring me clean blood. If he had, maybe Lydia be alive now. The thought make my stomach hurt. I feel a tear drop and it hit Lydia's baby on the cheek. She wiggle when she feel it. I wipe it away and don't let another fall. Smugglers be users, people who know what we need and make us pay for it *chère*. Too dear, sometime.

The smuggler quit his crying now, and it be sounding like static coming from his suit. He safe inside there, even crying like that and letting his nose run. Supposed to protect from the Fever, keep they blood clean, too, so they ain't be detected by chemical sniffers along the Wall. They can smell Delta Fever in you, even through an encounter suit. Enough fools found that out trying to cross the Wall in earlier days. But if you ain't got the Fever, the suit can keep you clean.

Blood hunters won't burn a smuggler. And they don't hardly ever use them for farming, neither. They too valuable a resource, able to get across the Wall, provide things we ain't got here. There be fewer smugglers these days, so this one be worth that much more if he go free. He just gotta show that suit and he can make a deal to walk. It be a wonder he don't know it. But maybe he afraid they take his suit. And then he be exposed, toxic like the rest of us, and he die anyway. That an asset for me, then. He still got a reason to be afraid.

I put Baby Girl in the sling and cradle her with me when I creep over to see him.

"*Eh la bas*," I say again real low. He be looking at me as I crab-crawl across the floor. I don't want to stand up 'less they see me through them windows. I crawl over and sit next to him on the floor. "*Ça va?*"

He stare at me, tilting his head like he listening to someone that ain't here. Then he sit up. "Yes?"

His voice pop a little like static.

"Hey, mister, you want to get out of here?"

The smuggler nod.

"Then we got to work together."

He hesitate, then nod again. "What's your name?"

I look at him and shake my head. A name ain't gonna save my skin. "You want to leave, we leave together. What you got?"

He stare at me like he don't understand, and I point to his coat, his rags, the pockets I can see in the dawning light. "What you got?" I ask again.

He follow my gaze and I see he understand. "Uh . . . a datalink, my suit. A compass and a chronometer." He look worried. "They took my duffel, and the rest of my gear is, uh . . . elsewhere."

I crab-walk back to my corner to think. He start to follow, but I wave him away. A compass and a watch ain't much, but they be assets, too. A datalink. We don't got that in Orleans, so I don't know what to make of it.

"Eh, mister, what the datalink do?" I whisper to him.

He push up his coat sleeve and show me a sheet of black plastic wrapped around his wrist like a cuff. "It's a computer. It translates for me, analyzes things, and acts as a guidebook."

"It got a rescue beacon?" I seen beacons in the bayou sometimes, marked with a smuggler's sign. If they left behind, it 'cause the smuggler either been rescued or they dead, but every smuggler got at least one, if he smart and he work with a team.

His face fall. "No. It's not a transmitter, just a guidebook. And a translator."

I shake my head. No use to me. I speak patois, French, English, and some Chinese and whatnot from trading with the Asians in Shangri-Lo. I be learning Spanish. And I know the city better than some. A rescue beacon be worth all that right now, but it ain't what we got.

The baby kick in my lap and I see she made a mess in her diaper. She be too young for it to stink yet, but it black and sticky. I wipe her down with a strip of my sack shirt and replace the moss with a rolled-up piece of sack.

The third rule of escape: Assess your weaknesses.

Well, I got a baby. I got a smuggler who be as useless as a baby. I ain't eaten proper since I vomited up that stew. I got no food and no diapers. And we running out of time. There got to be something else.

"What they call you?" I ask the smuggler.

He look surprised. "Daniel," he say without even thinking.

"Daniel and the lions' den."

"What?"

"That story, Daniel and the lions' den. He be thrown to the lions for keeping his faith, but they won't eat him 'cause he been doing right by his god."

Daniel sort of shudders and I think he laughing. "That's supposed to comfort me?"

I shrug. "Only if you doing right."

"What's your baby's name?" he ask. He be relaxing more, thinking I got a plan. I look down at Baby Girl and shake my head.

"Don't know yet." There a lot I don't know about Baby Girl right now. I don't even know if she an OP like me. She could take after her daddy, and I ain't knowing who he be, either.

"How old is she?" he ask. I know he being polite, but I ain't gonna say. Maybe he help me out of here, or maybe he just use me to get free. I sure be using him if I find a way. They won't know Baby Girl clean 'til they type her. That buy me some time.

He see me staring him down and look away. "It would be good to know a lion right now," he say. That make me snort. Then I think of what he say about his equipment.

"What you smuggling? Something worth a trade? Them hunters have lots of needs you can negotiate."

Daniel shake his head. "It's not like that. I—I'm not a smuggler. I'm . . ." He look at his lap and I feel my belly go sour.

"You a tourist? You buy a suit and come over the Wall for vacation?" I don't sound angry, but I am. I'ma die a blood slave, and this fool over here on holiday. Him and his damn fool datalink. If it ain't gonna call for help, it no use to us.

132

"I'm not a tourist," he say defiantly.

"Then what?"

He drop his head back against the wall and look up at the ceiling. "It's a long story," he say.

"You got somewhere to be?"

He straighten up. "Yes. Do you have a way out of here?"

I think of Daddy's lessons, and the rules of escaping, and how I just got myself a new asset. "Yeah."

"Care to share?"

I bounce Baby Girl on my knee. She fed and she be falling asleep again. The sun be rising, and soon it be full morning. "Everybody in bed now but the day shift. They doctors, nurses, not the big men. When they open that door, we going to walk out."

"How are we going to do that?"

"Easy," I tell him. "You a leper, and I got a baby. Do what I tell you when I say. Then we just gotta wait."

15

✦ DANIEL HAD HIS OWN WAY OUT. IT CAME IN SIX vials tucked away in his coat. If he just opened one of the vials and waited, it would kill everyone in this compound—the blood hunters, the other prisoners. The girl. Her baby. Everyone except him. One little vial and Daniel could go free. Part of him was almost scared enough to do it. He didn't owe Orleans anything. They were all as good as dead here anyway. He still had his work to do. He could return home and spend the rest of his life tucked away in a lab, looking for the cure, like so many great scientists before him. All he had to do was wipe the slate clean.

But he couldn't. Because there was a baby, and a girl. And enough dead in Orleans already. He almost wept in relief when she said she had a plan.

The girl looked so unconcerned, sitting there like this was an everyday occurrence for her, being kidnapped in the middle of the night. But maybe this was normal in Orleans.

Daniel thought over the girl's plan. It might work, but he doubted it. There were too many people with a reason to stop them for it to be that easy.

And even if it did work, what good would it do him? They had crossed the river getting here. He would never find his way to the Institute or the Wall on his own. He needed more information, or escape was moot.

"Where are we?" he asked the girl, hoping he didn't sound too desperate. If she thought she had something over him, it could make things more difficult.

The girl stuck her chin out, jabbing it toward the datalink cuff around his wrist. "Ain't that tell you?"

He shook his head. His maps were limited to the city, not wherever this place was, across the river.

"We in Algiers, best I can say. Edge of East Orleans."

Daniel tried to access his maps for anything outside the city center. Nothing came up. He sighed and hoped the girl was willing to bargain. "I'm looking for a place called the Institute of Post-Separation Studies. Have you heard of it? Can you take me there?"

The girl stared at him for a beat, then shook her head, laughing. "Boy, I got my own troubles. I ain't no tour guide."

Daniel clenched his fist in frustration. "I'll trade for it. I have supplies."

The look she gave him was appraising, but not friendly. "What you got you think I need?"

Daniel shrugged. "All sorts of things—bottled water, food packs. Clothes. I could give you a new shirt."

For the first time, the girl seemed to notice she was half

naked, with nothing more than a cloth sack for a shirt. She stuck her chin out defiantly. "Don't see none of that on you."

"Well, not on me. I left my stash in a building across the river, west of here. I don't have maps of this area. If . . . if we get out of here, and you take me to the Institute, then we can go to my stash and I'll give you whatever you need."

The girl snorted and looked away. She was just some dumb kid, Daniel realized. She'd probably never even heard of the Institute, let alone know how to get there.

"The Professors be all but dead," she said finally. Her eyes focused on him. Maybe she wasn't so dumb after all. "What you want with them?"

"That's . . . that's my business," he said. "The Institute? That's where these Professors live?"

"And die, too," she said. "Ain't no help for you there. Besides, that a long way to go for nothing but a new shirt. That ain't reason enough."

What else could he offer her? What more could she want? "I could get your baby over the Wall."

The girl's face faltered for a second, and Daniel held his breath. Then she frowned. "Fool, you locked up here and all but killed. What make you think I'ma trust this baby to you?"

Daniel thought of the vials of virus in his coat again. Using them would be genocide. He had to find another way. "You said you needed my help to escape. Well, I need you to get me to these Professors or I'm still stuck here. Help me and I'll help you."

She sighed, almost imperceptibly. "Where you put your stuff? You say west?"

Daniel's eyes narrowed. It was one thing to ask for help, another to ask for trust.

"Mister, look," the girl snapped. "Daniel," she said, softer this time. "I know you scared. Me too. And I got this baby to take care of. I got to do right by her, not just you and me."

We all have to do what's right, Daniel thought.

"You don't deserve to be here no more than we do, so we gonna work together and get out of here. Then I get you to the Professors. And that be that."

Daniel watched the girl and the baby in her lap, thinking of what doing the right thing had cost him so far.

"My name is Fen de la Guerre," she told him suddenly. "I am an O-Positive."

The way she said the words sounded formal, like a ritual.

INQUIRY: What is significance of blood type in the Delta?

RESPONSE: Blood type is identity in the Delta. It indicates tribe and potential value of blood, if type is rare or useful. It can imply a tribal challenge, or an act of trust. Type AB is the rarest, but O is a universal donor, and therefore of increased value.

"Fen . . ." Daniel sat up and cleared his throat. "Thank you," he said. Trust might come slowly, but they both needed it if they were going to get out of here alive.

"Mister—Daniel. You say that thing on your wrist ana-lyze stuff. Do it read blood types?"

Blood types, chemical compounds, air quality. The data-link was a very sophisticated computer, even if it was self-contained. "I suppose so," he said.

"Trade, then. You type Baby Girl, and I get you outta here, safe and sound."

"But we already—" he started to protest. How could he trust her if she kept changing their agreement?

"Keep your shirt, and your water. It don't matter to me as much as this."

He hesitated. "Bring her here."

Fen tucked the baby back in her sling and slid over to him. "Do it hurt?"

"No," he said, pulling up his coat sleeve to reveal the full datalink. Raising his arm, he showed her the scanning plate, a rectangle on the bottom like smooth green glass. "Look. It reads things from here without breaking the skin."

Daniel motioned to Fen and she held the baby's hand up. Gently, he pressed it to the scanning plate and his arm lit up like fireflies weaving in the dark as the datalink screened the baby's blood. Then it clicked softly and he let go of the baby's hand. The datalink whispered the information into his head.

"She's O positive. Like her mother," he said with a smile, wondering if the news was a relief. He couldn't tell by the look on Fen's face.

Suddenly, the door handle twisted, the lock clicking open with a heavy grinding noise. Daniel cowered and Fen flinched, setting the baby to crying again.

"Daniel," Fen hissed. "Get down." She motioned for him to lie down and feign sleep.

Between slitted eyelids, Daniel watched Fen reach into the hay pile behind her, pulling out the moss she had removed from the baby's diaper. And then he understood her plan. Newborns didn't process food into feces, but a black thick substance called meconium. Quickly, Fen smeared it into the corners of her eyes, mixing it with spit until she had streaks down her face.

Daniel recoiled, but lay still. Trust, he reminded himself. It wasn't like he had any other options.

The door swung open and a man in a dirty white lab coat appeared, needles in his hand.

Daniel saw the man glance in his direction, then turned to Fen, who sat with her head tucked down, face hidden from view.

"Come on, girl. We need to type your baby," he said, and reached for her. Fen rose, head down.

"Get me outta here, mister," she pleaded. "That man a leper. He making me sick."

She stepped closer. Daniel braced himself. Maybe he could rush the door, take the man off balance.

Then Fen screamed, "He killing me!"

She thrust her face into the lab man's, black ooze leaking from her eyes, and he screamed, falling out of the door. Daniel didn't hesitate. He leapt to his feet, moaning the way his brother had, ravaged by Delta Fever. They both groaned and stumbled out into the main room, but the man in the lab coat was nowhere to be seen. There was one other attendant, but he had no weapons. One look at Fen's face and Daniel's rags, and the man cursed and ran. The old smuggler had been right about the leper rags after all.

Daniel raced after Fen out of building 17. To the left lay the road into the camp toward the cook fires, all cold now in the morning light. A dog started to bark, and Daniel wondered how long it would be before the hunters woke up and caught them again. The lab men were halfway across the yard, calling for help, calling them infected. Daniel followed Fen's lead, staggering and moaning until they were close to the back fence, more a log pile than a real structure. They clambered over the logs, Daniel clumsily, Fen surprisingly agile even with the baby slung across her chest. Then they were out of the farm and in the woods. They ran.

16

WE LUCKY. THEY DON'T BE COMING AFTER US right away, and there be a stream right behind the farm. I splash into the water and run across it, then back again. "Follow me," I call. Daniel not so limber, but he do the same.

When our scent be on both sides of the stream, I run back into the middle where it deep enough to almost hit my waist, and I run best I can with water pulling at me. We go upstream, far away from the farm, and I don't be hearing no dogs because, as much as a new baby might be worth, they think we infected. In they mind, we a waste of fuel if they got to burn all three of us.

When we gone far enough I think we out of danger, I crouch by that stream to wash my face and scrub and scrub 'til I can stand to stop. Baby Girl be thinking it a game 'cause she waving her arms in the air and punching her fists and I think she be happy, maybe. If a body that young even know what happy be like.

Daniel sit on a log beside me and check his suit for tears.

"You alive, Daniel. I done my part."

He maybe grinning or scowling, the suit make it hard to see. But he nod a bunch of times and try to catch his breath. I look up at the sky. The sooner I be done with this fool, the sooner I can get Baby Girl to Father John. He the only one who can get her out of Orleans alive. Which be more than this boy can hope for. City always been easier to get into than out of for smugglers. But that be his problem, not mine.

"You still want the Professors? I can take you to your stash instead and you can get outta here."

He take a deep breath, like he making a big decision. "The Professors," he say, and his filtered voice sound even flatter out in the open with no walls to bounce off.

"Okay then." I wipe my hands on my pants and tighten Baby Girl's sling.

There be only a few ways to cross the Mississippi from here. One be that barge the hunters use. Too soon for me to get on that thing again, plus it likely they be waiting for us there if they waiting anywhere. The other way be a mud skiff. Sometimes there be crabbers and shrimpers in the river, but mostly they on the lake or the Gulf. What you see more of be them Chinamen and they junks, plying the river and mudflats for clams and oysters.

The shellfish beds be real big ever since Hurricane Jesus, like the mud been mixed up just right. First few years after the big ones, the water been poisoned. All them bottom-feeders been toxic. The military been dropping food supplies back then. Still, lots of folks got sick or starved. But the shellfish done they job eventually, cleaning up the river. Daddy told me there ain't been oysters this big since the white man first came to this country. Father John call it a gift from God. Mr. Go say it be Nature taking care of herself. I don't know 'bout that, but I know we can get a Chinaman to take us across the river for a fee. We just gotta find something worth trading.

"What part of the States you from?" I ask Daniel. If Baby Girl going over the Wall soon, it can't hurt to know what it be like.

"East coast," Daniel say. He still breathing kind of hard, and I wonder if it 'cause of the suit. "Delaware, Virginia, North Carolina. I've moved around."

I repeat the names in my head. "Sound exotic."

Daniel laugh. "Not like Orleans."

I shrug. "You got a nice place in East Coast?"

Daniel nod. "A two-bedroom apartment. It's okay. It's got parking."

I don't know what parking be, but it sound all right. "And schools? You got good schools, and enough to eat?"

Daniel rush to keep up with me. "Not everyone does, but yes. I mean, if you can afford it, there's plenty."

Every place you go got a price. I look down at Baby Girl and wish I still had that gold McCallan left me. Then Baby Girl be leaving with something to pay her way. "Don't sound so different from here," I say.

Daniel finally catch up, and look me in the eye. "Believe me, it is."

• • •

It be coming on afternoon when the trees give way to grass and marsh along the river. Soon we be at Shangri-Lo.

Nothing more than a row of shanties where the river men live. When the Fever hit, all the Asians in Orleans moved over here. The Fever ain't take to Asians the way it did the rest of us, so they like a tribe that way. They not like the rest of Orleans. They be mixing, for sure: Koreans and Japanese, Chinese and Vietnamese and Filipino. But nothing else. Folks in Orleans all be mutts except for the Asians.

"Why are we stopping?" Daniel almost run into me at the edge of the reeds. I point to the stick in the dirt with a red mark painted on it.

"Oyster beds," I say. "We almost there, but we need to work a plan."

"I thought you had a plan," he say.

It be enough to make me want to smack him, but Lydia always say there be more flies caught with honey. "I got us here, didn't I? Up to you to get us the rest of the way. The Chinamen got boats that go to the Market across the river, but they ain't taking us for free. You got any coin on you, or something for trade?"

Daniel look down at his coat. "I've got some cash," he say, and start to reach into a pocket. I shake my head.

"Man, Outer States paper no good down here. It just wash away. What else you got?"

"What's considered valuable?"

"Metal, fabric. Useful things. Glass? We don't get a lot of glass anymore."

Daniel shake his head.

Damn, this boy be useless. I think about my assets. I know a boatsman, used to study with the Ursulines, too, long time ago. We see each other time to time in the Market. His mama got a noodle stand there. Friendship don't count for much in Orleans, but maybe.

One good thing about these folks—they used to trading, so they ain't that territorial. Seafood and boats be bringing all kinds of folks to they door, and we ain't no exception.

"Follow me." I wave Daniel along, and we head across the mudflats into Shangri-Lo.

17

❧ DANIEL'S HEART CAUGHT IN HIS THROAT. THE shantytown spread out along the shoreline before him, huts of flotsam and lean-tos. Families lived here. Children. Life of a sort he hadn't expected to find. Thriving life. And to think he had the means to end it all in his pocket. He pulled his coat closer around him and self-consciously followed Fen into town.

"*Ni hao, konichiwa.*" Fen waved as she and Daniel entered the first row of shacks. A toothless old woman waved her away like a fly as they walked past her into the main thoroughfare. *Town* was too big a word for this place. It was more like a collection of shacks, some made with concrete walls and roofs, others just sheets of plywood. Sticky mud sucked at Daniel's boots as he picked his way after Fen. Small dirty dogs paced them through the row of sheds.

"How do they live like this, right on the water?" Daniel asked, ducking under a line of drying laundry. Fen shrugged, her back looking too thin beneath the fraying fabric of her sack shirt and the weight of the baby slung across her chest.

"How do anybody live?" she replied. "Concrete be good shelter in a storm, and it last if there be a flood. The rest of the wood be cheap. It blow away in the wind without breaking anything else, and float back when it over, so they put it back together again."

Daniel shook his head and stepped over an open gutter, wrinkling his nose at the filth that flowed through it.

"Is that a sewer?"

Fen laughed. "Naw, that be nasty. That the gutting canal. Where they throw all the oyster shells and fish guts. They wash back out to sea when the tide come in. It keep the place clean."

The sheds grew larger as they walked along the shore, deeper into Shangri-Lo. In some of the bigger huts, lanterns could be seen burning. Fen strode along confidently, forcing Daniel to jog to keep up.

"What's that up there?" he asked, pointing to a triangular wooden hut on stilts in the distance. "A watchtower?"

Fen paused. "Your datalink broken or something?"

"I was just . . . curious."

"Well, this ain't a tour, and I ain't your guide." She started off again, jouncing the baby, who had begun to cry. "I know, you hungry," she said to the baby. Daniel swallowed hard, feeling foolish, and mentally accessed the link.

INQUIRY: What is the purpose of a tall triangular hut on stilts in Orleans?
RESPONSE: Further data required. Describe hut.

INQUIRY: Slanted roof, wooden shingles. Cross of wood on top.

RESPONSE: Orleans contains places of worship, raised on stilts to protect congregation from floods. Possible match.

The church looked like a stork standing in the marshes. As he watched, someone was lowered from the little hut on a tire attached to a pulley.

"Hurry up, now," Fen called to him. "Rain coming."

For the first time, Daniel noticed the skies were darkening. He scurried to catch up to Fen, who had stopped at a three-sided shack facing the river.

"Kuan-Jen, *ni hao*, brother," Fen called into the shed.

The building was framed in signs Daniel could not read, but a drawing of a bowl of rice told him it was a food stall. Inside was a long table with two chairs on one side and a sleeping cot pulled up along the other side to serve as a bench. "Kuan-Jen!" Fen called again. There was no answer.

"Be right back," she said, but Daniel followed close on her heels. Fen slipped between the shed and its neighbor into a small alley backed by more marshland. Behind the shed, a big black pot balanced over a cooking fire. A thin older man tended the fire. Fen bent toward the man and began speaking a language Daniel didn't recognize.

INQUIRY: Identify language.

RESPONSE: A combination of French, Cantonese, Mandarin, and Tagalog.

Daniel tried to read Fen's face as she argued with the old man, who shook his head, laughing, and went back to stoking the fire.

"What's he saying?" Daniel asked.

Fen waved him off and dropped to her heels. She lifted up her bundle to show the man the baby. The man dropped his poker and jumped up suddenly with more energy than Daniel would have thought possible. Grabbing Fen by the elbow, the man marched off, pulling her along with him. Fen turned back to Daniel and winked.

They followed the older man out of the alleyway and down to the shore, where a young Chinese man was hauling in his sails on what looked like a windsurfer combined with an old Chinese fishing boat. The body of the craft was a shallow raft on runners, carved of wood, with empty plastic milk gallons attached for added ballast. Up top, a variegated sail was being drawn up a large beam like a window blind being raised to a top crossbar. The sail itself was cloth, segmented by thick bamboolike reeds. Daniel watched in bewilderment as the older man started shouting angrily. Whatever the argument, five minutes later, the young man lowered his sails again, the old man watching with crossed arms until Fen and Daniel boarded the junk.

"Thanks a lot, Fen," the young man complained. He looked to be about twenty, Daniel guessed. His smooth face was red with embarrassment as the wind whipped his ponytail across his mouth.

"How did she rope you into this, man?" he asked Daniel. Daniel shrugged and the man laughed. "Well, I'm Kuan-Jen. And apparently, this is my baby mama."

Daniel turned to Fen. "He's the father?"

"No," she said. "That the only way to get Kuan's dad to tell me where he be."

"That trick only works once," Kuan-Jen said. "And you picked a bad time to cross, Fen. Rain on the way and night falling. What Lydia got you doing up in Algiers, anyway?"

Fen's face closed tight, making Daniel wonder who Lydia might be. "My business, not yours" was all she said.

"Something up?" Kuan-Jen asked. "I heard rumors, but—"

"But nothing. Right now we need to get across this river, get some food for this baby. Mama-san got anything I can borrow?"

Kuan-Jen shrugged and finished tying his line. "You already owe me. How much more can you afford?" He jumped off the deck of the vessel and dragged it out into the water on a series of logs that turned like rollers beneath the bow. He climbed back aboard as it drifted into the river.

"I said *borrow*." Fen emphasized the word. "You know I be good for it."

"Hold on tight," Kuan-Jen said by way of reply. The boat jerked sharply as it was taken by the current. They angled down the river and Daniel could see tiny lights on the far shore. Midway, the water receded back into mudflats. Kuan-Jen tweaked the sails and the boat glided forward on its runners, tugged by the wind until it hit another deep channel of water.

"I had no idea the river was this wide," Daniel said under his breath. But Fen heard him.

"You got no idea 'bout a lot of things. You a tourist, pure and simple."

"Outlander, eh?" Kuan-Jen shouted from the far end of the boat. "Don't get many of those anymore." He turned to Fen. "This one got anything worth trading for?"

Fen looked at Daniel. "Do you?"

He thought of the things Fen said were of value—glass, metal. Useful things. With his duffel gone, all he had left were a few glow sticks, carbo food tubes for the encounter suit, and . . .

He felt inside his pockets. "Just candy," he said forlornly, pulling out one of the snack-size Snickers bars he'd taken from the front desk of his motel on the other side of the Wall.

Kuan-Jen's face lit up. "Candy bars? I miss candy bars. Missionaries used to bring them in, or airdrop them over the Wall." Even Fen looked impressed.

Daniel handed the thumb-size candy over. "It's kind of melty," he apologized.

The boatman accepted it reverently in his callused hands. He looked up at Fen, then Daniel. "Two more will get you dinner and a change of clothes for Fen."

Daniel reached back into his pocket, then hesitated. "What about diapers?"

Kuan-Jen gave him a suspicious look. "What about them?"

"I want a pack of diapers. And dinner, and a shirt for Fen."

Kuan-Jen lowered his outstretched hand and frowned. "For what?"

Daniel reached into another pocket. "For this." He held up a handful of mini candy bars. "Happy Halloween."

"Hey, tourist, heads up," Fen said.

Daniel followed her gaze. They were across the river now and lights stretched for a half mile in either direction. On the shore sprawled a village, covered in blue tarps and Christmas lights. Daniel looked up as a docksman waved them to a berth and the skiff bumped into the pier. Kuan-Jen threw the man a rope and they tied up to the shore.

"Welcome to the Market," Fen said. "This be the heart of Orleans."

18

THE RIVERFRONT WAS DEVOTED TO FISHING craft and boating supplies. Daniel followed Fen and Kuan-Jen through a rabbit's warren of stalls, cobbled together from driftwood, old beams, sheets of plastic, and the blue tarping that roofed it all. From above, he imagined it would look like a giant blue umbrella on a flat gray beach. The rain was starting to come down and the tiny lights of the Market—solar-powered holiday lights from the early days of the Wall, according to Fen—spread a warm firefly yellow against the slate gray sky.

Nets. Buckets. Shrimping baskets. Shucking knives. Broad hats worn by some of the denizens of Shangri-Lo. Leathery-faced men and women of Asian and less determinate race haggled in a dozen different languages with customers over their wares. This city was alive, and in such variety that it stunned Daniel. Did the government know about this? Did the military?

Fen was moving fast through the crowd. Daniel had to fight the urge to linger and observe. If he lost sight of her now, he was truly lost.

The fishing supply stalls gave way to fishmongers, long low booths with large tubs of live crab, catfish, shark, and shrimp skittering through murky water, drawn by the handful to be weighed and sold.

INQUIRY: What forms of currency are used in Orleans?
RESPONSE: Official currency of Orleans unknown. Barter and trade are most common. Postulating commodities to include food, tools, sexual favors, and blood.

Daniel balked at the thought, and found himself narrowing his field of vision to focus on Fen's retreating back rather than witness any of the muddy denizens of the Market in compromising positions.

Beyond the fishmongers, the stalls turned into food stands, with the sizzling sound of cooking fires and popping grease. The smoky stench of charcoal blended with the sweet, spicy tang of stews and fried seafood. Daniel looked up from the stall of a raw oyster bar—hand-size oyster shells split and served with wedges of lemon and red pepper—to see Fen turn an abrupt corner. He chased after her and found himself in a narrow lane of stalls with a hand-painted sign overhead that echoed the one he'd seen in Shangri-Lo—a bowl of noodles with chopsticks and a curl of painted steam.

Fen was glaring at him from beneath the awning of the

second shop on the right. She cradled the baby to her chest and scowled. "Keep up, man."

Daniel ducked into the open front of the stall behind her. Low crates had been set up to form seating along a narrow plank of driftwood, planed smooth on top. A short black man, blacker than anyone Daniel had ever seen, was crouched on the far side of the table, shoveling a bowl of hot noodles into his mouth. He ignored them completely, absorbed with his food.

"This be Mama-san's," Fen explained. Kuan-Jen had gone through a blue tarp draped across the back of the stall. A moment later, a small Chinese woman in a yellow rain slicker came through the curtain. She observed Daniel and Fen with bright small eyes, then looked at the baby.

"*Ni hao,* Mama-san," Fen said, and continued in a blend of languages.

Mama-san reached for the baby. Fen hesitated, then pulled her out of the sling. Mama-san gasped at the sight of the baby's makeshift diaper, the hay gone soft with urine and Fen's own sweat. Daniel didn't need a translator to know that Fen was being chastised.

Fen grabbed the baby and motioned for Daniel to sit down. Mama-san disappeared and returned a few minutes later with two bowls of plain noodles.

"No," Fen said sharply, startling Daniel. The word was in English, but the meaning was clear enough, even to Mama-san.

⚜ THEY TRYING TO BE CHEAP WITH ME NOW, after they got all that good chocolate the smuggler brought.

No way. We be needing real diapers, not just them cloth things. A bloodhound can scent a diaper as good as blood, and we ain't got time to stop and wash them. Best to throw them out quick. We also gonna get some hot food with meat in it. Kuan-Jen and his mama be arguing, but I don't care. I know what things be worth.

A minute later, we get a hot pot, a clay stove over a charcoal burner, with gumbo boiling away inside, chock-full of oysters and shrimp and thick slices of okra. We keep the noodles and get cups of rice, too.

"Eat," I say to Daniel, but he hesitate and I remember Delta food be like poison to him. He run his datalink over the pot to analyze, but it no good.

"Sorry, man," I tell him. "You ain't got no food on you, other than them candy bars?"

He make a face like he smell something bad. "Just carbo gel. For energy. It's too soon for another one."

"That a shame," I say, and pull his bowl of rice to me.

I don't know how hungry I be 'til Mama-san put everything on the table. Daniel look jealous, but that be his problem, not mine.

By the time I hit the bottom of the bowl, Kuan-Jen and his mama be back. They got what I need. Real diapers, the old disposable kind from before the storms, and a couple cloth ones that will last. And formula, a whole can of it, and some bottles of water to mix it with.

I offer Daniel a bottle. "Thirsty?"

He shake his head.

"It be clean," I tell him. "One thing we got a lot of down

here be bottled water. They been dropping it from the sky for ten years straight, and most of us drink what already here, so it like wine or something. For a special occasion."

"The suit . . ." He hesitate. "Recycles fluids. I'm fine."

I grimace at the thought of drinking your own fluids, but I guess it make some kind of sense.

I mix a bottle for Baby Girl and heat it over the coals. Mama-san keep looking at the baby like she something special, so I let her hold her for a while, and she be all smiling and happy and singing some Chinese song. It kind of nice, especially when we ready to leave and she act like we been doing her a favor. Kuan-Jen nod when I wave good-bye.

"She she," I say, and bow. Kuan-Jen laugh at me. Mama-san, she bow back and wave bye-bye to Baby Girl. It be like Daniel don't exist. He mumble good-bye and follow me out into the Market.

"Much better," I say when we out in the open. I got me a new shirt—new for me, at least—with long sleeves, and it made out of cotton, so it not as cold and scratchy as the sackcloth been. And my new backpack be full of baby diapers, formula, and bottled water. Mama-san even threw in a decent knife when she saw we was meaning to leave. Nobody who want to live in Orleans walk around without some kind of weapon. I be feeling kind of sleepy after all that food, but Lydia always say a good person pay they debts.

I head away from the river. "Come on, now. The Professors ain't far, but we don't want to be out too long after dark."

But Daniel ain't behind me. I turn around and see he stopped and watching one of them Ursuline girls head toward the hospital tent. Maybe it be a shock, seeing a girl that young, looking so clean and innocent in all this mess, but it ain't a reason to slow down. I got half a mind to leave him. Instead, I walk back and snap my fingers in his face.

"Hey, man, what you doing?"

Daniel look pale, like he seen a ghost. "Who is that?"

I shrug. "One of the Ursuline nuns' girls. Work at the hospital tent." Sure enough, she be ducking inside. A nun in full habit come out, white dress and veil glowing it be so clean, even by lamplight. Daniel blink like a bird stunned by a snake.

"I saw them," he say. "At the Superdome."

"Course you did. That be what they do, other than try to run a school, heal the sick, and raise the dead. They nuns, man. Ain't no different on your side, right?"

Daniel look at me real slow, and for a minute I think he be another Lydia, wanting to go into that tent. But I ain't letting him.

"Look, man, ain't nothing but the sick and dying in there. And the nuns. Nothing worth seeing, even for a tourist. Come on, it be getting dark."

Daniel hesitate. "They still try to save them? After everything?"

"After what? You think we be animals, just leaving folks to die?" I snap. "Well, sometimes it be that way. But not always. You ain't got a tribe to care for you, there be the nuns."

Daniel don't be listening to me, though. "Maybe we should—" he start to say.

"Do what you want. You on your own, then," I tell him, and walk away.

Hard to believe I been here just a couple days ago with Lydia, Harney, and the rest of them, and now they all captured or dead. Look like boys be fools on both sides of the Wall. They love the Market and they love looking for trouble. But I got more sense than that.

Seems Daniel do, too. He come jogging after me just like Harney. Maybe he won't die out here after all. If he learn to listen to me.

19

⚜ THE MARKET HAD SEEMED ENDLESS FROM THE inside, but after the hospital tent, it stopped abruptly. Daniel scanned the empty road beyond the Market. The pristine façades of the old French Quarter stared back. All thoughts of the nuns and their work, what data they could add to his own research, evaporated in the sudden silence.

INQUIRY: Last known status of New Orleans French Quarter architecture.
RESPONSE: Restoration to historical buildings of the French Quarter began after Hurricane Isaiah, utilizing reinforced composites designed to withstand a Category 4 storm.

Daniel stared at the buildings, with their balconies of intricate ironwork, the low sidewalk of short wooden planks laid alongside the muddy road. From the look of it, the composites had worked.

"Who lives here?" he asked Fen as she skirted the buildings, heading across the remains of St. Louis Cathedral and Jackson Square.

"A-Positives. They be a strong tribe here on the water. We got no business with them. Like in Shangri-Lo, folks got to come through here to shop the Market, but once they out, they best keep moving." She quickened her pace, thumbs hooked beneath her backpack straps. "Come on. We still got a ways to go."

They wove through the old French Quarter with its silent, watchful façades. "Where is everyone?" Daniel asked.

"They there," Fen said. Glancing around, Daniel thought he saw the gleam of eyes pulling back from an open doorway. The rain had stopped and the clouds were drifting apart, revealing patches of stars.

Fen pointed with her chin as they came to a wide stream, thick with broken pieces of concrete and rebar. "We got to go that way."

Daniel nodded and followed her up the street. The Quarter gave way to empty, shattered storefronts and the corpses of office buildings. They passed under a portico of rusting iron grillwork and the echoing steps of Gallier Hall, with its commanding staircase and stone columns now littered with dust and debris. Flooding had turned the steps into a dock for rescue boats. Craning his neck, Daniel could just make out the high water line marked around the pillars in mold.

Leaving the business district, they came to the edge of a broad lake. The empty hulk of an ancient skyscraper crumbled to Daniel's right. He was struck by the silence and the darkness. It felt like he, Fen, and the baby were the last three people on earth. But then he remembered those eyes in the doorway. The city was watching.

As they picked their way around the lake and onto a smaller road, he dialed up his night-vision goggles, wondering how Fen got along so well in the faint starlight. A quarter of a mile down the road, the remains of the interstate curved above them like the bones of an ancient whale. Fen sped up as they moved under the echoing expanse of the freeway. He followed close behind her, avoiding the black shadows of concrete pillars and rusted automobiles.

On the other side of the freeway, they returned to the remains of St. Charles Avenue, now a grassy meridian between two shallow streams that had once been roads. On the concrete shores, faded storefronts mingled with vine-choked apartment buildings. Fen stuck to the grassy lane in the center of the avenue, well away from the decaying stores, rotting houses, and whatever they might hide. Neutral ground, she called it. Daniel had read about the concept in history books. In the early days of the Louisiana Purchase, when the French residents of the Quarter clashed with the Americans in Uptown, these grassy areas were neutral territory. He wondered if tribes honored that these days, or if it was merely a name.

They moved into the Garden District, where the city had gone to seed, a cancerous jungle. Lush garden courtyards had burst like tumors, swallowing their outer buildings whole.

Entire families had perished in some of those buildings, drowned in their attics or consumed by Fever in their beds. Their remains fed the madly flourishing bougainvillea and morning glory vines, even in early winter.

The streets were quiet, waiting. Daniel shuddered. Orleans was a living city of the dead.

Half an hour later, Fen turned off the street toward a sagging building that looked like it had once been grand and white. Through his night-vision goggles, Daniel could see it clearly—an antebellum structure that had been flattened by Mother Nature's gargantuan fist.

"We can rest here," Fen said.

"Are you kidding? This place is falling down on itself," he hissed at her.

Fen cut him a look that made him take a step backward. "Fine. Then you choose."

Daniel looked around. There were so many ruins here, so few standing structures. He pointed toward a large two-story building that was somehow still standing at the intersection a quarter block away. Even the windows, geometric shapes in a modern stucco slab, were intact. "How about that place across the street?"

"Oh, perfect," she said, and he almost missed the sarcasm. "It look solid, don't it? You'd think a solid building already be full up of the tribe that live here. But maybe it ain't. And maybe that ain't a spotter on the roof looking at your fool self and thinking he gonna send somebody over for our blood before we come for his."

Daniel blanched. There *was* movement on the roof. How had he missed that, when he was the one with enhanced night vision? And there was something else he had missed.

"Wait," he said, but Fen was already clambering through the tumbled brick wall of her chosen hideout. He followed as quickly as he could without tripping, and they disappeared into the dank, slanting building.

"Was that a McDonald's?" he whispered into the dark. His goggles whirred, adjusting to the deeper shadows inside the building. It was as bad as he had expected inside. A few yards into the foyer, the floor gave way to a crater that took up most of the first floor. An explosion of vines and weeds burst from the hole, like intestines spilling from a knife wound. If there had been walls before, now there were only fallen beams, some shored up by the collapsed ceiling. Fen stopped just inside the front door and tucked herself into a corner to feed the baby.

"What are you doing?" Daniel asked.

"What it look like? We cross that intersection and we be in AB territory—La Bête Sauvage's ground. I ain't going in there with a hungry baby that gonna cry and tell them where we be." She gave him a hard look, laser sharp even in the gloom. "I feed her, she fall asleep, and we move fast enough, maybe we make it to the Professors okay."

Daniel shifted uneasily. "Can't we just wait until morning?"

Fen unwrapped the baby from her sling and cradled her in her lap while she mixed a bottle of formula. "You saw the spotter on the McDonald's. You think they gonna let us stay here all night? If you tired, we rest a few minutes, but not much more."

Daniel paced, his nerves getting the better of him. He needed food and rest. He needed to get out of here. The floor creaked alarmingly under his boots, and he shuffled quickly to the corner opposite Fen. The ground felt firmer here, the edges of the building holding together better than the center. He dropped carefully into a squat. "A McDonald's in Orleans. That's crazy," he said.

Fen shook her head. "You ain't left the planet, man. Course we got McDonald's. Starbucks, too, in some places. But it ain't like they open for business."

"Yeah." Daniel pulled a tube of whitish paste from one of his pockets. If she was going to feed the baby, he might as well have something, too. The baby was snuggled in Fen's arms now, and the girl looked as content as the child. Strange to seem so comfortable in such a dangerous place. But then again, the whole city was hostile. Daniel supposed you had to take your moments when they came.

He rolled up his sleeve and shoved the tube into a port in the arm of his suit.

"What it taste like?" Fen asked.

"Sorry?" The nutrient tubes were a high-calorie paste in a sterile casing that fed directly into his bloodstream by osmosis. Not exactly the same as eating, but it was that or starve.

"McDonald's," Fen said. "I know they made food, but what it like? I always been wanting to try a Big Mac."

Daniel smiled. "It's not like . . ." Not like what? Other burgers? "Do you have cows down here?"

"My tribe don't, but I hear some tribes do."

"So you've never had beef?"

"Just seafood and wild pig," she said. "What beef taste like?"

"I don't know how to describe it. Different from pork, but more like pork than fish. But a Big Mac is kind of its own thing. Sweet and hot, with two patties of ground meat, two slices of cheese, and this sauce that's supposed to be special, but I think it's just thousand island dressing."

The girl was staring at him with a little smile on her face. He blushed. "That made no sense, did it? You've never had cheese, have you? Or salad dressing."

She shook her head. "Sound like a rich place you come from. Maybe Baby Girl be having her first Big Mac for me one day." Fen smiled down at the baby as she drained the last of the bottle.

Daniel rifled through his coat pockets and found one last candy bar. Fen was watching him through half-closed eyes.

"Here." He tossed it to her.

Fen reached for it, smiling, and tucked it away.

"Snickers be good," she said. "Used to be I got them all the time for my birthday, for Christmas, too."

"No beef, but you've had a Snickers?" Daniel asked, surprised.

"I had a sponsor family in the States. Back when that used to be popular. They actually be adopting kids in the beginning, but by the time I been born, ain't no one allowed out the Delta 'cause of the Fever. So they be sending me care packages and clothes and whatnot. And I be sending them pictures through the mission what started the program.

Father John be the priest who ran it. He weren't afraid of the Fever and he stayed to help."

She cleared her throat. "That be a long time ago. His church be right at the border where the gates used to be for volunteers and tourists, like you." She chuckled when she said it, poking fun at him.

"He be a good man, Father John, and he make sure I always get my candy, and my pictures be scanned and sent to my people. The Coopers, 15527 West Arlington, San Diego, California. I remember the e-mail address if I think about it, too."

Daniel plugged a second nutrient pack into his suit and resealed his pockets. "It must have been hard growing up like that," he said. "Seeing what life was like on the other side."

Fen shrugged. "Ain't it be like that everywhere? Either you got it or somebody else do."

Daniel tried to get comfortable, resting his back against the spongy wall. "I suppose."

"It be true," Fen said. "You seen Orleans—how different can it be over the Wall?"

Daniel blinked. So different, he didn't know where to begin. "Well . . . for one thing, nobody's hunted me for my blood."

Fen snorted. "Yeah, we got special circumstances here in the Delta."

"But they did round up people with the Fever and keep them in hospital camps," Daniel explained. "Not so different, in a way. But there's so much more that's good. Schools and grocery stores and farms and amusement parks and movies."

"Amusement parks?"

Daniel smiled. "It's a place full of rides and crappy food that you go to for fun. You can ride roller coasters . . ." He trailed off, seeing her blank look. "It's kind of like a train that goes up and down a track."

"Where it take you?" Fen asked.

"Um . . . nowhere. It's just for fun. It's supposed to be scary and fun."

Fen shifted the baby in her arms and lay down on her side. "That be different from Orleans, then, for sure. We got scary, but it ain't no fun."

She closed her eyes and fell silent. Daniel looked at her—that young face and those terrible burns on her arms. In the Outer States, those scars would be repaired with plastic surgery. Fen should be in high school, not toting a baby around this nightmare of a city. Daniel shivered and looked away from the strange girl. He felt far from sleep, and very far from home.

20

❦ "DANIEL. DANIEL, WAKE UP." I KEEP BABY GIRL close to me and creep over to tap him on the foot. We been here less than fifteen minutes, and now there be a light coming in through the broken window. Firelight.

"Daniel!" He stir and suddenly sit upright. "Shhh . . ." I put a finger over my lips. He look around, nodding that he understand. I motion him to the front wall along where I been sleeping. "Come see."

Normally, I be giving him a hard time for being a tourist, but this be something special. Something I be real glad to see, too.

He shuffle over on his butt, keeping low like me. There be an opening in the wall that used to be a window, but the glass be long gone, and now it be open to the street below.

"Christ, what is that?" Daniel ask, and it sound funny through his filter, no expression, just words.

"All Saints' Day," I tell him. "Hurricane season be over today, and we still here."

In the street, riding toward us on lean brown horses, come an All Saints' krewe. They be decked out in all they finery— owl- and pheasant-feather headdresses, chains and bracelets made of shiny metal and glass mounded high on they wrists, and necks with strand after strand of old Mardi Gras beads, purple, green, and yellow, all sparkling and shining in the torchlight. The krewe be riding, holding they flambeaux high up to the sky. Like a thundercloud of fire, rolling toward us, they be singing and shouting at the clouds as they go by.

"Who are they?" Daniel whisper. I bounce Baby Girl in my arms.

"Anybody. Everybody. They wear masks over they eyes to keep from knowing. All Saints' krewes and the Market be the only times tribes come together. Folks just show up in they costumes, ready to ride."

The krewe outside be a big one, almost twenty riders. They wheel around in a circle at the widest point of the road and thrust they torches toward the center of the ring, moving to a trot as the ring shift shape and turn into a spiral 'stead of a sphere. Now they be like a hurricane, swirling and swirling, the smallest rider in the center at the eye.

The sound grow louder. I hear them and I mouth the words. "Katrina, Isaiah, Lorenzo. Olga, Laura, Paloma." Up and down, over and over, they be going faster and faster. "Jesus, Jesus, Hay-SEUS!" The Hurricane riders be stretching wider and wider in the street, and then they burst apart,

170

horses and riders shooting off in every direction, splashing through the streams and trampling over the neutral ground.

Some of they flambeaux go out, they be moving so fast. And they shout, hoot, holler, and I got to hold my tongue not to join them out loud. *"Nous sommes ici! Nous sommes ici! Encore! Encore! Encore! Nous restons ici!"*

Daniel be looking at me like he never seen me before. I want to laugh, but we got to stay quiet. All Saints' or no, it won't do to let them know we here. Maybe the riders ain't gonna bother us, but there be others that might.

"It be a good sign," I explain to Daniel as the torchlight fade and the riders gallop into the night. One rider play a trumpet. That old tune, "When the Saints Go Marching In." "Only time of year someone be fool enough to blow a horn like that. Ain't nobody hunting a Saints' Day krewe. Bad luck." The riders be gone now, but you can hear they song farther up the road.

"I don't understand," Daniel said.

I sigh and curl myself back into my corner. Daniel sit beside to listen. I wish Cinnamon Jones be here to tell it right, but I do my best. "In the beginning, Orleans be like this special place, back when it been New Orleans. Everybody knew about it. We tell the story all the time. It been beautiful back then, and there weren't no Wall, neither. It been part of Louisiana, and the whole Delta still been part of the United States. But then them hurricanes came, Rita and Katrina. And they break pieces off the land like eating cake. And they still rebuilding when Isaiah hit, and he ain't the

171

end. Laura and Paloma come along, and they be calling them the Two Sisters, 'cause they dance right on up the coast and drop skirts of rain on New Orleans like girls knocking over glass figurines with they spinning and twirling. And it almost over for the Delta. But the Government say they going to help us, they going to fix everything." I look up, suddenly shy. I been talking like one of Daddy's schoolbooks or Lydia, but I don't sound as good as they do. Did. Most likely Daniel done heard it all before, but he still be listening, so I carry on.

"Then Jesus came. It spelled like Jesus Christ, but it pronounced the Spanish way. I can't know why they named it that. Maybe somebody thought it funny. But it ain't. Jesus come so big, they ain't even able to measure it. They call it a Category Five because that been as big as they could get back then. But Olga been a Five, too, and Paloma. Jesus been way bigger, so the Government give up, say everybody evacuate. But can't everybody fit on a road out of town at the same time. Some people can't even get up outta they beds, so what *they* gonna do? No gas for the cars, and the roads be clogged, and people be needing they medicine and whatnot. And then some folks, well, they figure they born here, they gonna die here, too. The city been full of workers, immigrants who came here for jobs rebuilding since the Government been promising work and all. They stuck here, too, living in trailers and cheap housing, what the Government provide.

"And all them folks still here when Jesus come walking up the coast. West Florida to East Texas, he take his time, and he don't ever get weaker. He like a dog chewing on a leg bone, slowly eating it up. And so many people be dead when he finally fade and move north that survivors be getting sick, with bodies clogging the water and the pipes, and things all broken, and chemicals and sewage filling up the place.

"You probably know the rest. The Government say they can't save us. There ain't enough of us left to bother. Folks be given the chance to leave, and the first ones that do bring the sickness with them, and it turn out that the Fever kill more folks in the Outer States than it do in the Delta, so they be holding us off with soldiers. Then that checkpoint become a gate in the Wall, and we no longer part of Louisiana or even the United States. We just the Delta, and we been making our own way for half a hundred years.

"So that what they be singing about. How we the Delta, how we still Orleans. That first year after Jesus, when it been looking like we dead, that when the first krewe start. Somebody found an old Mardi Gras warehouse or something, and he pull out some costumes and go riding through the streets. Just one man holding up a lantern, saying 'We still here, we still here, thank Lord almighty, we still here.' I know somebody said he seen the man, riding like a damn fool, chest-deep through the floodwaters. And he couldn't help but follow. And other people started, too, 'til they all been wading along, with they flashlights and torches and all kinds of things, and they start singing and dancing, 'cause 'this be New Orleans and that be what we do,' he say. And every year, when the season for storms be over, somebody get out there and take up a torch and find theyselves a horse and do it all over again."

I ain't talked this much in a long time. Daniel looking at

me like he got too much on his plate and don't know how to eat it all.

"You got anything like that in the Outer States?"

Daniel don't answer.

"It be a good sign," I tell him again. "We gonna both get out of here okay."

I can see he don't believe me. He ain't got no tribe, no decent map, and nothing but me telling him so, but it gonna work out. Baby Girl back to sleeping in her sling again. Ain't no better time than now, so I stand up, stretch, and lead the way outside.

Night be thick around us. Daniel and I stick to the neutral ground. I tell him to watch for the trolley tracks running down the middle of the grass in either direction. Ain't been a trolley in more years than I been alive, but I seen pictures— pretty green boxes trimmed in red, used to carry a body from one end of the city to the other. Could use something like that now. A trolley'd take us right through A territory *and* La Bête's stomping grounds, drop us off right in front of the Professors' old school. But that ain't the way it be. We got to go on foot through the heart of it.

The As in the McDonald's don't stir. They ain't looking for trouble tonight. Maybe it be the sight of the krewe, or maybe enough folks be passing through on the way to and from the Market that they ain't trying to jump everybody that walk by. La Bête's people ain't quite so lenient.

Rain cleared up a while ago, but there still be clouds scudding across the sky. I hold up my hand to make Daniel wait and I think back to the last time I been here, with Lydia for another powwow, months ago, one that failed. This side of the road be mostly small trees, myrtle and magnolia, but once you cross into Uptown, St. Charles be a lot like a green cave. The road be lined with big old live oaks that done withstood even the worst of the storms. They make it darker than dark under there. La Bête had his people run signal torches all up and down the street, between the trees. Dried ropes soaked in pine tar and fat strung between them for fuses. One of his people have half a reason to suspect us, they light a torch and the whole place be bonfire-bright in minutes. I got good night eyes, but I ain't a cat. I pull Daniel back into the shadow of a crape myrtle.

"Daniel, listen. When I say run, we run. Cross the intersection to them trees on the other side. It gonna be dark over there, real dark. And I ain't got fancy goggles like you. I tell you where to go, you think you can lead us?"

He nod, but I know he ain't sure. He open his mouth, but I stop him.

"No. We can't wait 'til morning. Listen to me," I hiss. "They know we here. I guarantee La Bête got folks watching the street. We wait for a cloud to cross the moon and we run. Then it up to you. We heading to a big brick building on the right side, got an archway overhead say *Sacre Coeur.*"

"Sacred Heart?" he ask. "What's that got to do with the Institute?"

"That *be* the Institute."

I can see Daniel got questions, but we ain't got time.

"Okay. We going straight up the middle on the neutral ground, just like we been doing. Quiet but quick. They got

175

torches up and down this street, and if they hear us, they light them and it all be over. I'ma put my hand on your shoulder and follow you. But they come after us, you on your own. I got this baby to look after, and I'll do it however I can."

The All Saints' krewe feel like a fever dream now, the good omen feel more like wishful thinking. I look up at the sky. A fat mass of clouds be drifting right toward the moon. I hold up my hand, wait for them to block the moonlight. The intersection fall dark.

I grab Daniel with one hand, hold Baby Girl with the other, and we run, quiet as we can. Daniel be breathing heavy behind me, or maybe that my own breath in my ears. My heart pounding, that for sure.

The clouds clear the moon just as we plunge under the cover of trees. I can smell the pitch on the signal torches along the sidewalk. I know Daniel can see me, so I tap his arm and point to the neutral ground, three, maybe four yards away. I put a finger to my lips, point to the water. He go first, lowering one foot into the stream, then the other. I reach out and put my right hand on his shoulder, elbow stiff so I stop when he stop without bumping the baby. We take our time moving through the water. It ain't too high here, not even over the tops of my boots. We come out on the neutral ground and Daniel seem like he been listening, 'cause we don't stop.

We move through the dark and the back of my neck start tickling. I can't tell if it sweat or somebody got eyes on us. I want to push Daniel, tell him move faster, but I be guessing this the best he can do. Any faster and he'd be crashing along, calling down all sorts of hell on us.

I glance down and catch a gleam from the bundle in my arms. Baby Girl awake again, eyes shining in a dim shaft of moonlight. I hear her open her mouth in a yawn. Shit. In one of them books I got for Lydia, I read if I look scared, the baby gonna see me and get scared, too. Maybe even cry. So I look down at her and smile, even though it so dark under the trees, I ain't sure she can see me with them brand-new eyes. If I had any doubts before about giving her up and getting her out of this city, they gone now. This a hell of a way to spend your first few days alive.

Daniel slow down suddenly and I got to fight the need to cry out. Stupid. We at the end of the block. We step across another bit of stream as soft as we can and come up the other side before we pick up the pace. The dark be pressing down on me like a blanket. I strain my ears, but there ain't nothing but the wind in the leaves, little night creature sounds, and the call of a bird far off. Not every birdcall be a bird in Orleans, but it so far away I ain't worried.

And then Daniel stop so short that I bump into him. Baby Girl jump against me and I put my free hand over her mouth, praying she don't make a sound. Daniel reach around and grab my hand from his shoulder. He turn it over and tap the palm once. Twice. Suddenly I hear noise, the slap of footsteps on the broken sidewalk across the stream to my left. Two people. La Bête got his folks on patrol.

My heart start racing and I got to resist the urge to move, to look around when I know I can't see more than a foot in front of me. Any noise I make, any noise Baby Girl make, it all be over.

Daniel squeeze my hand and I hear him turn, watching. His gloves be rough on my skin, but his hands be my eyes right now. Sweat drip down my back. Then his grip relax. Whoever it been done come and gone. He put my hand onto his shoulder again and we move on. Two blocks down, two to go.

We less than a block away when it happen. Don't know if I stumbled or it just one of those things, but suddenly Baby Girl start wailing. A second later, I hear a whooshing sound and look behind me. The torches at the end of the block been lit and the fuses to the next set be starting to burn.

My hand fall from Daniel's shoulder. He on his own now.

But he don't let me go. He grab my hand and don't look back. We run.

It be a hard thing, running full tilt in the middle of the night, firelight racing to catch up with you. I hear the ABs screaming, hollering, but if they like me, the torchlight done ruined they night vision. All I see be grayness before me, orange light, heat, and shadows behind. Each torch that light send another whoosh of flame into the sky, and I try not to look back, but I can't help it. The light be gaining on us, and right behind it come La Bête's hunters, ready to take us down.

I hug Baby Girl to me and we running so fast that she stop crying and be gasping in little baby breaths. Then Daniel jerk me to the right and we splashing through the second creek and up onto the sidewalk. I see a torch looming and want to kick it out the ground, but if the fire stops here, that'd just tell them where we went, so I leave it and let Daniel lead.

He be smart, smarter than I thought, because we ain't come across right in front of the Institute. We run and the water on our boots runs dry on the concrete. Then we there, in front of the big wrought-iron archway, gold leaf turning to rust, but the words still visible: SACRE COEUR. I drag Daniel through a bend in the iron fence and out of sight in the overgrown yard just as the signal torches outside the gates burst to life.

21

❧ UNDER COVER OF THE ROAR OF FIRE, WE PUSH deeper into the courtyard. I lead Daniel around a corner of the building to where a little statue of Jesus's mother be lodged in the vines. We hide in the brambles and strain to hear La Bête's people run up the street as the torches ignite to the far end of the block. They moving past us, and I hear cursing and name-calling as blame being passed around. La Bête might be a sharp leader, but that don't mean his people be sharp, too. The drugs he use to make them fierce also make them stupid. And the blood they take mess with them in the head. Lucky for us.

We stay hidden 'til the torches burn theyselves out. It ain't far from here to the entrance of the building, but we got to cross the open yard, and even a drugged-up AB could see us then. So we wait. I make another bottle for the baby and she fall asleep without complaint. The whole time, I be remembering the feel of Daniel's hand. How he wouldn't let go, even though I told him to. Even though I'd have let go of him. Now Baby Girl and me owe him our lives, and I don't like it.

The sky be turning to dawn by the time we move again, a pearly gray peeking between them black-green leaves. I nudge Daniel and he don't jump, so I know he ain't been sleeping. Me neither. I take the lead, and we slip through the overgrown garden in the side yard, around the building where a brook flow beneath what used to be a covered walkway that led into the school. Now it more like a tunnel, an underground waterway.

"What is this place?" Daniel whisper. He be looking around like he seeing dinosaurs or something. I got to admit, I don't like the idea of going into that water. There ain't no boats tied up, and no way I be swimming down there with this baby in the dark. I turn to Daniel.

"You say you want the Professors. This be them."

Daniel frown up at the name carved into the stone archway above the water. "It's a Catholic school."

I shrug. "Used to be. Like you used to be a scientist, and now you a tourist."

"I . . ." he start to argue, but he can't, so he stop.

"The Professors started out at Tulane," I tell him. "But ain't a lot of buildings there after all the hurricanes. So they come over here once it dried out, after the Wall went up. Been here ever since."

Daniel nod like he understand and I wave at him to follow me. We move upstream from the school and cross where somebody laid down planks of wood for a bridge. Around

181

back, what used to be a playground now be overgrown with sweet potato and mirliton vines.

"Can you climb?" I ask him.

Daniel look down at his suit. "I don't think so."

"All right." I lead him around to the third side of the building. The door still be there, right up against a big crape myrtle tree, like someone plant it deliberately to hide the entrance. This be where smugglers drop deliveries. I squeeze past the tree and into the alcove.

I start to pull my knife to jimmy the lock open, but I don't need it. The door been left open, just a crack. I hold on to my knife anyway. "Watch yourself and stay quiet," I say, and we slip inside.

Or I do, at least. Daniel squeeze through that doorway like a baby being born. Just as noisy, too. I shake my head and move forward down the dark hallway. A little light be filtering in from stairwells at either end of the hall. The floor tiles be cracked marble, with seepage coming through, making them mossy. It be more like a natural cave than a hallway. A stranger ever make it this far inside, they be thinking the building abandoned and move on. But I know better.

Baby Girl look up at me like she know where we at, here where it all began. I want to touch that soft cheek of hers, but I don't want to rile her up. Instead, I give her a little smile and pad on up the hall to the right, all the way to the steps.

The light be stronger here; light shine in from a barred window in the upper stairwell. Daniel follow me up the marble steps, rubbed smooth from years of girls running up and down them. I stick to the wall where the stone still be level.

Harder to slip that way. We come out into another wide hallway, lit by dim fluorescents from above. The electricity still working here. That a good sign.

Halfway down the hall, I see the containment sheet still hanging. Ain't nobody messed with it, which mean ain't nobody here who don't belong. If an AB or some freesteader'd made it inside, they'd have torn the whole thing down, picked it over like an Ursuline cleaning a skull and bones. I resheath my knife and adjust my hold on Baby Girl.

"What is this place?" Daniel ask.

I cluck my tongue. "Ain't you got no new questions? You wanted the Professors. Sorry, your 'Institute of Post-Separation Studies.' I say it be useless, but you don't want to listen, so I'ma show you." We reach the containment sheet, a big wall made of plastic with a doorway in it. Instead of letting you through to the other side, it lead to a little chamber that curve in a tunnel to a door in the wall.

"This be sealed on both ends. You go through there into the infirmary. That where you'll find what be left of them."

"Like an air lock," Daniel say to himself. "How do you know all of this?"

I cut him a look. "How I know anything, man? I just do."

Daniel hesitate. "Aren't you coming?"

"I can't," I say, trying hard to be patient. "Anyone still alive in there, this protect them from the Fever. I be native, man. I be a carrier."

"They can't all be in there, can they?" Daniel ask, pressing his face up against the plastic. But there ain't nothing to see 'til he get inside.

I look around. "Didn't used to be, but it been some years since I been here, so maybe."

"You know them . . . the Professors?" he ask.

I shrug. "This ain't about me. You going in or not?"

"Come inside the air lock with me at least."

I shake my head. "Man, you a bigger baby than this little girl in my arms. Come on upstairs and we'll go around. There be a window on the other side."

We turn back to the stairwell and I be thinking about pulling my knife out again, but knives ain't no good against ghosts, and they the only thing waiting for me up them stairs.

22

⚜ *TODAY IS THE DAY WE SAY GOOD-BYE TO
everyone. Mommy and Daddy don't think that I know, but
I listen from under the table sometimes, and I heard them
say it. When we leave the Institute today, it will be the last
time I say good-bye to Priscilla, Dr. Warren, and the others.
I'm glad we are leaving. I don't like Dr. Warren's infirmary. I
don't like the beds or the lights or the sounds.*

*We live at the Institute on an Open floor, and Mommy
and Daddy work in the field. Priscilla lives on a Closed floor
with Dr. Warren. I only see her when we have our suits on,
or when she's behind a safe wall, but that's still too close for
me. She's pale as a fish belly, and mean. So when Mommy
says it's time to go to school today, and today is a Father
John day and not a Sister Mary Margaret day, I pick up my
schoolbag and I wave at Priscilla through the safe wall, and
when Mommy isn't looking, I stick my tongue out at Priscilla
before we leave. That makes me feel good.*

When I go say good-bye to Dr. Warren, I duck down real low so I don't have to look him in the face. Overhead, his screen blinks at me, green and black. When I wave, it blinks again.

GOOD-BYE, FEN. GOOD-BYE.

"Stay close to me, Fen," Mommy says.

"I always do, Mommy," I tell her, and she smiles. I am her good little girl. We leave the Institute and walk across the stream to the neutral ground.

Yesterday was my last day with Sister Mary Margaret and the other kids at the Ursuline convent. I made sure to pretend I'd see them again, but I won't. Daddy says we're going to visit Father John at the Catholic mission, but he's telling a story he must want everybody to believe. Because last night, I heard him talking to Mr. Go and Mommy. They said the Institute is a bad place and Dr. Warren is a bad man. They don't want to play with him anymore. Like I don't want to play with Priscilla. Just because she is older doesn't mean she's a grown-up, but she makes me do what she wants and I don't like it. Priscilla thinks she is special because Dr. Warren is her granddaddy and she was the first baby at the Institute. But I came second, and I was the last, and that makes me just as special, Mommy says.

Daddy is waiting for us in a jeep. It is Father John's jeep, the one he runs supplies with. We never get to ride in the jeep unless we are carrying Important Supplies from the Institute, or Mommy is bringing back samples of plants that are big. Jeeps run on Gas, and Gas is harder to find than a five-leaf clover, Mommy says. It comes from the Government in big yellow canisters, but Father John hasn't gotten any in a long, long time.

"Mommy, did the Government give Father John more Gas?" I ask.

Mommy shakes her head. "No, Fen. The Government isn't helping us out like that anymore."

"Why not?" I ask. Everyone is supposed to help everyone. That's what Sister Mary Margaret says. It's called the Golden Rule. It's not the same as Dr. Warren's Rules of Blood. Those are different. Those say everyone has to stay apart from everyone else. I'm lucky my mommy and daddy have the same blood as me, or else we would have to stay apart, too.

We get into the jeep and Daddy drives us the long way to Father John's mission. "Is Mr. Go coming?" I ask. Mommy gives me a look and I hold my tongue. I'm not supposed to know Mr. Go's leaving the Institute, too. That's a big secret. Mr. Go is like Priscilla. He lives on a Closed floor at the Institute and he hardly ever leaves. When he does go out, he wears an outside suit.

"Simeon's not coming with us today," Daddy says with a look at Mommy. I hold my tongue again. I remember last night when I was supposed to be sleeping. Mommy said Mr. Go is Not Right, either. She said, "We have to live in Orleans, not in Spite-of-it." I don't know where Spite-of-it is, but I don't want to live there. It must be where Mr. Go will live.

We drive and drive across the city, and some folks wave at us, and some hide. Mommy keeps her gun hidden, but I know it's there. Sometimes people get really hungry or really sick, she says, and they will try to take things from us. So Mommy carries a gun while Daddy drives, and he's such a good driver that she doesn't have to use it.

Soon we are at the mission and Father John sweeps me into a big hug. "Welcome back, Little Fen," he says. Father John smells like incense, like the nuns burn in the chapel at school. He is a big man, tall like a tree. Father John is my friend. Even though he is not a type O blood, I think he is part of our tribe.

Mommy and Daddy help Father John unload the jeep. There is medicine in white boxes with red crosses on the side and there are tools to help repair the computers in the mission. They run on electricity, which is hard to find. Mommy says you can make electricity with gasoline or wind or water, but you need the right machines to catch it. With these tools, Father John can keep his machines going even when the gasoline is gone.

I go inside and sit in the computer room and write a letter to Uncle Garrett and Aunt Cee. The Coopers are my family on the other side of the Wall. They asked to be friends with a little girl and send her letters and things, and they got to have me. I tell them good-bye. I don't know when I'll write again, but I don't say that because it's a secret.

"Fenny?" Daddy says to me when he's done helping carry supplies. "Do you remember what we talked about yesterday?"

I hang my head. Daddy got mad at me because I was talking like the other kids at the nun's school and the mission. "I'm sorry, Daddy," I say. "I was talking tribe. I won't do it again. But when I talk like you and Mommy, everyone makes fun of me. They say I'm a Professor, but I'm not. Professors are old people like Dr. Warren, and I'm just a little girl."

Daddy crouches down in front of me and takes me by the shoulders. "No, Fen, I'm glad you can talk tribe."

I think he's fooling with me. "You are?"

"Yes, honey. It's like that chameleon Mommy showed you."

I nod. "The lizard that looks like the leaf?"

"That's right, baby girl," Mommy says. "We're leaving now, Fen, and you've got to be like the lizard on the leaf."

"So no one can find me—and I'll be safe from owls and hawks?"

Daddy smiles, but Mommy is crying. "Yes, sweetie, so you'll be safe."

"I'll be invisible."

"That's right," Mommy says.

"Even to Father John and Mr. Go?" I ask. Mommy and Daddy look at each other.

"No, baby girl, they can see you. They're lizards, too."

"But not Priscilla?" I ask. I don't want to play lizards with Priscilla.

"Not Priscilla," Mommy says. "And not Dr. Warren or anybody at the Institute. And no tribes, either, unless they're Os or OPs, okay? Got it?"

That's a lot of people to be invisible to, but I nod because I will try.

"Got it," I say. And I talk tribe to show them I mean it. "They be Professors. But we be tribe."

Mommy take my hand then, and Daddy take the other,

and we wave good-bye to Father John and we walk into the woods to our new house, a little wooden house in a clearing.

It be just like a fairy story, only it scary, too, because we don't go back to the Institute when the sun go down, like we always used to do. We alone here, Mommy, Daddy, and me, and I know we ain't tribe at all.

We freesteaders. And freestead mean dead, the school kids say. But tribe, tribe is life.

23

⚜ "FEN?" DANIEL BE STANDING RIGHT UP BEHIND me, like I'ma give him a piggyback ride up them steps.

"Hold on, now," I say, and pretend to be adjusting the baby's sling around my shoulders instead of putting off seeing them ghosts. Baby Girl looking at me like she got something wise to tell me, but then she yawn and close her eyes. "All right," I say, and we climb.

The third floor of Sacre Coeur be like the first two—marble floors and a long hallway lined with classrooms, only these classes been over for fifty years or more, and since then the rooms been turned into housing. I stop at the third door on the right and look through the little window at the top of the door. It look like a storeroom now—cots and empty bookcases, boxes all shoved against the far wall, blocking the windows. My heart skip a beat in my chest and I take a quick breath. I be glad it ain't still the way it been when we left. Don't know if I could handle that.

"What's in there?" Daniel ask. I swear he be breathing down my neck, and I'm like to slap him, he bugging me so bad.

"You know, if I need to pull my knife suddenly, you'd be standing in the way."

He back up real quick then, hands up in front of his face. "Pull your knife for what?"

I snort. "You scare too easy. Back off. Three feet between you and me. Something come up, a body need some room to move." I point my arm out at him and draw a circle around me. "This, plus a blade. Leave room for it or you get cut. Got it?"

He back up a little more and nod. "Got it. But what's in that room?"

"Nothing now." I shrug and keep going down the hallway. "But I been born there."

I feel Daniel gape at the back of my head, but I keep my memories to myself. I ain't here to make friends and share my story. The sooner he see the Professors be a dead end, the sooner I be rid of him and get this baby over the Wall.

We descend to the second floor again, on the opposite side of the plastic doorway we been on before, and I stop in front of the infirmary. There be a window in the wall looking directly into the infirmary, not the lab room the air lock lead to. I don't like looking through that glass any more than I did when I been little, but I seen a lot of mess between here and there, so maybe this ain't as bad as all that.

On the other side of the window, the infirmary be dark,

except for the life-support systems lighting up the room in little halos of light, like flies swarming over each bed.

Some of the beds be empty. The rest be holding corpses.

Daniel gasp at the sight.

I turn Baby Girl away. She don't need to know about things like this, not if she gonna have a life over the Wall where things be normal and folks ain't trying to extend they lives beyond the natural span just so they can play king of the mountain. Like this room full of dried-out husks that used to be living, thinking people. Fools. I bounce Baby Girl against my skin and she feel so soft and warm and alive, it make me feel something close to glad.

"There you go," I tell Daniel. "They be the Professors."

Daniel stand quiet for a real long time, and I don't know if he accessing his datalink or just thinking. "Are they dead?" he ask at last.

"Not all of them. But they should be. Lot of these folks been old by Orleans standards when they got here. Dr. Warren over there"—I point with my chin to the first bed on the left—"got to be almost eighty, but I don't think age counts when it earned with pumps and force-feeding."

In the reflection we cast on the glass, I see Daniel blink back tears. He put a hand to the window. "Warren Abernathy James?" He press his head against the glass. "This was supposed to be . . . Oh my God, oh my God."

I don't say nothing, just let it sink in, let the sight convince him where my words can't.

"Fen . . . What am I supposed to do? How am I . . . ?"

"How you supposed to what, Daniel? What you come here for?"

He don't move back from the glass, but he turn his head to look at me. "I came to cure Delta Fever."

I laugh. "You and everybody else, I'm sure."

"Right. But what if I told you I've almost done it?" He reach into that big old coat of his and pull out a long black cylinder, lit up with green lights like the equipment on the other side of the glass.

Every muscle in my body go tight. Baby Girl wake up and start to cry. I shush her, but my eyes don't leave that cylinder.

"I call it the DF virus. My attempt at a vaccine for the Fever."

"Attempt?" I say.

"I was trying to kill the disease, but it kills the host, too. Carriers. Like you."

To think I thought I owed this fool my life and he been risking it the whole time. I swing Baby Girl's sling behind me and jump back from Daniel fast as a cat, my knife already in my hand.

"Fen—" he start to say, but I ain't listening. I take a swipe at him, and lucky for Daniel, he paid attention and be out of reach of my blade. But I ain't trying to kill him. I'ma let the city do that. I spit at him and back away to the stairwell. Swinging Baby Girl back in front of me, I get a good hold on her and run. There be a crack of light coming through the door we entered from. I squeeze back through the doorway and slam it shut behind me.

24

SHE PULLED A KNIFE ON ME, DANIEL THOUGHT. *She thinks I betrayed her.* But he had done the right thing. Leaving the virus in the lab would have been the same as giving up on a cure. Or worse, giving the military a weapon. At least that's what he told himself.

Daniel stood up, careful not to look back through the observation window that reminded him so much of Charlie's final days in quarantine. Careful not to think of what he would do now, without Fen.

The building was an eerie place, silent as a tomb. There had to be answers here somewhere. At the very least, there would be supplies, and a better map to help him find a way back over the Wall. There had to be.

Across the hall from the infirmary was a security room. A wall of monitors loomed above a workstation that looked like pictures he'd seen of the old mission control rooms at NASA. The Institute of Post-Separation Studies hadn't been well-funded. The loss of the Delta had hit the US economy hard. So the Institute had run on a patchwork of high-tech gear and dated equipment believed capable of withstanding the challenging environment in Orleans. A sensitive tool like Daniel's datalink wouldn't have lasted the first decade in the humidity here. So it made a sort of sense, even if the result was less than state-of-the-art.

The monitors were all cold and dark now, but labels beneath listed names of locations across the city—the Superdome, the Market. At some point, they must've had eyes everywhere. But there was nothing here for Daniel now. He moved back into the corridor and began peering through windows.

At last, he came to a room of filing cabinets. Daniel leaned against the door and listened. He dialed up his night-vision goggles. There was dust on the floorboards near the door that hadn't been disturbed in years. Relieved, he opened the door and went inside.

Green and beige filing cabinets lined the walls, four drawers high each. He opened the top drawer of the nearest cabinet. At least they had been clever. Instead of manila folders and paper files, the records within were recorded on thin sheets of plastic, organizing tabs running along the tops. Printed thermally, the words became a permanent part of the sheet. Even in a flood, these files would survive.

The windows on the outer wall were blocked by bookcases, and a thin gray light seeped in through the narrow cracks between them. He pulled out the first group of files and lowered himself to the ground, back up against the side of the cabinet. This way he could watch the door in case Fen came back.

"What have I gotten myself into?" Daniel muttered as his suit whirred to life, siphoning away the sudden sweat on his palms. Fen would come back, he told himself. She would realize she'd made a mistake, that he was the best hope for Orleans, and she'd come save him.

But it wasn't likely. Technically, she'd lived up to her part of the bargain. She had gotten him out of the blood farm and to the Institute, just as he'd asked. So he couldn't blame her for leaving, even if the Professors were in comas and he was still as lost as he had been the moment he arrived. He laughed, and it sounded high-pitched, nearly hysterical. He forced himself to stop, took a deep breath, and focused on the files in front of him.

First things first: He should find what he came for. And then, who knew? With a cure in hand, maybe he could bargain his way out of the Delta. What tribe would harm the man who could save them? Maybe the Institute still had working radios or other communications equipment. He could signal the States for help, call in the cavalry. With the DF virus turned into a cure, there would be no danger of genocide if he contacted the military. He would be a hero.

All he had to do was focus on the files.

They were personnel records, files for Warren Abernathy James and his crew of sociologists, biologists, botanists, and medical doctors, both psychological and physical. It read like a list of Nobel Prize winners, people who had consigned themselves to the quarantine city at the height of their careers, a dream team determined to find a cure. Then came the falling stars, once-renowned researchers whose willingness to join the one-way trip to Orleans was a Hail-Mary pass, a last, heroic attempt to make a name for themselves. Daniel recognized some of the names as former professors at his own university. They had thought the Institute would last a few years, a long sabbatical, and they would return, tenured and celebrated, the world once again united in good health. People still talked about those missing professors with reverence and the occasional head shake of disbelief.

There was nothing new to discover here. No research, just résumés and observational notes. At the back of the folder, he found the thinner résumés of graduate students who had treated a tenure at the Institute as the equivalent of a semester at sea. When he'd first heard of these students and their Peace Corps–like commitment to the people of the Delta, he had thought them ludicrous. It was one thing for a fifty-year-old scientist to make the move to Orleans, but what twenty-something student would willingly condemn themselves to life in a disease-ridden, dying city at the beginning of their own life? Even protected by the walls of the Institute, it had sounded idealistically shortsighted. But now he was here for the same reasons and not half the support or equipment that the Institute had begun with. Who was the fool now?

He stood up and shuffled the files together, ready to return them to the drawer, when a label caught his attention: DE LA GUERRE. Fen said she was born here. This file belonged to a Jerome de la Guerre. Fen's father? Daniel hesitated, fingering the top of the page. It didn't matter. He could read Fen's entire life history here, but it wouldn't help him cure the Fever or find his way back home. Shaking his head, Daniel returned the files to the drawer and moved to the next cabinet.

Inventories of food and equipment came next. The equipment lists were less useful than he had hoped. Much of the lab equipment was woefully unsophisticated and out of date. Only now were labs able to attempt the sort of viral engineering that had half a hope of beating the disease. And that required equipment that Orleans did not have.

So this was simply a data-gathering mission. Daniel would have to find his way home again to complete the work, no matter what.

The last drawer held newspaper clippings, medical journals, and the research that had gone into writing the articles. This was all first-year textbook reading for any biology student. Nothing helpful, nothing new. The rest of the filing cabinets were filled with the same sort of archival documentation.

At last, Daniel gave up. This room didn't hold any secrets. Except for one.

Feeling a bit like a voyeur, Daniel pulled the Jerome de la Guerre file from its drawer and began to read.

Jerome de la Guerre had been one of those idealistic graduate students, a doctoral candidate in social anthropology. Fen's mother, Sylvie, had studied botany. They both signed on for field duty. Their type O blood had made them more resistant to the Fever than some of the other Institute workers, and they had volunteered to work in the city, outside the protective walls of the Institute's old school building. They mimicked the lives of freesteaders at a time when freesteading was not as dangerous as it was today. There were still aide workers in the city then, church-run missions. Jerome and Sylvie had run a pipeline of information between a mission run by a Catholic priest, Father John Dunham, the Institute, and the Ursuline school. Together, the three organizations brought food, water, medical supplies, and structure to the struggling community of Orleans. Almost thirty-five years after the Wall had gone up, it seemed like a silver age, an age of hope. Somewhere along the way, Jerome and Sylvie fell in love, married, and had one daughter. Fen.

But something had happened. Fen's parents had left the Institute. A falling-out with the management, the file said. A change in the Institute's mission, a parting of the ways. If the Institute had been the de la Guerres' tribe, then at some point they, along with a five-year-old Fen, had made a break with Dr. James and his organization.

And they were not the only ones to leave. A senior researcher and a few other field operatives were said to have "gone native" as well.

Daniel closed the file and returned it to the cabinet drawer. This was politics and strife, not science. He was here for data, he reminded himself, not gossip. He had a world to save.

25

❧ I LEAN MY BACK AGAINST THE DOOR AND STAY hidden in the alcove behind that old crape myrtle, trying to think. *Fen, girl, you a fool.* So what if Daniel done pulled us through the dark? So what if he help us get out of that blood farm? He been using us. Like the swamp rats the Professors used to experiment on. Best thing I can do for Orleans be lock Daniel up inside. Him and his damned virus.

I be breathing heavy, feeling like a trapped animal. But I got away, I tell myself. We got away. Baby Girl make a noise in my arms and I look down at her little face. Her mama's eyes stare back at me.

"What you be looking at me like that for?"

She yawn, but this time she don't go to sleep. She just stare and I stare back. I can't help it. This baby got eyes like a sinkhole; they be pulling me in, and I let them.

"Can you believe that, Baby Girl? Fool trying to cure Delta Fever."

Ain't like a million other folks haven't tried. Before the Wall, Daddy say everybody with a test tube and a kitchen sink be trying to cook up a cure. A medicine like that make you rich for life. You could own the Delta.

But a cure mean other things, too. If Delta Fever be gone and all the sick folks over here be cured, there'd be no more blood hunting, no blue tarp room in the Ursulines' hospital. No Wall.

I be assessing my situation again, looking at my assets. I got Baby Girl. And I got a chance.

"You wouldn't have to leave me," I say softly. I think of Daniel again, dragging me after him through the night, torches on our heels. He a do-gooder. Maybe they all like that over the Wall. Daniel create a poison, but he ain't using it. He coulda opened that canister back at the blood farm, killed us all and gotten out. Hell, he could be using it now and we be dead where we stand. But he ain't. Daniel ain't a killer.

And now Baby Girl finally be talking to me with them eyes of hers. She be telling me what to do next. "Baby Girl, you don't know the world like I do. This gonna be more trouble than it worth."

She just look at me and yawn again like she bored. Like I ain't got any other excuses. Which I don't. I curse under my breath and look out through the branches of the myrtle tree. Baby Girl ain't never seen a crape myrtle in bloom, and she never will if she got to go to Father John and over the Wall.

"You want to see something pretty?" I ask her. "Maybe

one day you see flowers on this tree." She hiccup at me and I shake my head. Me, talking to this baby like it make some kind of sense. I don't make her any promises, 'cause I know this one gonna be real hard to keep, but I'ma try.

It take a little doing, but I get that door pried back open and I shuffle back up them stairs. Back to where I used to be someone with parents, good people who tried to make a difference.

Doors be open up and down the hallway. I find Daniel sitting in the middle of the hall, like a dog that don't know what to do without a master.

"You came back," he say.

I shrug. "You saved me and Baby Girl last night. I owe you for that." In my arms, Baby Girl gurgle and coo. I point to the open doors with my chin. "You find what you looking for?"

"There's nothing here." Daniel stand up, slow and stiff in his suit. "There's nothing here on the Fever at all," he say incredulously. "I don't understand. There should be research, records, data. Something."

I shake my head. "I told you it be useless. Come on, now."

"Where are we going?"

I look at the baby in my arms one last time, make sure I'm doing the right thing. "To the only person who might help you. The oldest man in the Delta, Mr. Go."

Daniel turn suddenly and look through the observation window into the infirmary. "My God," he say.

My feet don't want to move, but I make them, and I walk to see what he seeing. The screen over the first bed be lit up in big green letters: **WHO'S THERE?**

"Come on, Daniel," I whisper. But he don't move, and suddenly all the screens come alive with bright green lights. They blink at us like owls in a tree: **WHO? WHO? WHO?**

26

⚜ **FEN? FEN DE LA GUERRE?**

"Shit." I shake my head. "Yes, Dr. Warren," I say for the first time in eleven years.

FEN. ARE YOUR PARENTS HERE?

"You know they dead the minute they left you. We made it five years." Nobody survive as a freesteader for long.

I watch the screen. But it ain't like him to say sorry or nothing like that. On to the next thing, then. "Where Priscilla at?" I ask.

"Who's Priscilla?" Daniel whisper.

"His granddaughter. She twice my age but the closest thing to a kid the Professors ever had. When they got sick, she took over, caring for them and running the project. I thought she the one you been looking for."

Through the glass, Dr. Warren's screen lights up. **SHE LEFT US. IN THE NAME OF THE WORK.**

"Left you?" I think of the way the door been left cracked

205

open. She ain't planning on coming back here. Dr. Warren really be dead. He just don't know it.

"Is she coming back?" Daniel ask. I hear the hope in his voice, like he might still find what he looking for here.

I shake my head. "Man, you don't even know if she alive. Walk away, Daniel."

"But I have questions . . ."

I shake my head. He ain't gonna come with me 'til he ask. "Go ahead. But then we leaving."

Daniel face the glass, so close I think he about to hit his nose on the pane. "Dr. James, my name is Daniel Weaver. I'm a military research scientist from over the Wall. We're making progress on a cure for Delta Fever, but we still have questions. Where is your research kept?"

The screen stay blank for a long time. I shift Baby Girl to my other hip and wait.

THERE IS NO CURE.

"Not yet, but we're working on one . . . I'm working on one. And I'm very close. But I don't have access to samples in the States, the way you do here. Finding a cure was one of your objectives. Any work you've done on the subject might hold the key for me."

THERE IS NO CURE. PRISCILLA? ARE YOU THERE?

Daniel sigh and look at me. "Doesn't he understand?"

"Sure. You the one not understanding. Why you think my parents left? They ain't working on a cure here, Daniel. Orleans just a lab to them. We ain't people, we rats."

"If they weren't looking for a cure, what is all this for?"

"You from the other side of the Wall. Don't you know?" I

ask. He stare at me. "Dr. Warren's pet project," I prompt him. "He ain't interested in the Fever. He studying tribes."

Daniel frown. "Ending racism," he say. "For the most part, the rules of blood make race irrelevant. Blood types cross all ethnicities."

I nod. "If folks stop hating each other 'cause of skin color, the only difference be blood type."

"A new form of racism," Daniel say. His face go pale. "It's like Tuskegee all over again. They never wanted a cure."

I don't know nothing about Tuskegee, but if it mean folks with power always gonna abuse it, then I got to agree. "How else they gonna study tribes?" I say.

Daniel look back into the infirmary at them dried-up husks. His fist clench and unclench, and he drop his head against the window. Then he turn to me.

"What do we do now? Just leave them here?" He point at they IV bags, more than half empty. I shrug.

"Why not? They ain't tribe."

"That's insane," Daniel say.

"That the world they made," I say. "Now, I got a baby to take care of. You coming?"

Daniel hesitate. He maybe thinking how he saved me and Baby Girl out there just last night. And he be realizing I wouldn't have done it for him. It ain't wrong, but I don't like the way it make me feel, so I look away.

"All right, Baby Girl, we going," I whisper to Lydia's little girl. This time, when we leave, I make sure Daniel and his virus come with us. No more "every man for himself." If Orleans gonna have a better future, we in this together now.

Part Three

CHIEFTAIN

27

✦ "WE'RE GOING TO MR. GO'S?" DANIEL ASKED. He was moving slowly, weighed down by the visit to the Professors. Fen swept away the fallen leaves and flowers with her boot and shut the door firmly.

"Yeah, but I got to do something first," she said.

"What?" Daniel asked, adjusting the rags around his neck. The day was growing warmer, the sky so blue it was almost purple.

Fen tucked her thumbs into her pack straps and took off for the back road to avoid the avenue they'd come in on, and any lingering ABs.

"I had some people on the outside. I need to get a message to them."

"You can do that?" Daniel asked, hopping over the broken pavement. "Get a message over the Wall?"

"Don't always work, but it worth a shot."

Daniel hurried to catch up. "How do you do it? I mean, if I could do that, I could get help or something. I could—"

She gave him a hard look. "You could what? Don't take a genius to see you ain't supposed to be here. You got no idea what Orleans about. You here alone, not a single person got your back. So who you gonna contact, Daniel? Who gonna help you that didn't before?"

Daniel didn't say anything. There wasn't anything he could say. He'd made one mistake after another. Now it was up to Fen. Maybe it always had been. "I'll wait for your Mr. Go."

"All right," she said.

"You still haven't answered my question," Daniel said. "Where are we going?"

Fen skipped ahead and gave him an easy smile. "The library. Then, maybe church."

Daniel shook his head. "Oh. Of course."

The library was a beautiful building on the leafy avenue they had run down last night. Fen led him down a backstreet before risking the main road. This far into AB territory, there were no torches strung between the old live oaks, and sunlight sifted through the canopy overhead. They moved as quietly as possible. After last night's wild chase, Fen told him the ABs would sleep in. Daniel knew from his research that AB was the most Fever-susceptible blood type. Without constant transfusions, the Fever made ABs sluggish and weak.

Like his brother, Charlie. His sterile death in a hospital was cruel, but life in Orleans didn't seem much better.

They reached a place in the stream where chunks of concrete had been laid out like stepping stones. Fen jumped lightly across them to the green lawn on the opposite side, where the library squatted, an implacable building of red stone. Fen mounted the steps swiftly. Daniel followed her in, swinging the heavy steel doors shut behind him.

Inside, the library was a throwback to another age. Heavy wooden furniture, walls lined with thick dark bookshelves, stained oak floors. But it reeked of mildew and the bookcases themselves were empty.

"Used to be a librarian here when I been real little," Fen pointed out, breezing past the reception desk. The light leaching in through the windows was watery and thin, the old glass deep set into the walls of the building to protect them from storms. "An AB, since this be they turf. But she gone now. The computer be in the back."

"Working?" Daniel asked.

"Sometimes. That why I said maybe we could do it, maybe not. We not far from the Professors. My guess be one of them got this thing running. Someone did. Old car batteries and sometimes a generator. I don't know who been keeping it up. Here."

An ancient PC sat on a long oak table at the back of the ground floor, its casing filthy with age and use. The power cord snaked down to a box on the floor covered in black electrical tape.

"Don't be touching that," Fen snapped. She shifted the baby onto her lap so she could type. With one booted foot, she pumped a lever beneath the table, somehow attached to the box. Daniel recognized it as an antique sewing machine foot pedal.

"This is incredible," he said. "And it's communal? For everyone?"

Fen shrugged. "ABs had it to theyselves for a while and posted guards 'round the building. But they ain't knowing how to keep it running, and it died. So they abandon it 'til somebody come 'round and fix it." She peered at the blank screen. "That how it be. Share it, and it work. Mess with it and it don't. "

A few more pumps and the computer sprang to life.

"There we go," Fen said to herself. She wiped her nose with the back of her hand, opened a browser, and started to type.

"You have an e-mail account?" Daniel asked her.

"Every tribe do. Least the ones around before things got bad. They been set up by the missionaries. Supposed to keep folks in touch with they relatives on the other side. Only our chief ever used it, but I know the password. If they ain't changed it on me."

"What did your chief use it for?" It wasn't like they could go shopping online.

"Smugglers. Medicine and stuff too hard to get in Orleans. Beyond that be her business. I didn't ask."

⚜ HE BE ASKING TOO MANY QUESTIONS NOW, and I be letting my mouth run. I got business to take care of. I open the program and type in my e-mail. It be a hard thing to write, but I been thinking about it on the walk here:

Aunt Cee and Uncle Garrett, It's me, your little Fen. I am sorry it has been so long since you have heard from me. I hate to ask, but I need your help. You were always good sponsor parents to me. You would make good real parents too. If you would like to be please write me back. There is a child that needs your help. No Fever. DELTA-FREE. Love, Fen de la Guerre.

I feel silly writing it, using my best English how the Ursulines taught us, but I got to make sure they understand me. I hit send and wait to see that it go. My leg be getting tired from pumping the generator, but I keep it up.

"How does it get transmitted?" Daniel ask.

When it go through, I erase my password, clear the history, and log off.

"Maybe it don't," I say. "But I got to try. Now we wait and see."

Daniel be staring at me like I be crazy, but that ain't the first time. I stare right back. Then he say, "Can I send a message, too?"

Before I can answer, I hear the door open at the front of the building.

Hide, I mouth to Daniel. I put my hand over Baby Girl's mouth in case she start to cry and scurry away from the desk through a side door that be broken, into another room. Full of old furniture, it be all rotten sofas and flood-damaged stuff, covered with mold. I worry about Baby Girl breathing it in, so I cover her face with the sling. Daniel be right by my side, so I know he scared. I lead him around a mound of cushions and we stand behind an arch in the wall. My knife still in my boot, but I ain't starting nothing with this baby in my arms 'less I have to.

"Who?" Daniel whisper. I put my finger to his lips and mouth the letters *AB* and shrug. He nod. Then I lean forward and try to listen. Two men be talking.

"This thing don't even be working no more," First Man say. His voice be deep like his chest broad. He sound big.

"It work good enough to get what we want," Second Man say. He got a voice like a reed flute, the kind they sell at the Market for little kids. "Can't stop now, man," Second Man continue. "That raid on the Os, that a bold move, but you know what they say—you got to back it up with some serious action."

"You right, you right," First Man say in his deep voice.

My mind be spinning. These be the bastards attacked us at the powwow. Lydia be dead because of them.

That explain why there weren't no dogs after Lydia and me that night. It weren't just a blood raid. Tribes be attacking each other all the time, looking for fresh blood. But blood ain't enough for these bastards. They been looking to start a war.

Before I know it, I be bending down and my knife be in my hand. I grip it hard. My life be over because of them. Theirs 'bout to be over, too.

I wrap an arm around Baby Girl and edge toward the door, knife at the ready. They want a war, they got one.

I feel a hand touch my shoulder. "Fen?" Daniel whisper. I hesitate, shake my head. I got to do this. He grip my shoulder. I should shake him off, do what I gotta do, but if the baby cry from shaking, I ain't got no chance at all.

I look back at Daniel. His eyes be wide, scared. He shake his head no. Every muscle in my body screaming for me to go through that door.

In the next room, I hear somebody typing on the keyboard. They sending a message to someone, too. "A'ight, that done," Second Man say. "We can tell LB we sent it, let him worry if it gone work in time for tomorrow."

LB. La Bête Sauvage. That stop me. People say he crazy, but Lydia always treat him with respect. He a genius, she say, more going on behind one eye than most folks got in they whole head. I don't know about that, but I know he dangerous. He got ideas. He AB, and he bring As and Bs into his fold, too. But not everybody want to follow a crazy person.

I lower my knife, but don't be putting it away. The computer pings, and I know they e-mail been sent. "Two of two?" First Man say. "You send two messages on this thing?"

"Naw, man. It be a piece of junk. Let's go. What he got coming could make things a whole lot better, or a whole lot worse."

"Brother, war always be worse. And that what he got coming for us all."

We wait 'til I hear the front door slam. I motion for Daniel to wait a little longer. You never know who be playing you, and they not always as dumb as they sound.

After about ten minutes, when anybody waiting be getting bored, we slip out the lounge and see the computer room be clear. I put my knife back in my boot.

"War?" Daniel ask.

"Nothing to do with you, long as you leave Orleans quick. Bad times come and go here. Just means they coming back again," I say, and start pumping the computer pedal.

They ain't as smart as me. They don't be erasing they login or nothing. They ain't even signed out. "They cocky. Think they own the library," I say to myself, but Daniel nod like I meant it for him.

I memorize they account for future reference and open they e-mail addressed to orpheus@la.us.gov.

Daniel read the e-mail address over my shoulder. "Government? State of Louisiana."

"But there ain't no more Louisiana. Mr. Go say it became a military base after the storms."

"It did," Daniel say. "It's the first-response area for the entire Midwest."

"You come here through Louisiana?"

"No. Mississippi."

With that mess he carrying, I got to know. "Anybody know you here?"

Daniel don't blink or look away. "No. At least, I don't think so."

That ain't a good answer, but that be all he got. I turn back to the AB's e-mail. "Weird. There ain't no subject line and the message be blank."

"Look again," Daniel say, leaning over me. He drag the mouse over the e-mail and it highlight white letters.

SAMPLE WAS IMPRESSIVE. GUNS ACCEPTABLE. PAYMENT ON DELIVERY OF ORDER AT USUAL DROP. TOMORROW, 0600 HOURS.

I read it and read it again. Someone in the Outer States military sending guns to La Bête over the Wall. With Lydia dead and the Os scattered, he could take the city. It'd be unity like Lydia been wanting, but not peace.

"How is that possible?" Daniel breathes in my ear. "You said . . . Dr. James is bedridden. Could he do this from his bed?"

"Maybe Priscilla? Or might be something planned a long time back. Don't matter who, so long as it still happening." I close my eyes and think of Lydia. Things be worse in Orleans than she ever imagined. War again. ABs with guns. It one thing to be kidnapped and made a blood slave, but ABs get a frenzy once the blood start running. They shoot a body and catch that scent, nothing gonna stop them from killing everyone.

It only stop when the gunmetal go bad. And that could take years. Add a stupid tourist with a batch of poison, and it starting to look like the end of the world. Daniel and I need to get out of here, and now.

"How much you weigh?"

"What?"

"How much you weigh?" I look at him hard. "Hundred sixty pounds? Hundred seventy?"

Daniel blink behind that encounter suit. "Uh . . . one sixty-five. Plus the gear . . ."

I sigh. "Come on." I shut down the computer and grab my backpack. Hopefully Father John still got a computer running at the mission. I can see if the Coopers write me back. Otherwise, I got to trust that the nuns get them word, or McCallan on his way out the Delta. And then hope for the best.

Daniel head for the front door, but I shake my head and point left of the entrance. There another book room back here, with picture books I used to read when I been a kid. The best part be the window seat, used to look out on a garden, but that been ten years ago and things ain't the way they used to be. Good news be the yard so overgrown now, there be vines up over the windows. No one can see us from the street, or move fast to catch us if they did.

"Listen," I say, and point to the front door. "They might know we here. Probably waiting for us. We go out the back, we can still get to Mr. Go's, but it dangerous. Ground ain't what it should be this way, it ain't stable. That be good for us—nobody running after you on Rooftops. But watch your step. Follow me close. Got it?"

Daniel's eyes be big and wide. "Okay." His voice crack. I give him a smile to calm him down.

In my arms, Baby Girl make a little mewing sound, like a tiny cat. I look down at her and my heart beat harder. I never been through Rooftops with a baby before. She don't weigh nothing at all, but I still say a silent apology to Lydia. This ain't no kind of road for an infant.

"Shh." I jounce her a bit and hold her close. She still got that new smell, warm and soft. "I'ma get us out of this," I whisper into the top of her head. Curls soft and brown tickle my lips. I take a breath and lower her to rest in the sling.

"Help me," I say to Daniel. I get my fingers under one of the window sashes. Vines be growing between the window and the sill, holding it open and closed at the same time. I pull out my knife to saw through them. But the window too swollen with rain, wood too warped to raise right.

"Stand back," Daniel say. He kick hard at the window frame. It be so rotten, it come loose in two kicks and fall out onto the weeds below.

"*Pas mal,*" I say to him. Not bad. We move out into the jungle quick, and I be glad we did, 'cause the front door open and I hear voices again. But we in the garden now, moving to the old fence, and there be alleys enough to hide in. This be the edge of AB territory, so we stay low and I try not to think about the message in the e-mail.

Instead, I think about Baby Girl, and how time be running out for both of us.

28

❧DANIEL RAN. HE HAD A STITCH IN HIS SIDE, but he kept running. The air stank of methane and garbage behind these old houses, rotted streets turned into shallow, stinking canals.

They had left the library far behind, crisscrossing St. Charles and climbing a long, shallow hill to make their way north. Daniel craned his neck to see behind him. No sounds of splashing, no footsteps. For whatever reason, the two ABs hadn't followed them. Daniel gasped for breath as Fen finally began to slow down to a fast walk.

He needed time to think. All of his plans had gone to dust.

INQUIRY: Directory, pre-storm New Orleans. Resident, male, last name: Go.

RESPONSE: Three residents on file: Octavian Go, Kelvin Go, and Han Go.

INQUIRY: Cross-reference results with storm deaths.

RESPONSE: Go, Octavian, resident of Austin, Texas. Go, Kelvin, and Go, Han, deceased.

INQUIRY: Any other records of a Mr. Go in New Orleans, Louisiana?

RESPONSE: Records exist for MRGO, Mississippi River Gulf Outlet.

INQUIRY: What is the Mississippi River Gulf Outlet?

RESPONSE: MRGO was created to allow drainage and better flow to the Gulf from the Mississippi flood basin. It is cited as a major cause of the flooding post–Hurricane Katrina. A second outlet was created after Hurricane Olga, but never completed.

The datalink's audio crackled at the base of his skull and faded into silence.

"No," Daniel groaned, pounding the buttons on his wristband.

"What now?" Fen asked, clutching the baby to her. He had almost forgotten she was there. The baby hardly ever cried. Fen barely made a sound, even on these broken sidewalks, even in the boot-sucking mud. Now they were on grass, and she moved like a ghost.

"My datalink," he replied. "It's acting up."

"It be a computer. How can it act like anything?" Fen asked.

"No, I mean . . . never mind."

Fen glanced back at him. " 'Cause of the humidity."

Daniel covered his datalink band with his coat sleeve again. If she was right, it was a useless piece of junk now, as useful as having a battery strapped to his wrist. "You might be right."

"No worries. We be there soon."

"Where is there, exactly?" He tripped over a hummock of marsh grass and caught himself. "Nobody's following us. Can we stop? I'm kind of tired."

Without waiting for a reply, Daniel dropped to the ground and sat down.

"Daniel!" Fen barked. "Listen to me, fool, or I be leaving you behind."

Daniel opened his mouth to protest. "Look, I'm following you like you said, staying close, and we're fine, all right? We're—"

"We still being followed," she said quietly. "Now get up before you sink."

"What?" Daniel blinked. Followed? Sink? He looked down to see the grass beneath him starting to give way to bubbling mud. Above him, Fen shook her head.

"You think you got trouble with your link, you gonna be real sorry if that box you carrying be in your coat pockets."

"Shit." Daniel jumped up, lifting his coat around his waist. Fortunately, the vial case was scratch-, water-, acid-, and fire-resistant. His coat was another story. "It's supposed to be waterproof," he said, but the fabric was clearly soaked through.

"This be Orleans water. It ain't the same. Higher pH," Fen said.

Daniel stopped trying to wipe himself clean. "How do you know things like that?"

"Why wouldn't I?" Fen asked indignantly. "We ain't all tourists here, and we ain't all ignorant."

"I never said you were," Daniel said by way of apology. Fen snorted and swung the baby sling onto her hip. He looked around again, but couldn't see anyone behind them. Still, the girl had been right about everything else. No point in doubting her now.

"Stay close, and move careful," she warned. "We about to enter Rooftops. No one gonna follow us there."

The canals gave way to rolling grassland, vivid green beneath the blue, cloud-dotted sky. It reminded Daniel of a golf course, with new greenery revealed over each successive rise. But there was no clue to explain the odd name.

A warbling birdcall made Daniel look up. "What was that? The people following us?"

"The *person* following us," Fen corrected. "I only seen one. And no. That call be scavengers."

"Is that a type of bird?"

"No, it be a type of person," she said, rolling her eyes. "They be hunting for scrap here."

"What kind of scrap can you find in a marsh?"

"All kinds," Fen said. "This ain't always been marshland. There be houses under here, silt and mud on top. Acting like a natural levee for us, but used to be somebody's home. Now it be they crypt. Things inside them houses float up in a rainstorm. Furniture, food, bones. You name it."

Daniel looked down at the ground he was walking on. The hummocks that had tripped him were more than just grass. He kicked a little mound with his toe. A metallic clang answered back. He tapped it again.

"It's a chimney cap," he said incredulously.

Fen nodded. "That why they call this place Rooftops. Now stop kicking at it and stick with me so you won't fall through."

"Fall through?"

If words were curses, Daniel thought. The last thing he saw was Fen turning around at the sound of the ground caving in around him.

Everything hurt. And it was dark. Pitch-dark, except for the patch of blue high above his head. Daniel groaned and took inventory of his body. He remembered breaking through something that tore like rotted wood or carpet . . . something. He moaned and the smell of mildew filtered in through his suit. He was protected from mold at least, but the scent warned him, reminded him where he was. A storm-drowned house, buried under fifty years of muck and forgotten.

Inventory, focus. Daniel wiggled his fingers. That worked. He did the same with his toes. Rotated his wrists and ankles, his head. Stiff neck, but fine. He patted his coat pockets.

"No, no, no!" He sat up too quickly, but it didn't matter. Nausea rolled over him, and it increased as he felt his inner pockets. The one that held the case of virus was open.

The box had been hermetically sealed, lined with protective cushioning, holding the six small vials. The world's entire supply of DF virus. The case would have survived the fall. He just had to find the green light, the one that meant the case was sealed. He closed his eyes, cursing, then opened them again to scan the darkness.

A few feet away, a red light blinked.

Daniel's heart stopped. He crawled over to the box, reaching for it with careful fingers.

The compartment was open, the seal smashed by the impact of the fall. He felt around, belatedly remembering his night-vision goggles. They were smeared with muck from the fall. He wiped them as best he could and dialed up the intensity, turning the blackness around him into a murky green. He was in a small bedroom, having fallen through the attic of a house. Tatters of carpet and splintered floorboards framed the hole above him. The walls were black with mold. Mushrooms grew on what might once have been a bed, the brass framework poking through like bones. He looked down.

The inner case with its six vials was gone, dropped into the depths of Orleans. The edges of the empty compartment glinted in the negative view of his goggles.

"Dear God," he said. He had lost the virus. And there were scavengers here. *Anybody* could find it. He needed to tell Fen. For all he knew, she had fallen with him.

"Fen?" he called out.

He heard a sound overhead. "Fen!"

It came again. A dragging sound from above. It wasn't Fen. But it was nearby. "Hello?" he said, and started to stand, panicking. And then he saw something move above him, dragging a heavy, long body in front of the hole his fall had created, blocking out the light.

29

❧ "AW, HELL." I START TO RUN BEFORE THE sinkhole take me with it. The ground be too damn soft here to be messing around like this. So I keep moving, watching my feet, and finally the soft fall of sod stop behind me.

It look bad. The roof done give way over a row of houses, long skinny things a couple stories high. Everything be rotten under the earth. If I be lucky, Daniel broke his neck. Then I don't got to risk my life saving him. Then again, he carrying that virus. If that broke, I be good as dead, too.

"Daniel?" My voice echo back to me from the dark hole. I look hard, but all I see be broken roof and blackness down below. "Can you hear me?"

Silence. *Please let him be on the top floor,* I think. Then maybe a rope or something can get him out. If he any lower, there be worse things than a broken neck to kill him.

"Daniel!" Baby Girl be crying again. She scared from the crash, and the smell coming from the hole be almost as bad as the blood farm. "It be all right, Baby, everything all right," I croon to her, searching the dark with my eyes.

"Fen."

It sound real weak, like he far away, but Daniel alive. Maybe he got a broken leg or arm or something, or maybe that suit hold him together better than regular clothes do, but he alive.

It make me happier than it should to hear his voice. The Fen I used to be woulda been glad to be rid of a nuisance. But it different now. Just the three of us. We be like a tribe.

"You hurt?" I call.

"Yes." He sound like he talking into a tin can.

My stomach twist. "Bad?"

"I don't know."

I wait, but he don't say more than that. "I can't see you. Hold on." I tiptoe around the sinkhole 'til I find a place firm enough to stand on at the edge. It be the top of another chimney, something solid enough for the time being.

"Daniel?" There be a long pause.

"Yes?"

"You passing out?" Another long pause. What that boy doing? I look around for rope or something to help him climb out. Finally, he answer.

"No. I . . . There's something down here."

Shit. Course there is. There be things living in every damn nook and cranny of this place. Like a city beneath the city here in Rooftops. They say there even be roads down there, but you got to be a damn fool or a fish to reach them. "Can you climb out?"

"Uh . . . no."

"Then I'ma come down and get you."

"How?"

I look around. I could jump down and find a way for both of us to climb back, but I got the baby to think of, too. "You got a rope? I can pull you out."

"In one of my pockets. Hold on . . . I . . . Christ, it's dark down here," I hear him say.

I hear more whistling behind us and know there be scavengers about. They'd have a rope I could use, but they ain't gonna be loaning it to me out of the kindness of they hearts.

"Daniel, talk to me," I say.

"Um . . . I'd rather not," he answer. And I hear a sound that ain't like Daniel, and I know for sure he ain't alone.

"Be right back," I say, and run off, light as I can, to find them scavengers. I whistle like they whistle and keep looking over the fields, but it be hard to see over so many little hills and piles of trash. I whistle louder.

"Who are you?"

I spin around. Three of them be standing right behind me. Little ones. Scavengers in Rooftops be either children or people the size of kids. They got to be awful light on they feet for this kind of work, so I ain't heard 'em coming. They staring at me with they hard eyes, two skinny boys the color of river mud and a woman, an old lady with a back like a crow, all hunched in half, shoulder blades like wings. They be dressed in pocket coats down to they ankles, waterproof sailcloth with pockets up and down to hold what they find.

"Who are you?" the woman say again. She sound like a

crow, too, and her hair be gray and wild, like a bird nest on her head. She got to be close to fifty. That mean she crafty, living this long.

"That ain't your business," I say. "Strike me a deal."

The three of them lean forward, peering at Baby Girl with greedy eyes. Scavengers usually go for scraps and findings, but they ain't above trading with blood hunters if they hungry enough. Judging from the skinny on these boys, they plenty hungry for sure.

"A deal for the baby?" the old woman say.

I shake my head. "Something better."

"What be better than that?" one of the boys ask. "Baby worth an awful lot to some folks."

"A treasure be worth more," I say. "We got a house full of it."

"What treasure? There ain't no treasure here but bottle caps and chimney ends," the old lady say with a wave of her hand.

"Nobody goes in them houses!" the boy exclaims. "Death be in them houses. We take from the tops."

True, Rooftops be dangerous enough without going underground. Don't take much rain to make things float to the surface, even through the mud and grass, if you know where to look.

I shrug and walk away. "All right, be like that. I'ma find someone else to carry it."

I can feel 'em looking at each other behind me. "Wait, wait, wait!" the old lady call. I stop, but don't turn around.

"I have two fine boys here, strapping boys, they help carry anything you got, for a price."

Now I turn around, swinging Baby Girl onto my hip, and give them the once-over. "I don't know. Maybe they ain't light enough on they feet for my kind of treasure."

"We light. We like feathers," one of the boys insist, and step forward.

"Like a bubble," the other say.

"We don't want no treasure from under below," the old lady say. "But them braids of yours be fine. Mighty fine."

She come closer and snake out a hand. I slap it away, but she reach with her free hand and grab a hold of my hair anyway. "Yes. This gone do just fine."

❧DANIEL STOPPED BREATHING. THE DARKNESS was suffocating and his goggles were useless without a light source. They could amplify even starlight a thousandfold, but the thing above him was blocking the hole to the upper world. He willed himself into silence, but his heart was jolting against his ribs so loudly, he was sure it could be heard. Any predator worth its salt would scent him out.

But Daniel was wearing an encounter suit. Would he still smell like food? He hoped not. Up above, Fen was saying something. He ignored it, wishing she would shut up. Maybe the thing in the room would go away if she was quiet. Maybe it would move again and the patch of daylight would come back. Then he could find a way to climb out.

Unable to stop himself, Daniel took a quick breath. Above him, the creature shifted. He couldn't see well enough to know where or how, but he heard the creak of broken floorboards, the slow drag of a body against the floor. He could *feel* it, an enormous presence, filling up the attic, taking what little air there was out of the room. A musty smell pressed down on him, making his stomach flip with fear. He knew that smell. Had come across it in the lab where they kept the reptiles. Snake, or something like it. Alligator?

Daniel pissed himself. A second later, he felt the skin of the encounter suit compress, and a soft whir as it processed the urine, filling a catch pocket with drinking water.

Then something touched his face.

Flickering against the outer skin of the suit, it fluttered against him and retreated. Fluttered again. A tongue?

Alligator or snake, even if this thing *couldn't* smell him, it had found him and was coming in for a better look. Daniel thought about praying, but he was a scientist. He didn't know where to begin.

He wondered what the virus would do in the belly of this beast, and he closed his eyes. The afterimage of the hole in the sky filled his blackened lids.

Glow sticks.

It popped into his head just like that. He had taken them from his duffel before climbing the Wall, had used one to light the Dome. Slowly, he moved his hand down to the right pocket and reached inside. He could feel them with his fingertips. Closing a hand around the tube, he pulled one out.

The tongue had stopped touching his face, but it was close. Any sudden movement might cause it to strike, but he had no choice.

Daniel shook the glow stick, snapping it to ignite the chemical light. Green light flooded from his hands, searing his night vision, causing the thing in the room to shriek. He screamed along with it, not wanting to see what it was. A giant reptilian eye glared at him, no more than a foot away. He saw the inner eyelid snap shut, protecting the eye. A pupil the size of his fist disappeared, and the thing, whatever it was, dragged itself out of the light.

"Fen!" Daniel yelled.

She didn't respond.

30

❧ I STEP BACK TO PULL MY HAIR OUT OF HER grasp. "Back off."

The old lady shrug and point her chin back at the boys. "I got two strong boys. Used to have three, but one gone now. Down underneath. The rope come back." She reach into a pack on her back and pull out a coil of rope made from vines, fibers, and locks of human hair. I look at her and realize for the first time her head be nearly shaved bald. Them boys, too. Nothing but blond and brown stubble, same color as the rope. She hold it up to me. "See? Three feet short. Cost me a house diver. But you . . . you got more braid than you need. Give it to me, and we help with your treasure."

I hesitate. Don't know why. Ain't like I be uppity about my looks or nothing. I been bald before, I been all kinds of things. But I reach up and feel my braids tied on top my head, and my eyes start to sting. Lydia done this for me. From the first day, she took me in, cleaned me up, got the tangles out.

My hair softer and shinier than it got a right to be 'cause of her. Uncle Rom say she treat me like a doll, always brushing and smoothing it down. I say she treat me better than that. She treat me like a person. Like a person she love. These braids all I got left of that.

Then I think of Daniel down there with whatever it be bit off the end of this woman's rope. These braids gonna have to come out sometime. Might as well be now.

I sigh. "Follow me."

The old lady nod and the boys come scampering around me like a pack of street dogs, bounding in front and behind, stepping in places I be too afraid to go. Like they got bubbles on they feet, for sure. When they see where I be heading, though, they slow down.

"You afraid?" I ask.

The boys look at each other, then at the old lady. I know they be missing friends what fell down these holes before, so I try to act casual. "Daniel?" I call into the hole.

I can see a pale light way down inside, but not much else.

"Fen?" he call back. He don't sound so good. "Thank God," he say.

"You find that rope?"

"No. For God's sake, hurry."

"I will." I turn to the old woman and pull my knife out of my boot. "How much?"

She shrug and hold her hands out a length. I stretch out my braids and lop them off at the string holding them in a tail. The string come undone and little bits of black curls fall around my shoulders. My hair be sticking up all over the place. I still smell the palm oil Lydia use to keep the braids soft. I hand them to the woman. She grin without all her teeth.

"Good. Good. Now." She drop to the ground, cross-legged, like Daniel, only she don't seem to mind the mud bubbling up around her. She be quick with them old fingers, undoing the braids and weaving them back around her rope 'til she got what she came for and then some. It don't take long at all. I watch, trying hard not to touch my head and feel the missing hair. I blow a bit of broken stubble off Baby Girl's face. She wave a fist at me. The woman hand me the rope and I tie it around my waist. The boys come up to the edge of the hole.

"There be monsters down there," one of the boys say, and I see he just a little kid, younger than I thought.

"And the old dead," the other boy say with a nod. "That be a hole to Hell."

"True," I tell them. "So we best get him out while we can."

That make some kind of sense, so they hold on to the rope behind me and I call for Daniel to be ready to climb. I drop the rest of the rope down into the hole and the old lady watch us pull in the slack as Daniel haul himself up. Then the pale little light be rising, and finally Daniel come up out of that hole.

When I finally drag him over the edge, he fall to the ground, coughing through his suit filter.

"You okay?" I ask. I can't say more with the scavengers listening, but I hope he brought up everything he went down with, including that damned black case.

"Where the treasure at?" the old lady ask. Daniel look up at me, confused.

"What it be to you now?" I ask her. "You been paid."

The little boys back up, but the old lady look at me, suspicious. Daniel sit up. "There's something down there," he say.

It dark as pitch down there now, without Daniel's glow stick.

The lady shake her head. "That's what took my rope, and my other boy," she say.

Then it move, whatever it be, a dry rasp below the earth. The boys scream, high and loud, "The Devil!" They run away. Baby Girl start to cry. The old lady give me the evil eye, but she don't come any closer. She spit at me, then scurry away.

"What was that?" Daniel ask. I shake my head, bouncing Baby Girl to calm her down. She gonna need a bottle soon, and a new diaper, and I wonder how I be managing any of this, let alone the two of them at once.

"Nothing. You all in one piece?" He hesitate, then nod. I help him to his feet easy enough.

"Come on, then," I say, soothing Baby Girl's tears into hiccups and sighs. When she quiet down again, we pick our way out of Rooftops toward the lake where the Ursulines live.

31

ORLEANS AIN'T EXACTLY GOT A RELIABLE MAIL system these days. Best way to get a message to anybody be to cover your bases. Lydia call it the rule of three—send it three different ways, and if you lucky, one of them might get there. Looking up at the sun, I see the time be about right, so the Ursuline convent be my first stop. If I get a chance, I'ma leave a note for the old smuggler, McCallan. He got a couple drop points near here and might do a final round before leaving town.

Daniel be following me all quiet now, and he don't say nothing when I pause to make another bottle for Baby Girl. She just sleep and eat and mess her diaper, nothing more. If I keep her from crying, we maybe do okay. But she a baby and the only cure for that be growing up, so I hold her bottle, burp her when she done, and keep on walking, trying not to think of Lydia every time I look at her face. Soon enough we make it to the edge of the Academy grounds. I take a look around, but we alone now, so we climb up top the concrete wall around what used to be the parking lot.

"What is this?" Daniel ask, looking around from the top of the wall. We be sitting a short three feet above a concrete pebble shore, broken pieces of asphalt and sidewalk still jagged 'cause there ain't no waves to grind them smooth.

"Convent Lake," I say, and point across the water. It big as two parking lots maybe, and still and calm, reflecting back the bright blue sky. Daniel follow my hand and see what I be pointing at—the Ursulines' convent, half underwater, across this big old pond. "When Katrina came, they say it flooded parts of the buildings here." I sweep my arm to show the whole campus, what used to be a girls' school, with a chapel and everything. "That the last time it drained all the way. Next storm came and the pavement broke up some, but not enough to drain completely. Now it be like this all the time."

"What's that in the middle?" Daniel ask, squinting at the white shape halfway between the shore and the mossy walls of the nun's home.

"That be Jesus Christ. This the parking lot, then there a courtyard under there somewhere. When the nuns saw the water weren't gonna drain, they raised the statue. In the right light, it look like he walking on water."

❧ DANIEL KICKED HIS BOOTS AGAINST THE concrete wall, letting his heels rebound lightly until the blood moved into the tips of his toes.

INQUIRY: Why did the Ursuline nuns stay in Orleans?

RESPONSE: The Ursuline Sisters have devoted their lives to the education of young girls. The convent is the site of a holy relic believed to have turned back danger from the city time and again. They believe they are protected.

INQUIRY: Who protects the Ursulines?

RESPONSE: Data not available at this time.

The datalink was working again. That was something, at least. They had been on the wall for a quarter of an hour. He felt like vomiting. He had lied to Fen, back in Rooftops, about being in one piece. The vial case was back in his pocket, the seal broken, the light blinking red, but the vials of the DF virus were lost somewhere beneath Rooftops.

For the first time, Daniel was glad of his disguise, of the rags and hat, the thick mucus layer of the encounter suit. He couldn't have hidden the guilt on his face otherwise. If the ABs hunting them had followed them here, Daniel didn't notice and didn't care. He just wanted to keep moving in the daylight and not think of what had happened underground. The vials remained unbroken; the scanners on his datalink would have alerted him otherwise. Daniel wasn't a mass murderer, just a clumsy, unlucky fool. It was the best news he could hope for, given the circumstances.

He should tell her, he knew. But then what? He couldn't go back underground again. The thought made him break into a sweat, his suit whirring to life to compensate. And if not go back, then what? Fen didn't need him. She'd left the men and women of the Institute to die in that school back there, abandoned in their beds. She would leave him, too. He imagined her knife at his throat, the suit slit open, his blood running out as Delta Fever raced in to claim him.

No. Better to hold his tongue and keep pace. She would help him get to the Wall and never be the wiser.

"You being awful quiet," Fen said, startling him. He jumped and had to force himself to steady his breathing.

"What are we waiting for?" he asked.

Fen shook her head and smiled at the bouncing baby in her arms. "For a miracle, Daniel. We just a bit early."

Just then, bells rang out from the towers of the convent. "Angelus," Fen explained. "Noontime prayers."

Daniel looked around expecting the bells to draw people, but no one came. They rang eight times and the pond in front of them, the woods behind them, fell silent.

"'Round here, folks ignore the bells," Fen said. "They be ringing all the time. Nuns be the only fools willing to draw attention to theyselves with that kind of noise." Daniel might have imagined the hint of respect in her voice. "They think God'll protect them."

"Does he?" Daniel asked. It was a comforting thought. But Fen snorted, a short, harsh laugh.

"No way, man. This *moat* protect them; and they sheer numbers, sometimes that protect them. Ursulines take in girls from all over the Delta. They separate them in dorms to keep the Fever down. But that be all they got, that and the walls of that church. But not God. Some tribes 'round here ain't against rape. Blood hunters, neither. A nun just as like to find herself in a brothel as a convent. If she make it out alive, she stuck raising her rapist's bastard. Where be God then?"

Daniel shook his head, his heart sinking. He had tried to save this unsalvageable place, and he had failed. He swung his feet in their short arc from knee to wall and back again. "I wonder how they keep their faith."

Fen shrugged and jumped off the wall, one arm wrapped beneath the baby on her chest. "Who's to say?"

And then she stepped out onto the water and walked away, barely disturbing the surface as she strode toward the open arms of the statue in the middle of the lake.

❦ IT TAKE HIM A FULL HALF MINUTE TO PICK HIS jaw up again. That boy be so blind sometimes, I don't know how he make it on his own. "Stay there," I call back to him. "You too heavy to be following me."

Beneath my feet, the hard top of a car shift enough to make me glad he be listening and stay on the wall. I clutch Baby Girl to me and catch my balance.

Noon be the time when the pond go down just enough to make the cars left behind come to the surface. Some days, when the sun ain't so bright, you can see them under the lake. Today it just look like blue sky under my feet, except where my shadow fall. The nuns lined up sunken trucks and buses, all of a height, to make a path to the statue.

The cars come to a stop right in front of Jesus, and so do I. He be standing like he waiting for us. Baby Girl reach out her little hand to touch the statue's marble one. She grab his finger while I take my note to the Coopers and tie it to his right wrist, the one facing the convent. If they see it, they paddle a boat out. The nuns be good about things like that—delivering notes, teaching little ones, and looking after the dead. No kind of life for me, but I appreciate they work just the same.

"This be another step, Baby Girl," I say. "Tell 'em to set up the nursery in California. We gonna get you a nice new home."

Message sent, I pick my way back across the lake before it get too deep again. Daniel be waiting for me without a word to say for once. I hustle him back over the wall and we continue on to Mr. Go.

⚜ DANIEL PAUSED AND PLACED A HAND ON THE tree in front of him.

INQUIRY: Analyze compound sample.
RESPONSE: Desiccated live oak.
INQUIRY: Contaminants?
RESPONSE: High concentration of sodium nitrate.

Like the other live oaks he had seen, this one was tall, spreading its branches overhead in an umbrella canopy that blocked the sky. But instead of the gray-green spread of leaves and hairlike Spanish moss draped in their boughs, the tops of these trees were reddish brown, bleeding into a dry, powdery orange shade that faded to dun at the roots. In spite of everything, he could not quell his curiosity about this place.

After leaving the lake, they had wound their way silently through neighborhoods of crumbled buildings and wild greenery, and now this forsaken bit of woodland. All of the trees were orange, rising improbably out of the marshy earth. To Daniel, it seemed like they were standing in a forest of rust.

"What is this place?" he asked her. Fen was already foraging ahead along some unseen route through the mucky forest floor. Her narrow shoulders rose and fell in a shrug.

"A place, like any other."

She paused by a tree made even more distinctive by the hole in its trunk and dropped something inside.

"But the trees?"

Fen looked at him, one hand cradling the baby's bottom, the other at her shoulder, thumb tucked into the sling. "Boy, didn't you ever hear curiosity killed the cat?"

Daniel half smiled beneath his encounter suit. It was a good warning for him.

"What did you just do there?" he asked, nodding toward the tree.

"What did I say about the cat?" she shot back, moving forward again.

Daniel grimaced. "Strike that."

Surprisingly, she didn't. "Smuggler drop. Leave a note, they pick it up, get you what you want."

Daniel's eyebrows rose in surprise. "Does it work?"

She shrugged. "Sometimes."

"What did you ask for?"

"A home for Baby Girl," I say. "That about all I want. A good home."

Daniel followed in silence a moment longer, but found he couldn't help himself. "Why are the trees covered in rust?"

"You the one with the fancy datalink, you tell me," Fen said.

"I think it's got something to do with the water here," Daniel guessed. He sniffed the air, splortching forward through the soft mud. "It's briny. Like seawater. Like maybe there was a breach in the levees and the water from the Gulf came up too far and killed the trees."

"Maybe, tourist. You got all the answers," Fen muttered.

Daniel hurried to catch up with her. "Sorry. I didn't mean to upset you," he said.

Fen didn't look at him. "I ain't upset."

Daniel slowed his pace and let her go back to leading him. He didn't want to aggravate her. Instead, he turned to the trees, wondering at the flaking lacework of brittle, fire-colored branches beneath the pale blue sky. *Such a strange place to live.* He thought back to the men on horseback, swirling and chanting, waving their torches in the air. Yes, the Delta was dangerous, but it was still very much alive.

Ever since the Separation, the Outer States had been decaying. Back home, riots were more common than parades, protests over food and clean water. Torches were used to fire-bomb empty storefronts rather than light the night. Yes, there were still schools and grocery stores and amusement parks in the States, buildings without trees growing through their roofs. The Outer States had almost everything that Orleans didn't. But the Delta still lived on.

32

THIS BOY BE DRIVING ME CRAZY. I REACH UP to tug at my braids but they ain't there. Traded for this fool's life. I shake my head. No point in regrets. Even with all his questions and jabbering, Daniel done put his neck out for me like nobody but Lydia'd ever do. And now I be doing it for him, too. I look down at Baby Girl dozing in my arms and wonder if being a baby mama making me soft. But I know we wouldn't have made it this far without him.

We leave the dead forest and move into greenery again. Ain't far now. I smell the water before I see it, heavy with salt and dead leaves. Mr. Go's bayou be just up ahead. The woods around us be quiet, the sun softer as it head to the horizon. I wait and listen. This ain't nobody's territory, which make it everybody's. I scan the trees, but we alone.

"This is the same river?" Daniel ask.

"Same as what?"

"The Mississippi. That the hunters took us across."

I shake my head. The wind around my hacked hair feel strange and I take a minute to run a hand over my head again.

"We got more rivers than land these days," I say. "But this ain't part of the old river. It be Mr. Go's bayou."

I stop and point ahead. The river ain't more than thirty yards across here, and in the middle of the water be a lemon-shaped bunker with the river flowing fast around either side. The roof covered in baby trees like the ones close to shore for camouflage. It be hard to find if you don't know what you be looking for. But I do.

I walk over to a tree stump a few feet from the shore. It be wide enough for one person to sit on. But it ain't for sitting. I knock on the pale exposed surface of the inner wood and Daniel's jaw drop for the second time today.

"Who's that knocking at my door?" a man's voice say from the stump.

"Fen," I say.

"And who's that with you, Fenny Fen Fen?" Daniel be looking around for cameras, I guess.

I lean toward the stump. "A friend."

Suddenly, the water level drop, like Moses parting the Red Sea, 'til the canal bed be damp, but not dry. I scramble down the bank and across the mucky river bottom, Baby Girl in my arms and Daniel right behind me. Together we scale the mound of land in the middle of the river, like a beaver's dam, where Mr. Go make his home.

The minute we top the sloping walls of the island, the protective waters swirl back into place. Mr. Go designed the canal, and I see Daniel be impressed. I lead him around to a set of stairs and a doorway that weren't visible from shore. The door slide open and Mr. Go be standing there, smiling.

"Welcome," he say, his square teeth bright in his mahogany face. Mr. Go's hair be almost as white as his teeth, but streaked with gray, in a springy bush that be higher on top than the sides. If I ain't careful, my hair be looking like his soon.

Dressed in a pale gray tunic and loose pants, he make Daniel and me look sloppy in our dirty clothes. Daniel peek around me, trying to look inside. Mr. Go smile even wider.

"Please, come in. Make yourselves at home."

"Home" be a massive greenhouse dense with life. It run the length of two hogans and be full of fruits, vegetables, trees, and flowers. The old man point to a funny set of white wrought-iron chairs and a small table holding a wooden tray of food. "Fen, I see you've brought a smuggler with you," he say. "And, is that a child?"

"This one been a help," I tell him, with a nod toward Daniel, who look surprised. Telling him about Baby Girl gone be a bigger conversation. Mr. Go give me one of his studying looks. He know I'm stalling, but he let me.

"I'm sure he has," he say smoothly. "Please, have a seat, sir." He point to the table. "I know I have some bottled water and packaged food here somewhere, if you are tired of your nutrient packs. I assure you it is quite safe in here without your suit on." He point to the plants—banana trees with they upside-down bouquets of fruit, sweet potato vines snaking along the wall, tomatoes, roses, and a dozen other kinds of flowers, fruits, and vegetables in these first few yards. "You see, the flora in here acts as a filter for the toxins in the water. The first generation cleansed and the next purified. My garden is fourth generation now, and purely hydroponic." He show Daniel the roots of the plants, rising out of glass basins, roots like white worms in a swamp. "Quite independent of the outside world. Quite safe."

"Thank you," Daniel say in his filtered voice, but he don't remove his mask.

"As you wish." Mr. Go give him a little bow and take a seat. "At least sit with me. I haven't dined yet. And Fen, you certainly are welcome to eat your fill. Then you can tell me about your little companion and what brings you here today."

"Can I use your bathroom first?" I ask. I ain't got a suit like Daniel, but I didn't want to stop with evening coming on. And I ain't talking to Mr. Go about Lydia until I'm straight. I see Daniel looking at me and Mr. Go, like he trying to figure something out, but that can wait.

"No need to stand on formality here, Fen," Mr. Go say, taking a bite of sliced mango. It sure smell good and sweet to me, but that can wait, too. "We're old friends. Please." He wave me down the long hall before turning his full attention to his meal.

🜂 DANIEL STOOD IN THE MIDDLE OF THE ROOM, uncertain what to do once Fen was gone. Things tended to go badly when she wasn't around. *Stupid, Daniel.* All of the danger they had faced and now he was afraid of a smiling old man. An old Orleanian who had no record of existing.

"Mr. Go is not your real name," Daniel said.

Mr. Go wiped his mouth with a cloth napkin. "No, it's not."

"Um . . . my name is Daniel," he offered belatedly, and slowly pulled out a chair across from the other man.

"Daniel, a pleasure," Mr. Go said, not accepting Daniel's proffered gloved hand. He indicated the fruit juice on his own hands and gave an apologetic shrug. "I'd rather not make a mess of things," he said. "Daniel. A good name, by the way. Strong. It means *God is my judge,* like Daniel and the lions' den."

Daniel laughed, an odd burst of static through the suit's filters. "That's what Fen said."

"Ah, that's because Fen was a student of mine years ago. It's good to know she remembers the old stories."

"A student?" Daniel asked.

"Yes, but let's not get ahead of ourselves. First, I should introduce myself properly. My Christian name is Simeon Wells. I hail from Chicago, Illinois, in the Outer States of America. I used to work for the Department of Agriculture. This would have been before you were born, before the great storms, even before Katrina." He wiped the juices from his mouth with his napkin, then folded it in half to draw his knife through, wiping it clean. "And then after the storm years, I joined the Army Corps of Engineers."

Placing his napkin down, he selected an apple from a bowl on the table, and methodically sliced it into wedges, scooping the seeds from the core as he continued. "The people here affectionately call me Mr. Go because I helped redesign this canal we are sitting in. It drains the surrounding areas the way the original Mississippi River Gulf Outlet, or MRGO, was meant to."

"It was supposed to drain off floodwaters," Daniel said.

"Indeed it was. A miracle of modern engineering. But it failed in Katrina, burst like an aneurysm, flooding the surrounding area with raging toxic waters. So we widened this bayou before the Two Sisters struck, hoping to hold off the lake water from the north. As they say, history will teach us nothing. It proved the fatal blow." He chewed thoughtfully on a piece of apple, his eyes distant, seeing the past. After a moment, he started and came back to himself with a chuckle. He poured some honey onto his plate from a small jar. "But it makes a good home. I keep bees here, too, Daniel. I shall have to show you the apiary. They make germinating the plants so much easier."

"Bees?" Daniel repeated. "But honeybees are extinct."

It was one of the reasons for the riots back home and the slow migration of people on the freeways, fleeing the countryside in search of jobs and food. Daniel had assumed the honey on Mr. Go's plate was synthetic. The man expected him to believe it was real?

Mr. Go gave him an amused smile. "Not here, Daniel, not in the Delta. You see"—he mopped up some of the honey with a piece of apple—"despite our failings, the Delta is the Promised Land. The land of milk and, quite literally, honey." The golden syrup dripped from the white and red apple slice, forming viscous tears as it fell to the plate and coated Mr. Go's fingers. Daniel hadn't had real honey since he was a small boy. His mouth watered and he licked his lips. The suit responded by recycling his saliva away.

"I hate to waste it," Mr. Go said by way of apology, and tilted his head beneath the fruit, eating it whole, licking his fingers afterward.

"In some ways, by killing New Orleans, it seems we have saved it," he theorized. "Now, I am no saint, and indeed when I moved to Orleans before the Wall went up, I knew what the government had planned. I simply could not let them seal the Delta off without trying, *trying* to fix what went wrong." For a moment, a look of pained anger flashed across the weathered old face, and Mr. Go stopped to sip some water before he continued.

"To understand Orleans today, you must understand what happened in the beginning, son. In 2005, 2015, 2018. The chain of events that led to the downfall of the greatest city in the greatest nation on earth. Don't believe for a minute that the rest of the United States has survived any of this deep tragedy. Oh no, for we are no longer a nation. There is the Delta on the one hand, and the Outer States of America on the other." He tapped the table with the edge of either hand as he spoke. "As our great president Abraham Lincoln knew, a house divided cannot stand. We are divided, young Daniel, and so your homeland dies, while ours flourishes, and yet we die, too, every day, for want of the things your world could provide. The land of milk and honey, Daniel. What will it take for them to see it?

"We are the offspring of our own making; the way a potato vine can self-propagate into a mirror image of itself, so have we done. And that was New Orleans before the Wall, and that is the Outer States and Orleans now. Our children are thieves and murderers first by necessity, then by a self-determined sense of right. Where is the rule of law? After the first storm, Rita, there was looting, even without making landfall in the city. Then came Katrina, and when New Orleans was still on her knees, her children were killing one another. Killing out of petty dispute and personal gain when they should have been helping one another, lifting one another up, raising their city, their *mother,* out of the muck and the mire and rebuilding her anew.

"Is it any wonder that Orleans is a wasteland today? As much as Nature takes back and rebuilds, it is in her own image, and not those of the people of New Orleans. And the ones who survive, no better than vampires, waging war against one another for blood in order to live another day. What is a day in the life of a live oak tree, Daniel? What is one human day in the life of an ecosystem? Nothing. And still, we cannot see."

He looked sad then, and patted Daniel on the knee. "You can't build a future when no one lives to be older than fifty-five."

Daniel paused, unsure how to reply to the old man's sudden outburst. "Fen said you are the oldest man in the Delta." *Except for Warren Abernathy James,* he thought. Not that the scientist in his chemically sustained twilight could truly be called alive.

Mr. Go stood up. "I am an anomaly. I live here for the protections it gives me, and I hold these plants, these life-forms, in trust for the Delta, for the world. This is Noah's Ark," he said with a smile, and walked over to a gardening table half covered in vines. He pulled a crate from beneath it and made himself busy lining it with moss. When he was done, he brought it over to the table, along with a stool to set the crate on. "As I recall, Noah lived to the ripe old age of nine hundred." Again, the bright smile in the dark face. "But for me, the floodwaters have yet to recede."

INQUIRY: Database search, Simeon Wells.
RESPONSE: Wells, Simeon. Doctor of Biology, University of Chicago. Doctor of Environmental Engineering, University of Chicago. Rhodes Scholar. Dr. Simeon Wells is believed dead. Last known location, New Orleans, Louisiana, 2015. There is an outstanding warrant for his arrest.
INQUIRY: Recite warrant charges.
RESPONSE: Crimes against the citizens of the state of Louisiana. Crimes against the citizens of the United States. Crimes against humanity.
INQUIRY: State evidence.
RESPONSE: Data error 4401.

The digital voice faded, replaced by a thin crackle of static. Daniel shook his head and checked his wristband. The battery still worked, but the chip inside had crapped out again. Daniel switched the datalink to the off position, disengaging it from his earpiece.

With all the vials lost, he'd been ready to give up, just find his way back over the Wall. Warning Fen would gain her nothing but worry. She might even risk going back down the hole. This way, the virus was at least hidden from the world. But now this. Honeybees, cultivated by a wanted criminal.

Little wings of hope tickled at Daniel's middle. What would Mr. Go do if Daniel told him about the lost virus? What *could* he do? Help cure the Fever? Keep the virus safe?

Or finish destroying the city, the way the datalink implied he had done years before. Mr. Go was a mystery, not an ally. He didn't seem dangerous, but the datalink's last words had given Daniel just enough reason to doubt him. If only he could access the Internet.

"Son, are you all right?"

The interface with the broken datalink had only taken a moment. He nodded. "Sorry. Just some sort of . . . suit issue."

Mr. Go gave him a considering look and nodded. "Are you sure you wouldn't like something to eat or drink?"

"I'm sure," Daniel replied. Inwardly, he cursed his equipment, his doubts, and everything that had brought him here. Orleans had been a mistake, his mission a failure. The sooner he got back over the Wall, the better.

Just then, Fen came back into the room, the baby cradled in her arms. "Okay, Daniel," she said. "Show him the virus."

33

✤ DANIEL DON'T MOVE. HE JUST STARING AT ME like a stunned bird. I roll my eyes. My plan for Baby Girl always been to get her to Father John so he get her out of Orleans. But Daniel showed up with his virus, saying it be halfway to a cure, and I can't help but stop a second and think. Maybe between the two of them, Daniel and Mr. Go can turn the virus into a cure. No more Delta Fever mean no more blood hunters, no more blood whoring like Mama Gentille. No more Wall. With a cure, we just a step away from Lydia's dream. And her baby could stay with me, be my family. A new tribe.

"Go on, Daniel. Tell him about the virus. You can trust him," I say, but Daniel look away from me and my stomach start to sink. "What?" I ask.

Daniel's mouth open and close again without making a sound. Then Mr. Go stand up. "Here, child, let him be for now. We have other things to attend to." Mr. Go wave me over, and I see he done set up a crate for the baby. I watch him lay a clean cloth over the bed of moss inside. "Let us see this child of God."

I lay her down and she seem to like it okay, but it feel strange to not be having her in my arms. Mr. Go bend over the cradle. Out the corner of my eye, I see Daniel relax, and I cut him a look so he know he still got some talking to do. But first, we gonna talk about Lydia.

"Hello, baby," Mr. Go say. "Is it a boy or a girl?"

"Girl."

"Well then, hello, Daughter of Eve," Mr. Go say. He lift Baby Girl in the air and I be glad I changed her diaper. "Thank goodness it's not cold in here," he say. "We shall have to find you some clothes." He look at me, then point to his worktable with his chin. "I have a present for your chieftain in the workbench over there." I open the drawer below the tabletop and pull out a package wrapped in brown paper. I unwrap it and find three soft white baby shirts, two with long sleeves, one without.

"I've been working on creating a variety of silks from plant fibers. Unlike the honeybees, silkworms have proven more difficult to encourage," he say with a chuckle. "Still, the milkweed silk is quite durable, as are certain breeds of corn silk. I've taken the liberty of making what we used to call a layette."

"They beautiful," I tell him. "And so soft."

Mr. Go smile, satisfied. Baby Girl be all settled in his arms like it a natural place to be. "Indeed. Washable, too. Durable as the Delta itself." He run a long finger down the baby's cheek and smile again. "I do find crochet to be relaxing. So, now I have met the child. I presume she belongs to Lydia. Where is the mother herself?"

My face grow hot and I take my time answering. Saying it out loud gonna make it feel real, so I put it off as long as I can. I stuff two of the baby shirts in my pack and put the third on Baby Girl. I take her from Mr. Go to thread her little arms through the sleeves. When I look up at Mr. Go again, my eyes be burning, but I don't cry.

"She be dead. Baby coming killed her."

Mr. Go's head drop to his chest. "I see," he say softly. "Why didn't she come to me? We had talked about having the birth here. Perhaps I could have—"

"ABs attacked our powwow with the O-Negs," I tell him. "La Bête be on the warpath. He got weapons coming in over the Wall."

Mr. Go look like he the one who gonna cry now. That a lot of bad news to take all at once. "I suppose it is that time again," he say. For a minute, he look even older. "Your whole tribe is gone, then?" he ask.

I shrug and shift Baby Girl to my other arm. "Far as I know."

He look at me for a long time with them old eyes of his. Only other eyes look that old and wise to me be Baby Girl's. I wonder if she ever gone grow to be his age.

"Where will you go, Fen? Where will *she* go?"

Don't know about me, but for Baby Girl, at least, I have an answer. "I'ma take her to Father John, have him get her out of the Delta. She young enough for it. And that what Lydia would want."

"Father John . . . did you contact the Coopers? You always did love your sponsor family." He smile and I know we both thinking how Orleans used to be.

"You got any better ideas?" I ask him. "You looking to take on a baby girl?"

Mr. Go shake his head. "I'm old, Fen, too old to become a father now, or even a guardian to one so young. By Orleans standards, I should be dead already. And we both know what happens to young freesteaders who lose their parents."

I look down at the little girl in my arms—my seared, twisted skin—and swallow hard. "Yeah," I agree.

"But a baby and a young woman," Mr. Go continue. "There might be a place for both of them here."

It ain't the first time he offered it. Shoot, if Mr. Go had his way, my folks woulda come here when they left the Professors, and maybe all three of us still be living here today.

Mr. Go's place be nice enough, and secure, too. But it ain't nothing but a big containment suit in the end. He stuck in here just like Dr. Warren and them others be stuck in the infirmary at the Institute. Being OP, we ain't as likely to spread Fever to him, long as we ain't mixing blood. But I ain't never been able to picture that as my kind of life. Sure, I can come and go, but we a long way from anywhere I'd be headed, like the Market. If I leave here, I'd be going alone. And if something happen and I don't come back? Baby Girl got no one but Mr. Go, and like he said, he ain't gonna be around forever.

"No," I say finally. "The three of us ain't enough. A baby need more than two folks watching her. She need a tribe." If I had a tribe when I been younger, if my folks stayed with the Professors, or even Father John, things mighta been different. "Tribe is life," I tell him.

Mr. Go don't look too surprised, but he ain't happy about it, neither. "Well, at least stay with me 'til this war blows over. The ABs can't sustain their violence forever."

I hold Baby Girl to me. Got to feed her soon, got to lay her down for some real sleep. I count the days she been alive. "I ain't risking Baby Girl catching the Fever. I gotta get her to Father John first thing tomorrow, before she stuck here forever."

Mr. Go nod and turn away, wiping his eyes. Then he clear his throat and his eyes go sharp, focusing on Daniel. "Now, where were we? There's some sort of virus?"

Daniel grimace and pull off his hat. "My name is Daniel Weaver. I'm a scientist."

"*The* Daniel Weaver?" Mr. Go ask.

I shift Baby Girl to my hip and frown. "What that supposed to mean—*the* Daniel Weaver?"

Mr. Go break into a big smile. "It means that I have heard of your friend. You see, Dr. Weaver, we are not completely cut off from civilization. I have followed your work, albeit I'm a tad behind the times." He leave the room and come back with a stack of disks. He hold them up and show Daniel the titles. "Not exactly the latest medical journals and scientific trade papers, but recent enough to include some of your work. Smugglers are my librarians, you see," Mr. Go say with a laugh. "I'm something of a Delta Fever buff myself, as you can imagine. And while I do my work in Orleans, I find it's always useful to see what they are working on over the Wall."

He drop the disks onto the table and sit down again. "But you seemed to have slipped off the map in recent years, Dr. Weaver. Perhaps that is where you should begin."

Daniel crush his hat in his hands. He look trapped in that encounter suit. Like a chick in an egg that broke too soon, and he all curled up inside.

"I've been working on a cure for years now. I kept hitting dead ends 'til I created a retargeted virus designed to attack the Fever from the inside out." He look up and Mr. Go nod, which he seem happy to see. He drop his hat to use his hands when he talk.

"I was there, Dr. Wells. I thought I had the cure. But it went wrong somehow. In the lab, it kills the Fever. In test subjects, though . . . it does more than that. It turns the Fever against itself. Eradicating the Fever, but . . ."

Mr. Go sigh. "But also killing the host."

"Yes," Daniel say.

I watch them, waiting for what come next.

"A virus like that could be weaponized," the old man say. Daniel got the good sense to blush at that. Mr. Go may be the oldest man in the Delta, but he also one of the sharpest.

"The military doesn't know about it," Daniel say quickly. "When I saw how dangerous it was, I took it off the books. I needed more data, firsthand, if I was going to move forward. I couldn't rely on the lab to supply me and keep it secret. So I gathered all my samples and data, and here I am."

"Where is the virus now?" Mr. Go ask, but Daniel don't move.

"Show him," I say. This be what it all about.

Daniel take a deep breath and blow it out slowly into his suit. He reach into his coat and pull out the case he showed me back at the Institute. But it ain't the same shape. I lean forward for a better look. There be a little red light on the black box, clear as day.

I swear under my breath. "That supposed to be green, ain't it?"

Daniel nod. "With six vials inside." He hold the box out, show that it be empty.

I lean back, pulling Baby Girl away from him. My face be getting hot and my head be spinning. "Where it at?"

Mr. Go slump in his chair and run a hand over his face. Daniel look at his feet.

"Lost in Rooftops. The fall broke the case open."

"Jesus wept," Mr. Go say. "Did it break the vials? Is the virus out?"

Daniel shake his head. "No. I would have known. I've got . . . My datalink has scanners. It would have told me. They're just . . . gone. Maybe swallowed by that thing down there. I don't know. I was scared. I just wanted to get out."

"You. Was. Scared." I bite off the words, my eyes watering. He don't know from scared, a guy who ride a roller coaster 'cause being scared be fun. I *saved* this fool. I gave my braids for him. But he ain't worth shit.

Daniel look up at me. "I'm sorry."

"Oh, well, then I guess it be okay," I say.

Daniel clear his throat in a burst of static and turn to Mr. Go. "Dr. Wells, you're a scientist. Maybe you can help?"

Before Mr. Go can do more than open his mouth, I be in Daniel's face.

"Help?" I bark at him like a swamp fox. "Help what, man? Turn your weapon into sunshine? He ain't a magician, Daniel. He just an old man. And you. You been carrying this mess with you since day one *knowing* I got a baby I be trying to protect. But you made me think we had a chance, a chance for something better down here. And then you just *leave* it in that hole there—that hole *you* made. And you don't tell me? I should kill you. I should cut you wide open and leave you for hunters to find."

"It's not like I meant to—" Daniel start to say, but I raise my hand to stop him.

"It be *exactly* like that, Daniel. You come into my town, my *home,* with this mess and be looking to do Lord knows what. Now what? You just gonna leave it here and walk away? Hell no, man. You don't walk away from this. You take your shit with you when you leave. You hear me? All of it."

"Fen," Mr. Go say so soft, I almost don't hear him. Daniel be hanging his head like a whipped dog, and Mr. Go looking at me like I be the one done something wrong.

"Dr. Wells *is* a scientist," Daniel say. "Maybe . . . maybe he can—"

"Damn it, man, you been asking other folks what to do since before you even got here. Now pack up. I'ma take this child to that priest, then I'ma take you back to Rooftops.

You going in that hole and finding that virus. Then you take it and your no-good, virus-carrying ass back over that Wall. Damn." I squeeze Baby Girl to me so tight, she be squirming, and I start to leave the room. But Mr. Go speak up.

"Forget the virus."

I whirl on the old man and see he got a hand on Daniel's shoulder now. "How we supposed to do that, exactly?"

"What else can we do?" he ask back.

Daniel look at his raggedy clothes, still gunked up with the muck of Rooftops. "She's right. I could go back. To Rooftops. Find the cave-in and the virus."

"Could you, now?" Mr. Go ask. "One sinkhole in the midst of a dozen to crawl around in the dark and hope the things that live there don't find you first? And then what?"

Daniel slam his hand on the table. "I don't know. I don't know! This city was supposed to be dead."

Mr. Go smile a crazy hard smile, white teeth flashing like a warning. "Oh, far from it, I'm afraid. Look around you, Daniel. This island, this greenhouse, is one big containment suit. Instead of pumps and filters, I rely on plants to clean the air, siphon the poisons and disease. A fragile ecosystem, but one that works. And bears fruit—not stale recycled urine and carbo gel. It's why I live here. But outside, in the city, the same process is happening. Orleans is healing itself."

"No thanks to me," Daniel say bitterly, and I hear his guilt. Good. Guilt be the start of knowing right from wrong, Daddy used to say. But that all it be. A start.

Mr. Go shrug, palms up. "Show me this virus. You have your data, I presume?"

Daniel nod. "I'll need something to write with."

"Maybe two heads will be better than one," Mr. Go say. "In the meantime, Fen, the vials are lost. God willing, they will stay buried long enough to dissolve into the mire. You are right, Daniel, I am a scientist, and I say that the virus you've created, and the cure that you've sought, are both inconsequential in the face of God's work. Nature knows what to do with a poison. She dilutes it. Your sealed vials won't last forever in the ground here—they will disperse, leeching out in a manner that the land can control. But you've got the child to consider. So we'll take a look at what Daniel has tonight and, in the morning, you will leave. And may God be with you."

Daniel blink and I hear the tears in his eyes being sucked away into drinking water by his suit. I just can't bring myself to care.

Part Four

SHEPHERD

34

❧ "CHILDREN," MR. GO SAY SOFTLY. I WAKE UP like a shot, scaring the baby. She cry out, and I jerk myself into a sitting position. Got to feed her, change her so she be quiet. I can't let her cry.

I don't remember falling asleep, but I remember my dream—me sharpening my knife to use on Daniel, and Mr. Go dulling the blade, over and over again.

Maybe Mr. Go get something from talking with Daniel. Maybe one day there be a chance for a cure, but not soon enough to keep Baby Girl with me. Not soon enough to save us both from Orleans.

"We up, we up," I say. I take a deep breath and feel a lump in my belly I don't expect. The same lump I felt when them ABs attacked. Ain't 'til now I realized that lump been easing since Daniel showed up. Now it back and I don't know who I be angrier at, that fool tourist or me.

Mr. Go be standing in the doorway, smiling like we ain't

both been bit by a rabbit and found it been a snake. "It's near sunrise, Fen. Time for you and that healthy little girl to get a move on. I've set aside some purified water for her formula. I can give you more, if you are running low."

"Thank you," I say, but water ain't all we running low on. Common sense in short supply, too. I been going since before Lydia died and don't know how much more I got in me. I already been stupid with Daniel. Any more mistakes and Baby Girl and I both be dead. Still, I stand up and get Baby Girl ready to go. The sooner this be over, the safer for us both.

When we pulled together, Mr. Go lead us down to the water. Daniel follow, all silent and sulky. He ain't too happy about yesterday, but I don't really care long as we get to the end of this thing.

"Have you thought of a name for her yet?" Mr. Go ask, nodding at Baby Girl.

I make a face. It be a big deal, naming someone. But I been thinking Nola, for New Orleans, or Enola, for East Orleans. "Enola," I tell him. "Enola Jeanne Marie, so she always know where she come from."

"Enola," Mr. Go repeat, rolling the word in his mouth like he be drinking it. "I think that sounds just fine."

We follow him to the air lock at the bottom of the stairs.

"Your ship awaits," he say, waving his hand like he a showman or something. The door be made of glass. Through it, we can see the "ship" bobbing up against a small dock. It be just a little round bark, like a saucer, made from woven reeds. Two paddles that look like logs be lying in the bottom.

"This?" Daniel ask. "This is a basket."

Mr. Go nod. "A well-*made* basket; to be precise. Water-proof in every way, easy to camouflage, and, best of all, completely biodegradable. Now, I'll be using the locks to reverse the flow of the river here in order to send you upstream. The moment you feel yourselves pulled backward, get to shore. That's as far as the locks have influence. Otherwise, you'll just end up back here. Daniel, I've drawn you a map. Fen will get you part of the way, and this will lead you to a break in the Wall." He turn to me. "By the Old Gate," he say, so I can point Daniel in the right direction.

"What's the Old Gate?" Daniel ask as he fold up the map and tuck it away in his coat.

"One of the last entrances through the Wall, sealed up about a decade ago. Aide workers and supply trucks used it to deliver goods into the city. You came across, so you are familiar with the moat formed by the bayou along the Wall? The Gate served as a drawbridge. Then it was a watchtower for the military. Unoccupied, as I understand it, for many years."

Daniel pat his pocket and give his thank-yous.

"Mr. Go." I tuck Baby Girl in my arms and reach into my pack. The candy bar Daniel gave me be melted into a different shape and hardened again, but it still good. I put it in Mr. Go's hand.

"Well, I'll be," he say, and break into another smile. "I sure do love a Snickers."

We say our farewells and I climb into the boat with Enola. We be bobbing in the water 'til a hatch lift to one side of us and we use the oars to push off from the steps.

The locks be like wooden gates all along the canal. We float between two hatches and the water start to rise around us. Then a hatch in front of us open and we go whooshing forward, down to the next level. It be like steps made of water. Daniel and I use the paddles to keep from knocking the walls too bad. The last set of locks angle west, and we set off on a smaller stream that flow into the river. Soon we be under the trees and the sun be shimmering through all green and yellow, and it feel like a day in paradise. And it would be, too, if this fool hadn't gone and dropped a time bomb in the middle of our city. And Orleans not been going to war.

We ride upstream in silence, passing the ruins of rotted houses and empty patches with trees that be showing where driveways used to be. The air be cool today, but humid still, and it stick to my skin like a wet shirt. I look down at Baby Girl, glad she got Mr. Go's new clothes on her. She stare back at me like she waiting for me to say something, so I do.

"Once upon a time, there was a magical place called New Orleans. There was magic in the water, magic in the trees, and magic in the people. But most magical of all was a woman named Jeanne Marie," I say. The story Lydia used to tell me when I first came to her. It make me glad I can give it to Enola now. "Jeanne Marie was clever as a clock and pretty as a sunset. She was smart as a whip and pretty as a new moon," I say.

Daniel sit behind me and I know he be listening. He be making my back itch, like a spider crawling by. So I try not to think about it. Instead, I tell Baby Girl stories her mama used to be telling me, the same stories I be telling Lydia while she giving birth. This one about the time Jeanne Marie tricked the Devil into giving her back the moon. Enola seem to like the sound of my voice and be waving her little legs as I talk. It make me glad Jeanne Marie part of her name. I think Lydia woulda liked it.

By the time the story done, Enola be asleep again. Babies don't be doing much more than that, it seem. We drift awhile in silence, pushing along with an oar every so often.

"What was that?" Daniel ask. His voice sound like crunching leaves in the soft air. This boy ain't never gonna win no staring contests. He can't stay still long enough. "The story you just told?"

I shrug. "Just a story. Enola's mama used to tell them to me."

"I liked it," he say. For some reason, that make me feel good.

"It gonna be strange not traveling with you and all your fool questions," I say.

I look over my shoulder at him. He crazy dumb, but he been there for me since the blood farm, and on St. Charles Avenue. I ain't gonna forget that.

It take a minute, but he almost smile through that mask of his. "It's been . . . fun," he say.

I snort and shake my head. "Don't know about that, but it been interesting."

We quiet for a little while, then Daniel speak up again. "I'm sorry," he say. "You were right about what you said last night. I've made a lot of mistakes, Fen. I'd never want to hurt you, or . . . Enola." He say her name for the first time and it sound right to me.

"Well. You ain't been all bad," I tell him.

Suddenly, I sit up straighter and tell him we here. The boat be pulling back downstream. We pole our way to the side of the canal and climb out on shore. Daniel hold us in place with the oars while I climb out with Enola and my pack. Dropping the oars into the boat, we watch it drift back the way we came, returning to Mr. Go.

❦ SHE BELONGED HERE.

Daniel watched Fen as she swung the baby into her sling and tossed her pack onto her back. Her posture changed the moment they were on dry land. She didn't stand, but moved in a crouch, wary, listening for things he couldn't hear. Looking for signs he couldn't read.

This way, she mouthed.

Daniel itched to log into his datalink, missing it like an amputated limb, but it couldn't help him anymore. He had taken it off last night after a final attempt to get it working. He felt for it now in his pocket, like a security blanket that could no longer keep him warm.

"Daniel," Fen whispered. She pointed to the edge of the trees, where the crumbled hulks of buildings could be seen. "These be old housing projects, according to Mr. Go," she said.

She pointed at a fluorescent orange X graffitied on the wall, with numbers and symbols in the crooks of the crossed lines.

"What is that?" he asked.

"Directions," she replied. "Used to be they marked the houses like this after a storm, tell you how many in the house, alive and dead. Now it be a way to tell whose land this be and, if it your own tribe, it tell you where they next camp be. O-Negs must've made these."

Daniel studied the marking, but it made no sense to him. "Do you know the code?"

Fen shook her head. "Nope, I ain't an O-Neg. But I know they been this way and . . ." She moved past the markings on the wall to look at the far side of the building. "If they only be putting it on this side, it be the direction they headed. So we go the other way and steer clear of them. Or they find us, and I can't say what happen next."

Daniel nodded and followed her in silence as they set out across the broken courtyard of what once might have been low brick apartment buildings.

Fen scowled. "Shh. Something in the trees," she whispered. She waved him behind a section of tumbled wall. "Get down. Stay still."

Where? Daniel mouthed, dropping down beside her and the baby. Fen pointed with her chin to the north, back the way they had come. Did something flicker in the trees? It looked like a man. But just as quickly, the shape was gone.

Fen reached into her waistband and pulled out a small knife.

"Take this," she whispered, and shoved it into his hands. "You got to get out of here. I'ma go out there, you wait and head the other way. Follow that map now, make it to the Wall."

She turned and looked at him. Her eyes were serious. "Be safe, tourist. I ain't got your back after this."

Daniel nodded, fumbling the knife into an outer pocket where it couldn't harm his encounter suit. Fen would be all right, he told himself. She still had a blade of her own, the hilt sticking out of her boot. He wanted to say something, anything to tell her how grateful he was to have known her.

Suddenly, a piercing cry shattered the hushed ruins. It bounced around the old buildings, coming from everywhere at once.

"Shit," Fen swore. "Stay down, then go," she said again, and then she was up and walking out into the clearing. Daniel crouched low, peering through a crack in the wall.

Fen stood in the tumbledown courtyard, her hands up in the air, a little smile on her face.

"My name is Fen de la Guerre. I am an O-Positive. I come for counsel. This child is Enola. She is an O-Positive, too. Her daddy be one of you."

Daniel listened to the ritualized words as he looked around, trying not to make a sound. And then he saw, in the hollowed-out buildings, shadows pulling away from shadows. Fen was surrounded. Lithe, tall men and women appeared in the openings, peering through the crumbled mortar. Daniel's heart beat faster, the sweat from his palms making the encounter suit sticky and unbearably hot, as he realized the O-Negatives were armed. Small, flexible bows with brightly fletched arrows were aimed at her from all sides. Yet Fen seemed unafraid.

As one, the bows lifted into the air. There was a shuffling sound, and then a man stepped forward from behind a free-standing doorway, little more than an arch connecting two sections of wall. His eyes were the green of agates. His braids twisted around his head, giving him the look of a lion.

"*Comment ça va,* Fen? We feared you were dead."

Fen shrugged, at ease. "Not yet, Brother Davis," she said.

Brother Davis. Daniel exhaled in silent relief. Fen knew this man. With that assurance, and Fen's knife in his pocket, Daniel turned to face the woods. He wormed his way out of the ruins from a crouch, to a crawl, to a run into the woods, leaving Fen and Enola behind.

Heart and legs pumping, Daniel headed away from the ruins. When they were no longer in sight, he stopped to catch his breath and reorient himself. He pulled out the map Mr. Go had drawn him and read it by the early afternoon sunlight filtering through the trees. The woods were ghostly here, young trees like overgrown weeds pushing up through the foundations of what once were wooden houses and carefully tended yards. If he squinted, Daniel imagined he could see the old New Orleans, what it looked like before the storms.

He peered down at the map in his hands and chose his direction. The Wall lay to the west, but he had amends to make. He turned and headed south, back toward Rooftops.

35

❧ "YOU HAVE MUCH TO ANSWER FOR," DAVIS TELL me as we follow an unmarked path past a jumble of fallen houses. He got his arm around my shoulder, but not in a friendly way.

"Do I?" I ask. I feel sick seeing him again, and the lump in my belly be growing bigger. "Seem to me we in the same boat. Only it look like most of your tribe got out alive."

Davis smile like an alligator. "Now, Fen." He look around the ring of folks surrounding us, and I see what going on here. He ain't got Natasha to back him, but he still in charge. And now he got to show it. Davis spread his arms wide. "My people had no weapons—we turned them over to your tribe to honor the parley. Under those rules, Lydia was sworn to protect us. She did not."

My face go hard. Lydia ain't one to dodge responsibility. "Romulus gave you back your arrows. I saw him."

"Be that as it may, blood was lost. O-Neg blood. It must be repaid. Where is Lydia?"

I shake my head and laugh. "She dead, you fool. Like the rest of them. She died giving birth to this baby during the raid. She done paid the only blood price she gonna pay."

Davis's face go ashen. "This child is hers?"

"She mine, now," I say, hugging Enola to me. How a baby can smell so sweet in the middle of all this mess, I don't know, but for half a second, it give me some peace.

We in a deeper part of the woods now, full of shadows and broken buildings. I hear water and guess it be the lower stream where Mr. Go sent us up. We pass through a line of trees, and then we suddenly in the O-Neg camp.

The camp look like a tent city, a row of teepees in a half-moon-shape clearing, backed up against trees so dense, they be hard to squeeze between without getting scraped bloody. The teepees face a grassy lawn with that stream running through, so they got fresh water, and the trees be tall enough to hide smoke for miles. It look like they been here awhile. The grass be wearing thin and show where folks be going into the trees to relieve theyselves, and in and out of the food and hospital tents.

Davis's people peel away from whatever they be doing to form a circle around us. A group of women down by the stream soaking reeds for baskets come up out the water. A couple of boys net-fishing in the stream pull they nets. It peaceful. And too easy to find, once you know about the stream.

"You been here too long," I tell him. "La Bête's people gonna come for you."

Davis nod. "We won't be here long enough for it to matter. At least, not to you."

He stand in the center of the ring his people make and face me. "As I said, Lydia owes us a blood price. Give me the child, and it will be paid."

My face go cold as stone. "She ain't for sale."

Davis smile, like he being reasonable. "She is Lydia's child; this is Lydia's debt. Natasha is dead. And half a dozen of our men and women while in her protection. This is owed to us."

"Like hell," I spit. "You gonna sell her to blood hunters? Exchange her for weapons? You think they gonna take this baby's little cup of blood when they got a full-grown O-Neg in front of them with ten pints for the taking?"

Davis's smile turn into an angry scowl. "Child, don't speak to me as if we are equals. You were nothing but Lydia's pet. I do not hear you."

I can't help but laugh now. It stupid, me in the middle of this ring, this man calling for blood, when all hell about to break loose. I ain't never been good with fools, and while everything else be changing, that still be the same.

"Davis, listen to me. Them ABs that attacked us? They coming, you know. This be the start of another war." I speak loud so everyone hear me. Davis may be they chieftain, but he ain't all that without Natasha telling him what to do. Maybe someone else here can make him listen to truth.

"They be coming for you, and soon," I warn him. "This time, it won't just be clubs and nets. They got guns."

Davis laugh, but it mostly for show. His people laugh with him. "Guns? That's ridiculous. Everybody knows guns don't last in the Delta. The air will eat them up."

"Guns don't got to last long to be deadly. They just got to last for today. And they been here since this morning."

He shake his head in disbelief. "Well, thank you for the warning. We'd best not tarry. Give me the child, and you can be on your way."

"She ain't mine to give," I tell him true. "I made a promise to Lydia and I'ma keep it. You want blood? It gotta come from you or me, but not her."

Davis raise an eyebrow, reading my face. He see I mean it. "Very well. Will you let us move her to safety?"

"Say it first," I tell him. "You accept blood payment from Fen de la Guerre. Say it."

"I accept your payment, Fen," he say, and I know he live by that. Every tribe got its own way of dealing with things, but one thing for sure, in front of all his people, Davis got to keep his word or he ain't worth the clothes he standing in.

I unstrap Enola and one of them basket-weaving women come forward and take her. Baby Girl start fussing, but that can't be helped. The first rule of escape be assess your situation. Baby Girl and I gotta get out of this camp, and soon. The only way be through Davis. I got a baby, I got a plan, and I got a knife. It'll have to do. I crouch down and pull the blade from my boot.

36

❦ DAVIS LOOK LIKE A PEACOCK, STRUTTING around me. He got his own blade, and it a good size, but ceremonial, like his clothes and everything else—bits of feathers and beads, mess that just get in the way. Maybe it ain't never come down to it for Davis. Maybe the first time be at the powwow when he come out of hiding long enough to see his own folks get cut and bleed. Seems to me this blood fight he wanting be mostly for show, and from the way his O-Negs be cheering him on, they think it for show, too.

But it ain't. I watch the way I step, keeping low enough to stay balanced if he come at me. The ground ain't too even here by the stream, and it soft in places. I forget that and I might stumble. Davis, on the other hand, know the shift of the soil here. He be standing up tall like you win a fight by being of a size, not a mind.

I be of a mind. Let him showboat if he got to. But I ain't got all day. Them ABs be coming, and if Enola and I ain't gone by the time they get here, then it all been for nothing. So I got to find a way to force his hand. I stop circling. Davis stop a second later, but he closer to me than he been and it make him nervous. He hefting the knife in his right hand, blade up, looking to stab at me. Stabs be killing blows. Me, I just got to make a point.

I hold my knife blade down, ready to slash, and rush him. Davis suddenly drop to a crouch and thrust his knife at me. I sidestep and hook my left arm around his knife arm, hold it tight to my side. With my own knife, I cut off one of his braids. I push through and hope he trip on the uneven ground.

He don't go down, but I do, 'cause somehow he use my hold to throw me past him. I tuck and roll, keeping my knife out and away from my body. When I come up, knife ready, eyes back on Davis, I be almost up against the watching crowd. They know they place, though, and leave me be.

"This is a blood price, Fen," Davis say, reaching up to feel where his lock used to be.

"For you, Brother Davis. I ain't asking nothing from you but to let me be on my way with that baby. I cut you now, them ABs be on us all the faster. You ready for that?"

"Are you?"

He come at me so fast, I ain't got time to do more than bend to the side, arms out for balance. I feel his blade, but it cut my arm, my scar tissue, and that don't bleed so easy. Davis turn on me, angry to see his blade ain't running red. So maybe this ain't a game for him after all.

He rush me, and this time, our blades connect. I block

him, knife against knife, stepping into the blow. If I jump back, he gonna stab me. If I step in, he gotta change the way he holding the knife, or give ground. He gives and I slice him, whirling away. Blood come pouring down the cut on his cheek, pouring down good. He don't cry out, but he wipe his face, smearing it.

"Enough?" I ask.

Davis's blood look like war paint on his face, like them folks on All Saints' Day, decked out for they krewes. He growl at me, "No. This is for Natasha."

He rush me again. This time, I step forward, past his blade, and hit him in the chin with the top of my head. It don't pay to be standing so tall after all. His jaw snap shut and his head fly back. He stagger away from me, but I don't let him get far. I drive my knife into his right shoulder and jump into his body, kneeing his gut.

Davis grunt and hit the ground. His knife go flying across the clearing. My own knife done cut through his vest. It tough leather, made from deer or boar hide, but there be blood darkening the entry hole. I hold my blade against him and lean in close. Around us, his people be muttering and shouting. They ain't happy. "Davis," I say. "I ain't looking to kill another O-blood today. Flip me. Take my knife, and I'll call mercy."

"No," Davis say, gritting his teeth. "Natasha—"

"Natasha weren't no fool. She'd know these folks need a leader. That gonna be you or no? War coming whether you like it or not. If I call mercy, you let me and the baby go. I'ma get her out of this city. I promised Lydia. I'ma do that. After that . . . you and me can settle up. Whenever and however you want. But we both got to live to do it."

Davis look at me with them gray-green eyes I used to think be so beautiful. He don't nod, but I feel his body shift beneath me and I let it. He toss me over and onto my back. I release my grip and he take my knife, pressing it to my throat. Around us, the O-Negs roar in triumph.

"And this is how the price is paid!" he say, loud enough for everyone to hear. I lower my eyes. "Mercy," I say. It don't come out half as loud as his words, but it don't come easy to me, even in a play. Instead, I start to shake, try to say it again. "I yield," I say so soft it be a whisper. Davis sneer at me.

"Your blood won't do," he say to the crowd, to me. "It's too thin. Natasha had the blood of a warrior," he roars. I want to laugh in his face. That woman had the hands of a baby and the eyes of a fox. Sly and cold. He right. We ain't the same quality stock at all.

He get up off me a minute later and wipe his blood off my knife. He throw it over the heads of the crowd, into the woods.

"Bring the child," he call to the basket weaver. He take the baby from her. Davis bounce Enola in his arms for half a second. "Leave us," he say. "Your blood would weaken our tribe. This child would weaken our tribe. Do not return."

I take Enola and wrap her sling around her like a blanket. I look Davis in the eye and wonder who Enola's daddy really be. Got to be an OP or an O-Neg, and I know it ain't one of our boys, or old Uncle Rom. I hope it ain't Davis. But anything possible.

The crowd part and I walk into the woods where he threw my blade. I find my knife in the dirt and rub it clean on some leaves to get rid of the last of Davis's scent.

Ain't much later when I hear a howl split the air. Blood hounds or bloodthirsty ABs, it don't make a difference. With all them O-Negs close by, they won't be looking for me right away. Even so, I start to run.

37

THE AIR GREW MORE HUMID AS NIGHT CAME on. Daniel felt exposed on the flat expanse of grass. Rooftops at night was even more frightening than during the day. He should have waited, he knew, waited until morning. He should have listened to Mr. Go and not come at all. They had stayed up for hours, going over Daniel's formulas, swapping theories, but made little progress. The tools Daniel had used to make the DF virus didn't exist in Orleans, just as the samples available in the Delta could not be found in the Outer States. Without the missing vials, they might hit on a cure eventually. But it would take years. Time that Fen's city did not have.

And so he'd had Mr. Go draw a second map, one that would allow him to retrace his steps. The map had done its part. The rest was up to Daniel.

He looked out across the gently rolling landscape. It was insanity to walk the hazards of this field in the dark, let alone attempt to go spelunking, even with his night-vision goggles. They'd be next to useless, but time was running out. Gingerly, he edged from the trees and onto the soft earth.

Fen. She kept popping into his head, unbidden. Fen. Enola. The reasons he was back here. What was it Fen and Mr. Go had both said? Daniel in the lions' den. They couldn't have been more right. He took another step onto the damp earth.

A high-pitched scream filled the air. Daniel dropped to his stomach like a frightened mouse, freezing in terror. The cry came again, like the hunting call of an owl, and he recognized it as human. His encounter suit reacted as he broke into a fear-induced sweat, his heart pounding faster. The war that Fen feared was already beginning. Now that he was still, Daniel could hear other bodies in the field, moving silently except for the susurration of grass as they passed.

Daniel withdrew into the tree line and dialed his goggles up higher. When he rose to his knees, he could see the hunting party. Fearlessly, they were dancing across Rooftops, whooping occasionally. Daniel recalled what Fen had said about the man named La Bête Sauvage, how he drugged his hunters to make them brave. *Or suicidal,* Daniel thought. But the grass beneath them did not give way. Like a joke in a child's cartoon, unaware of the danger, they defied gravity. Across their backs were slung bows and bigger weapons: the guns that Fen said were on their way.

Daniel pressed his back to a rough tree trunk and tried to think. He was so close, but where there was one group of ABs, there might be more. Daniel's heart sank. He couldn't risk them finding the virus. If he managed to find it and they caught him . . . In the wrong hands, the virus would devastate Orleans, sweeping across the Delta like an avenging angel.

Again he thought of Charlie. Happy-go-lucky Charlie, scrabbling to eat the dirt from his potted plant. Even at his worst, with gums bleeding and teeth ground down to nubs, Daniel never once thought of euthanizing his little brother. Charlie had been alive, like Orleans. And that was the first, most important thing.

Daniel stared out across the field, alive now with hoots and burning lights. The DF virus was almost a cure, but almost was not enough. Mr. Go was right. Better to leave it buried and escape the city. Better to live and start again.

Torchlight moved toward him like a will-o'-the-wisp, driving him to hide in the scrub brush beneath the trees. He looked again at Mr. Go's map, at the directions that would lead him to a breach in the Wall. He was less than a mile away from the area Mr. Go described on the map, but the war for Orleans had started, and the streets were filling with tribes. His only hope was to hide.

Daniel's heart pounded in his chest. Panic fluttered inside him and he saw Charlie's face again. Charlie when he was healthy and strong. Enola's little face, so delicate and tender. Fen scowling, smirking at him.

What was it Fen had said? Churches are sacred. They are sanctuary.

Daniel looked at his map. Father John's church was just west of him, and slightly north. Closer than the Wall. The church would have to do for now.

38

✤ THE SUN LOOK LIKE A DYING CANDLE ON THE western edge of the treetops. My eyes be adjusting to the dark as I walk. Leaves and pine needles crunch beneath my feet. Father John's mission ain't far from here, and it won't be in danger of the ABs, the Os, or nobody. He ain't like Mama Gentille. Father John's church still be sacred ground. Like the Ursuline Sisters with they schooling and praying, Father John put his faith to work. When he come down with his missionaries and open up the old Super Saver food store as his church, people start to come. There been food and water there when the Red Cross and the feds weren't nowhere to be found. He brought in clothes, shoes, medicines for tribe and freesteader alike.

When the first round of Fever struck, he turned his mission into a hospital. Bed against bed, full of people moaning and dying, but Father John and his folks, they stay. That is, 'til some of them nuns and other priests be getting sick, and they go home. But they take the Fever with them. I guess there be a real crisis of faith in the Outer States when the ministry start dying. All them Catholic hospitals and Presbyterian hospitals and Methodist hospitals, the Jewish ones, too—all of them been infected with Delta Fever. Nobody be going to church when the pulpit be empty. Mr. Go say religious folks be right in line with the government when it come to building the Wall. Two thousand some years ain't killed Christianity, or Islam, or Buddhism. I guess they be damned if some little Fever gonna do it in less than a decade.

But down here be different, 'cause some of us got immunities. Some of us learned to live. Father John survived and he kept on caring for us. When the borders closed, he still helped by getting us sponsor families. That been how I came to have the Coopers, with they care packages and pictures of a real house, with painted walls and glass windows, and a dog that weren't a blood hound. That why I be having faith in them, and in Father John now.

The trees be thinning, but it true dark now. Good thing, too, because there be a road up ahead, and I see people coming. They carrying lights, but the lights go dark as they get close, and I hear whispers and I know they part of the AB raid. I stay in the trees 'til they gone past me. Then I see Father John's mission up the road a ways. I stop and hold Baby Girl close in my arms, get to my knees, and say a prayer for them O-Negs, and for the O-Positives, too, if any still be alive. They don't deserve what about to happen. Nobody do. And to think I used to want to be a chieftain. I be lucky if I can help this baby, but that be about it.

The Super Saver look just like I remember—a big one-story brick of a building that take up most of a block. You can see the edges of other stores that used to be next to it, but they gone now. Just this big old red thing left behind. The SUPER SAVER sign be broken where it attached over the double doors to the inside. Somebody gone and repaired it with a piece of plywood, and they changed the word *saver* to *savior.*

Behind me, far away, I hear faint pops and shouts, like there be a celebration in the woods. It make me break into a run. I reach the doors and pull hard, but they locked. Chained from the inside. Father John ain't never locked his door. Churches be sacred.

I be too exposed standing here like this, so I run down the steps and around the building, away from the woods, to look for another way in. At the back of the store there be a loading dock with two trucks what used to bring food over the border. They empty now, but it look like somebody been sleeping in one. There be a little nest of clothes inside. The truck be parked so close to the dock, you could walk from the truck through the bay doors and back without getting wet in the rain. Maybe Father John be living back here now.

"Father?" I call out softly, and brace myself in case I need to run.

I try the back door. It be unlocked, so I walk in and call out. "Father John?"

My voice echo down the back hall of the church. I feel guilty, sneaking in the back way, but it ain't safe out front. A few torches flicker on the wall. They been added after the generator died years ago. It always strike me how churchlike they make the place feel, since it really be an oversize grocery store. The hallway be dotted with office doors that say MANAGER, ASSISTANT MANAGER, but somebody, maybe the same joker who did the sign out front, done changed *Manager* to *Manger*.

Most of the rooms be empty. I look through the little glass windows set in the doors. Nothing but darkness.

"Hello?"

The lunchroom be next. When Father John took over, it been a classroom for us, with computers to e-mail our sponsors. Father John used to set out our care packages on the long tables, and we kids be going crazy trying to see who getting what. I got my first pair of rain boots that way. But they too soft to be walking around in Orleans back then, with debris so high and nails and pieces of glass cutting up everything. Daddy say I'd be dead of tetanus if I try wearing them. They too small to fit over my work boots, but they bright yellow with little white daisies on them. I ain't never seen daisies for real. I loved them.

The hallway end in a set of closed double doors. Back here be where the nuns used to live, and the priests, and volunteers. Father John, too. Out there be the chapel. I put a hand to the left-side door and push.

"Hello?"

I hear somebody scuffling, like they rushing to hide, then some softer sounds. A man clears his throat.

"Welcome, child, and all who enter here." The voice be

booming softly, like a storm in the distance. It like Mr. Go that way, like Lydia, too, with her important voice. I relax. I know that voice, those words.

"Father John, it be me, Fen de la Guerre. You knew me a long time ago."

It seem like I always be giving the same speech these days, telling people who I be, why they know me. Like something in the air here erase who you been and you got to keep saying it so you don't forget.

"Fen?" He don't sound so strong now, like the man I knew. He sound old. I step through the door. The room be lit with stubs of candles all around, making it hard to see. I stand by the altar, on a little stage. Rows of hard metal folding chairs fill the floor in front of me. A thin maroon rug run down the steps of the altar between the chairs to the front doors, with they heavy chain crisscrossing the handles. Things have changed. But not everything. The smell of old incense be strongest here, sharp with wild sage and other herbs. The real incense ran out before I been born.

"Father, where you at?"

"Here, child." And then I see him in the corner by the nave. He reach into the old desk for matches and start to light the rows of devotional candles. Father John be tall, one of the tallest men I know. He be wearing long robes today, not his priest robes, the pretty black thing with the embroidered collar he used to do service in. These look more like the robes of a monk, rough-woven and dark brown. The kind of cloth we be making in the O-Positive camp. Easy to weave.

He light the last candle and turn to face me. The glow

from the nave light up more of the room, but it keep his face in the dark. "Good to see you, Father," I say.

He move into the light then, and I see him, older and with more gray in his hair than used to be, but his skin pink and healthy, and he smile at me like old times. He sweep me into a big hug, and I smell the sage, even stronger now, and something beneath it, sharp, like kerosene. I pull back.

"I'm sorry for the smell. You caught me cleaning up a spill from the generator. It runs on ethanol now. Some tribes in the area run a still and bring it to me. Made from potatoes or some such, I understand."

"It ain't bothering me," I tell him, even if Baby Girl be wrinkling her nose like she fit to sneeze. "I just be happy to see you," I say again.

"And you, Fen. And your child, is it?" he ask, catching sight of Enola. "You've both picked an interesting night to visit us. There seems to be an . . . altercation in the woods."

I don't know how to tell him it be worse than that, so I say nothing.

"Tell me, child, how are your parents?"

My breath hitch in my throat. "They dead, Father John. Long time ago, too."

He nod and fold his hands into his sleeves. "We never had a service for them." He don't say it like he be judging me, but I feel bad all the same. Just because I ain't got much use for God don't mean my parents never did.

"That true," I admit, hugging Enola to my chest. "They been killed by hunters. Ain't nothing I could do to stop it. They told me to run, and I ran."

"I am very sorry," he say, but I can't look him in the eye or I might let these tears fall. He put a hand on my back and push me into a seat. I can't stop telling the story.

"They say, 'Run, Fen, and don't look back.' And I don't want to run, but there be dogs and whips and I don't know what else to do, so I run and then I be in the swamp, swimming and running, and I couldn't go back. I couldn't." I look up and I be crying again and angry about it but I can't stop. "And I'd've come here to you, but you been so far away and them dogs been chasing me and then they stop and I know they got Mama and Daddy. So I just kept going and I fell in with some bad folks, and it take a while, but then I find the OPs like Daddy say and they test me and take me in."

Father John don't say nothing. He just sit next to me, so solid and safe and steady that I start to breathe again and my eyes stop leaking and I sink into my seat and let some of it go.

Baby Enola be looking up at me with her eyes bigger than anything, like they hold the whole world. She yawn real big and Father John shift beside me.

"Tell me about your little one."

I smile, but it be sad to say it. "This be Baby Girl Enola, Father John. She ain't mine," I tell him. "She the daughter of my chieftain, but her mama be dead and we need your help."

"Shall I baptize her?" Father John ask.

I hesitate. I don't know what Lydia'd be wanting there, but then I think of that Delta water running down Enola's clean face and I say, "No. But you can give her a new life. Outside the Delta."

"What are you saying?"

I turn to him. "Remember my foster family, the Coopers? I know it been a long time, but they sponsored me 'cause they wanted kids and couldn't have one of they own. They good people and they wanted to help me. Now I need it. Enola, she brand-new, Father, born just a few days ago. She type O and she clean, healthy as can be. She can go over the Wall, if you help."

Father John look at Enola for a long time, then he look away, toward the lights burning in the nave.

"Can you do it?" I ask.

He clear his throat. "I'd have to test her," he say. "And contact my diocese in the States. They might have a family . . . or contacts to your Coopers."

A knot I ain't known been in my stomach relax. I be sorry to let Enola go, but I be glad for her.

"There be a war out there," I tell Father John. "That fighting outside be just the beginning, so the sooner, the better."

Father John tense up. "Another war?" He sound distant and I know he thinking of the last time things been bad. Bad times be like the tide in Orleans. Now the tide be coming in again.

"I have feared this day," he say, and it sound like he read it from the Bible.

He stand up quick. "Well, let us make haste, then. Bring the child to the altar. I will get my instruments."

Testing Enola take some time. He swab the inside of her cheek to check for Fever in one of the offices with medical equipment. She drink two whole bottles while we wait. I change her and we sleep in one of the rooms the nuns used to share. The walls of the Super Saver be thick, but not so thick that I can't hear fighting outside. It make me wonder if Daniel got enough sense in him to make it over the Wall on his own. But it too late to worry about that now. All I got to think about be this baby in my arms.

I must have fallen asleep, 'cause Father John wake me from a dream about the cottage in the glade.

"I am so sorry," he say to me in that deep, important voice. "But the child is unclean."

39

✠ I ASK HIM TO SAY IT AGAIN.

I make him run the test three more times, but the answer always be the same.

It don't matter that Enola be only four days old. That she ain't had nothing but pure water and pure formula.

"I don't know who told you she was O positive, Fen," Father John say. "She's B positive. She had the Fever even before she was born."

It don't make sense. Daniel lied to me. But why? It don't matter to him one way or the other what type Enola be. Unless he trying to get on my good side. What'd he say? "O positive, like her mother." Like that be good news. And it was, enough to get him out of that blood farm and safe to where he want to go.

I sit down hard on the bench next to Father John's equipment. Baby Girl in my arms don't like the drop and she start to cry. She ain't the only one be wanting to cry.

The world ain't what it been to me an hour ago. Nothing make sense.

Lydia would never be with an AB. She knew ABs and Os make A and B babies. Any child she had would belong to La Bête . . .

But then I think of how them ABs attacked us right when it been her time. And how she tried to talk peace with them months ago and failed. Maybe La Bête been coming for her and got the powwow instead.

I feel sick. Ain't no way for me to raise a B baby. Ain't no way. Enola look healthy now, but that ain't gonna last. She gonna be needing transfusions, and I ain't able to give her my blood. She gonna get sick and die like that boy in the Ursuline hospital tent. Or she gonna be one of them girls at the Market, owned by La Bête and flirting with whatever trash come her way.

She look so small and innocent against the ugly scars on my arms. I kiss her on the forehead and she wriggle her little legs. She looking more like her mama every day. But she type B. There ain't nothing I can do to save her.

"Father—" I have to stop because my voice break and I clear my throat, start again. "Father, will you raise her here for me? This be a sacred place. You give her protection and she be all right. You can get her the blood she gonna be needing. You got equipment and folks willing to trade. You hear me? That's more than I can do."

I got no tribe, no home. I could keep her, I suppose, take her back to Mr. Go and we raise her on that little island. But she infected. She sick, and it only a matter of time before she pass that on to Mr. Go.

"Sorry, Baby Girl. This church be the safest place for you. Safer than being with me." She be looking at me, the only person she know in this world. But I ain't exactly been good luck.

I put my face close to her, breathe in that warm baby smell. "I love you, Baby Girl. Remember that, if you can." She be watching me with old eyes. I touch her cheek and she pull a little half smile. Not a real smile, I know. She too young for that. But it break my heart just the same. "Bye-bye, Enola. Bye-bye."

And then I hand her to Father John, along with the baby formula, the bottles of water, the two extra shirts Mr. Go made.

"When she old enough, send her to the Ursulines for schooling."

"I will," Father John say. "And I'll be glad for the company in the meantime, child. But what about you?"

"I don't know," I confess. I feel like I done used up all I got to give to this life. Maybe this be why we don't grow old in the Delta. There just ain't no point.

I don't take long saying good-bye 'cause it hurt. Like Daddy say: Run, Fen, and don't look back. So I don't. Even when Baby Girl start to fuss and be crying, I keep walking. Father John take the chains off the doors, now that the sun be fixing to rise. Baby Girl wailing for all she worth. She ain't used to Father John. She ain't used to nobody but me. Then I hear him start humming to her, a real old song he used to play when we been here long ago. He a good man. She gonna be all right with him. I shut the door behind me.

40

❦ *I DONE THE BEST I COULD.* I SAY IT TO LYDIA,
though I just be talking to myself. She ain't here. It just me now.
I did my best, and this gonna be a better life for Enola than
what she woulda had with me on our own. Or the O-Negs,
too stupid to take good advice, be on they guard. Better than
with Mr. Go and his little island, locked up like a tomb. I head
up the road, away from the O-Negs and the Super Saver and
the woods, like the last time I say good-bye to Father John. My
parents been with me then, and we walked together into the
trees. I follow our footsteps, back to the heart of Orleans and
a glade in the swamps.

The clearing be smaller than I remember, and the house
ain't even a house no more, just a half-burnt, vine-covered
wall. The rest gone back to the swamps. Even the ground be
softer than it used to, marshland claiming its own. Daddy
had pumps going to keep it solid for us. That all gone to
rust now, too. I walk around the edge of the glade, touch

the trees, and remember how Mama had a hammock tied between these two trees on sunny days in the middle of summer, and how Daddy got so angry when he saw me carving my name into that trunk because it be a sign someone live here. Could be dangerous, even after we moved on. Could give a hunter my scent, and a reason to follow. We been so careful out here. Freesteaders have to be.

I be glad the swamp so alive here, full of gators and foxes and all. 'Cause my parents be dead, and there ain't no trace of them left, no bones, no nothing. Nothing to cry over. No one to blame. Two young people chose to come over the Wall. They fell in love, had a baby, and left her behind.

I be tired of running and hiding, tired of just trying to survive. How can Orleans be a home if it always trying to kill you? How can it be living if you ain't allowed to live? What did Lydia say? The City takes. Well, I ain't got nothing left to give.

I plant a cross of twigs in the dirt by the cottage wall, pick some yellow primroses, and twist them into the twigs. "Sorry it ain't a real funeral, Mama," I say.

The flowers be pretty. I tuck one behind my ear. Mama used to do that. She used to do a lot of nice things. Enola shoulda had a mother like that.

When the sun be bright in the sky, I get up to go. The place look so small; hard to believe it used to be my whole world.

I don't pray, but I kiss the cross and I say good-bye. Then I walk into the swamp and the trees be so tall, it like a cathedral from a photograph, high arches, cool and deep and green. The water be warmer than it look. It feel good to the touch, so I step in, lower and lower, ignoring the moss and the green scum on the surface. I drag my hands behind me and I start to feel so light. I start humming that song Father John be singing to Enola. It be soothing and I need that, so I be humming, then I be singing: *"Would you be free from your passion and pride? There's power in the blood, power in the blood."* I lay back in the water like a baptism, and the swamp be dancing around my ears, little sounds like clinking glass, and it smell of earth and water, and it feel warm, like blood. *"Come for a cleansing to Calvary's tide; there's wonderful power in the blood."*

The City takes. Well, if She want me, She can have me. Maybe then She leave Enola alone. I lie in the water and let the current carry me away.

41

IT TOOK HOURS OF CAREFUL AVOIDANCE, BUT Daniel made his way to the broken field outside of Father John's church. Unlike Rooftops, this field was clear. The Super Saver squatted at the far end of the field, solid, safe. Candlelight twinkled through a gap in the curtains along the one high, narrow window set in the western wall, barely visible in the late morning light.

Daniel sprang from his hiding place and ran.

The rear of the store-turned-church was closest. He ignored the trucks parked there and mounted the loading dock, two steps at a time, praying that the back door was open. It was. He was safe. But not alone. The long hallway flickered with guttering torches. At the end, beyond the double doors, a baby was crying. Enola.

He slowed down, resisting the urge to call out to Fen, and eased his way down the hall. The doorways to the left and right were dark and empty. The second to last door swung open and a tall man stepped out, dressed in a dark monk's robe, hood pulled back, face streaked, pink and yellowed gray. Daniel froze. The man was wearing makeup to conceal the telltale scars from Delta Fever. A syringe in his hand caught the light.

"Ah, you've found me in disarray, I'm afraid. I've been cleaning, you see." He wiped a sleeve across his face, smearing the rest of the concealing makeup in a grotesque streak on his forehead. "Welcome, my son," the man said brightly. "All God's children are welcome here."

Daniel hesitated. "I'm looking for Fen."

Confusion flickered across the scarred face. He gave Daniel a once-over, and his face brightened. "An outlander. Yes? Is that an encounter suit? What a wonderful invention. Would that they had had them when I first came to Orleans." He chuckled. "Never mind that, though. Come along, we were just about to get started."

The priest turned back through the double doors.

Daniel followed him. "Fen?"

Enola was there at the altar, a machine next to her warming up with the help of a small generator. He stared. It was a dialysis machine, designed to clean blood. Or harvest it.

Before Daniel could react, a dull pain pounded at his temple, and everything went black.

42

WATER LILIES AND SWAMP FLOWERS WRAP around me. I glide in slow circles, watching the sun through the trees. It beautiful, the mist lifting like the veil of a nun, trees dappled in shadow and light even as the sky grow cloudy. Peaceful. The most peace I ever found in Orleans.

I drift and sing to myself, wanting to sink under, to bury myself deep. *"Would you be whiter, whiter than the snow? There's power in the blood, power in the blood."* I been tempting fate, dangling in the water like an alligator snack, and I ain't dead. *"Sin stains are lost in its life-giving flow. There's wonderful power in the blood."*

Why ain't I dead?

"There is power, power, wonder-working power in the blood of the Lamb."

I think about Lydia, how her life be over so fast. She the most alive person I ever knew, and she gone like that. Mama and Daddy, they be gone in the blink of an eye, too. But

Enola, little Enola, she perfect. Perfect little Baby Girl. Little baby lamb. She come into the world just as fast as everybody else be leaving.

"There's wonderful power in the blood."

And Father John, like Mr. Go, he been around forever. Like these trees in this swamp, ancient and strong. Mr. Go rooted like a tree, but Father John be like the chameleon, the lizard on the leaf. He know how to blend in. How to survive. Mr. Go be brown and rough, like the trees, and Father John be smooth and fresh, like he just been born.

It be like time stop ticking. The sun don't move in the sky. And I ain't floating anymore, waiting to drown. The world stop breathing and I think: Father John's face, all pink and healthy. Not a line or a wrinkle in all these years. How could that be?

Unless it ain't.

I be out of the water so fast, it startle a heron nearby. I climb out, hauling myself up the roots of a cypress tree. Daniel ain't the liar. It be Father John. Right in front of me, like that chameleon, he blend himself in, make himself look healthy. Too healthy for his age.

Those test results he showed me ain't Enola's. They his.

He the one with B blood.

He the one with Delta Fever.

You can't trust no one in Orleans. But Daniel ain't from here. I shoulda trusted him.

Now Father John got my Enola. He got my Baby Girl.

43

✣ *"WOULD YOU BE WHITER, MUCH WHITER THAN the snow? There's power in the blood, power in the blood. Sin stains are lost in its life-giving flow. There's wonderful power in the blood."*

INQUIRY: Who is singing?

Daniel's head was throbbing. His datalink was broken. A baby was crying. Nothing made sense. Slowly, he opened his eyes only to close them again. Dizziness threatened to make him ill.

"Power, power, power in the blood, there's wonder-working power in the precious blood of the Lamb." The singing was deep, sonorous, and annoying as hell.

Daniel tried to sit up. The room dipped dimly, then resurfaced. He was in the chapel of the Super Saver on a cot placed on the stage next to the altar. Enola lay on the altar, wailing her heart out. The singer spoke. "Hush, child. All will be well soon."

Daniel forced himself to focus. Nearby, a man wearing the tattered robes of a monk leaned over the altar, fiddling with something small—a butterfly needle. Daniel looked down at his own arms and groaned in fear and relief. He was strapped to a gurney, but his suit was still on. He hadn't been compromised. Not yet.

The priest turned to him and smiled. "Ah, you're awake," the man said. "Welcome back. I'm Father John, and you are welcome to stay with us as long as you like."

"What are you doing?" Daniel asked.

"Right now, I'm trying to find a needle small enough for an infant. It's been many years since I've treated one so young. But her blood is pure, pure as snow. It has the power to wash away all sins," he said by way of explanation.

"And you, young man, you are proof that the good Lord shall provide for all his honest servants. You see, there was a time when I was prideful and thought that I could single-handedly save the people of this parish. But I failed." He stopped sorting his needles, a faraway look coming over him. "Instead, my helpmates grew sick and died. But still I stayed. I was healthy, and in my pride, I stayed. When the churches and the government decreed the Delta be cast out, I chose to stay, as if I could minister to fallen angels, to Lucifer himself. I let myself fall into Hell in the belief that I could pray my way out."

He looked at his Fever-scarred hands, the makeup washed from his skin. "I have been punished for my sins. 'But though

I have wept and fasted, wept and prayed, though I have seen my head, grown slightly bald, brought in upon a platter, I am no prophet—and here's no great matter.'"

Daniel struggled to get off the gurney, but he was strapped down at the waist as well.

"And now," Father John said, ignoring Daniel's struggles as much as Enola's cries, "I've been forgiven!" He said it with such joy that Daniel almost wanted to be happy for him. The blue eyes in his scarred face were bright and clear.

"'And a child shall lead them,'" he quoted. "And so she shall. This child will cleanse me. But you, my son, you are the truest answer. While her blood might purify me slowly, sustain me for a few days or weeks—you, with your pints and pints of glorious, wonder-working blood—" He stopped, overcome with emotion. He wiped his eyes with the back of his hand. The skin of his fingers cracked, slowly leaking dull brown ichor. "I can cast out my demons. I can refresh my soul."

He leaned closer, and Daniel could see that the brightness in his eyes was caused as much by the Fever as by his faith.

"You have given me the keys to the kingdom. I just have to sacrifice you, my son, and this child. Then God will welcome me home."

He began to sing again. *"Would you do service for Jesus, your king? There's power in the blood, power in the blood."*

The song was punctuated by a small gasp. He had found an infant-size needle at last. Father John attached it to the IV tube and pressed Enola's head to the altar, turning her neck to find the artery.

"No!" Daniel screamed.

The door banged open.

Fen stood there, clothes streaming with mud, leaves twisted in her hair like a madwoman. And Daniel's voice was her voice. "No!" she screamed, and she flew at the priest.

Father John raised his hands in defense, singing louder and louder. Fen tackled him, sweeping a hand across the tray of instruments. Needles, scalpels, knives, she cut her own flesh gathering them into her fist, and she thrust them with one angry, desperate motion into the priest's heart.

The singing stopped so abruptly that the silence was deafening to Daniel. Then Fen's breathing came to him, hard and fast. She clambered off of Father John's body and pulled a knife free from the thicket in his chest. She wiped it on his robes and cut Daniel loose. Then she stood over Enola, not picking her up, rubbing her hands on her clothes.

"I'm not clean." She looked at Daniel. "Help her. Stop her from crying. Now!" she snapped, shocking Daniel into action. He couldn't move fast enough to pick up the baby, to cradle her and let Fen know she was okay.

"Here, clean off. You can take her." He tried to hand her a cloth from the tray of instruments.

"No, no, I can't," Fen insisted. "I don't want her to be sick, Daniel. I'm covered in it. Fever be in the water, the air. In me." She shivered with horror. "I won't risk it now. We too close."

She looked so young. Daniel wanted to hold her, to tell her she was okay, too, but he couldn't. Instead, he waited for her to be Fen again.

He watched her grow calm and, in another minute, she was.

"What you doing here, Daniel? You supposed to be gone by now," she asked.

Daniel took a breath, trying to replace the air that had been knocked out of him. He was surprised to feel himself blushing. "I tried to go back to Rooftops, but there were ABs everywhere."

Fen looked at him and made a choking sound, like a laugh. "Rooftops? You trying to be a hero?" she asked.

"No. I'm just trying to set things right."

"You want to set things right, you take Enola with you over the Wall," she told him. "You find the Coopers. You get her to a good home."

Daniel closed his eyes. He would do it, he already knew. He tried to read her face as he warned her, "It's not perfect over there."

Fen did laugh this time, harsh and sad. "Anything be better than this," she said. "Now, don't stand there looking at me, tourist. We gotta go."

Fen shoved aside the lab equipment and knelt by the generator on the floor. She turned the machine off and yanked a hose from the casing, pouring clear ethanol fuel onto the floor.

Daniel watched as it spread across the church, toward Father John's prone body. Fen ushered Daniel toward the door, then knocked over the stand of devotional candles on their way out of the chapel. The old priest's robes caught light quickly. The flames roared across the pool of fuel, spreading to the altar cloth, the carpet, the walls. They left the Super Saver to quietly burn.

44

❧ "WHAT ARE WE LOOKING FOR?" DANIEL ASK. We be winding our way through the woods, the Super Saver behind us. The trees be bigger the deeper into the woods we get. Soon we be coming out the other side.

"The Charity Gate," I say. "You ready to go?"

"We're ready."

He say *we* and it hit me that Enola don't belong to me no more. She ain't looking up at me with her mama's big brown eyes; she looking at him. It make me fold my arms against my empty chest. I want to hold her again, but then I might not let her go. *It gonna be all right,* I tell myself. Daniel know what to do. He got the Coopers' address in San Diego. He got they e-mail address, too, so they can know he coming. Baby Girl be all right, as long as we get them out of Orleans.

We hear the Wall before we see it. The trees be so close together here, there ain't no leaves on they trunks except for at the top. Ain't nothing to muffle sounds, so we extra quiet, in case there still be ABs around. That be the only reason I hear it: a burst of radio, like a louder version of Daniel's voice filter.

"Hold up," I hiss, putting my hand up for him to stop. Radio static. Only folks I know who got radios be Mr. Go, Father John, the Ursulines, and the Professors. None of them be here now. Daniel crouch next to me and I signal for him to stay put. He nod, and I inch my way out to the edge of the trees 'til I can see it. The Wall.

Surprise me every time, how short it be. Maybe twenty, thirty feet high. Look like you could climb it with rope or something. But it almost as wide as it be high, and between the soldiers and the razor wire, you'd be stopped before you made it across. That be why Mr. Go so clever. The Wall ain't as kept up as it could be, this close to the gate, and a crack in the mortar be enough to get a body through.

No more than a couple yards downslope from us be the moat, where they dug a channel for the bayou to go along the Wall. To my right, across the muddy channel, be the Old Charity Gate. The army checkpoint still there, a big concrete bunker squat in the middle of the Wall, like a frog sitting on a log. It look like it always do, covered in vines and crumbling around the edges. There still be searchlights mounted on the roof on both sides of the gate, and a drawbridge, too, where there used to be a road out of the city. The old highway been blown to bits long ago to make way for the moat. I used to come here with my parents when I been little, just to look at it all. I liked to see the people, the soldiers in they black jumpsuits and camouflage hats, they guns strapped across they chests, new ones every month 'cause they don't be last-ing out here for long. The outpost been empty for a long time, with just a sniffer drone to keep watch. At least, it sup-posed to be.

I guess we been wrong about that.

Soldiers. Two of 'em I can see, and that burst of radio mean there be more somewhere I can't lay eyes on. Cigarette smoke drift toward me. There be more of them, all right. The two on the Wall ain't smoking.

Then the searchlights come 'round, bright as stars against the gloomy afternoon. I scuttle back into the trees.

"Fen?" Daniel ask when he see me coming back.

I shake my head. "Change of plan."

I lead him deeper into the trees so we can talk without being heard. "Mr. Go say there be a way through just south of the gate."

Daniel pull out his map. He point at a spot on the drawing of the Wall, marked on the paper with an *X*. He take a deep breath. "What aren't you telling me?"

"It's what I *be* telling you that you got to listen to, Daniel. The gate being watched. Not just drones, neither."

Daniel don't say nothing, and I know it 'cause he scared. But I need him not to be. I need him to do this for me, for Enola. I squat down next to him.

"Listen to me. You take Enola back downstream outta sight of the gate and wade across. The moat ain't too deep. If it was, they'd risk losing stuff that fall in by accident. I seen it happen."

Daniel shake his head. "They'll see us. I heard their radios, too, Fen. This place must be crawling with soldiers. Jesus, this is stupid." He run a hand over his hat, like he be smoothing his hair if he not been in the suit. He be worrying like an old woman. I want to slap this boy. I close my eyes.

"Course it be dangerous, but it be necessary. Look at the Wall. You see what Mr. Go be talking about?" I point through the trees. Maybe thirty yards downstream from the gate with its old drawbridge welded shut in the raised position, the Wall ain't reinforced with steel sheeting like the gate. Whatever been there done rusted away and it be just concrete now. Vines be growing, eating at the Wall like acid. Where the vines be thickest, Mr. Go found a hole.

Daniel nod and look at me. "Fen? Don't make me do this. I'll stay. We can find a cure together. I promise."

I look at him; I look at Baby Girl. She be sleeping in her sling. I fight the urge to wake her, have her look at me one last time. I didn't know I had any heart left to break 'til she come along. But there ain't no use in crying on it now.

"Say you stay here, you and Enola. And them vials you dropped in Rooftops break open. We all be dead then. Say they don't break, and we stay the same. You been in a blood farm once. You think it can't happen again?"

Daniel hang his head and nod, like he be convincing himself. He know I'm right. We both do.

"It ain't what I want, Daniel. But it got to be. Now, give me your coat."

"What?"

"Give me your coat. But don't wake the baby."

Daniel hesitate a second, but he do it without asking why.

That a first. I smile at him, but I don't feel it. I glance at his encounter suit, seeing it fully for the first time. Thick as gator skin, with fluids that be pulsing and pumping inside. It nasty and uncomfortable-looking, but it going to save two lives. I bundle Daniel's jacket up 'til it just about Enola's size. Then I tuck it into my arms.

"Wait for my signal. The moat ain't wide. Just start moving. When you hear me, run."

"What are you going to do?" he ask, looking at the bundle.

I sigh. This boy never learn, but I forgive him this last time. "They won't shoot a woman carrying a baby. Now, listen for me, and hustle."

Slowly, Daniel rise to his feet. "Keep her above the water," I tell him, and I squeeze his arm through the bulk of his suit. "It been nice knowing you, tourist. Take care of your souvenir." I nod at Enola and head north, toward the gate.

Away from my tribe.

45

FEN WAS GONE. DANIEL LOOKED AT THE ridiculously small child in his arms and swallowed hard. He moved through the trees downstream, and into the tall standing cattails on the edge of the moat. *Wait for her signal.*

The moat wasn't that impressive here, not like the wide swampland he pressed through on his jetskip. It was like a canal, a concrete culvert maybe fifteen feet across. A token blockade, really, this close to the Wall. The water was too murky to see the bottom, but Fen and Mr. Go had both said it wasn't deep. Nothing to worry about. He edged closer to the water, as close as he dared, allowing the reeds on the bank to conceal him from the soldiers upstream. A soft rain was starting to fall, further darkening the cloudy sky. The tiny raindrops were almost beautiful, flashing brightly in beams from the searchlight on the Wall as they swung across the treetops and shoreline. Daniel ducked down flat as lights washed over his head in a lazy arc.

He adjusted his grip on Enola. *Wait for the signal,* he thought, but what would it be?

Daniel flinched when it came. A splashing sounded from farther upstream and the searchlights passed him over, converging on one spot. Daniel risked a look upriver.

Fen was in the water, lit up like the midday sun. One arm tucked under the bundle of his coat, the other waving in the air. She was shouting, drawing the attention of every soldier at the post. She hollered the way she had at the blood farm, like a madwoman. Insane.

Daniel's heart leapt into his throat. His stomach dropped. As fast as he could, he lowered himself into the water, trying not to splash. It was chest-deep, deeper than where Fen was wading waist-high in the muddy water. Daniel scooped Enola up, away from his body, over his head, and willed himself across the moat.

His splashing was drowned out by the frantic squawks of the soldiers' radios along the wall. "Stop where you are! Stop where you are! Hands in the air! You are in a restricted military zone!"

He broke into a cold sweat beneath his suit and felt the industrious suck of the equipment as it pulled the sweat back in to be recycled for later. His hands, his face felt like they were on fire. He pushed on. The soldiers were not shouting at him.

At last, Daniel pulled himself along the shoreline to where the vines grew up and over the Wall.

There. The vines gave way in the center. There was a crevice, maybe three feet to the other side, where he could see gray daylight again. Taking a deep breath, Daniel pushed an arm through the vines. He could feel it, the crack in the wall, like a tunnel hidden from view. Behind him, Fen stood silhouetted against the searchlights, rain spattering the water around her. Her arms were raised, her face turned up, the bundle held high in the air. She rotated in a slow circle as the rain washed the mud from her skin.

For an instant, she looked at him. The moment hung in the air, Fen's mouth curving into a smile, seeing Daniel and the baby almost there. Almost there. She turned away.

A shot rang out. The bundle fell from her hands.

Daniel jumped, pushing himself desperately through the vines. *Don't stop, don't stop.* He had made a promise to protect this child. To take her to a better life. And that's what he was going to do.

The vines fell back into place as he pressed into the crack, all but crushing Enola to him as he passed beyond the dead city and the madness of the Delta. He was sucked into darkness smelling of green and loam, the sharp bite of asphalt and stone and, somewhere up ahead, a cool breeze.

They had made it.

Daniel stumbled through the last stretch of narrow tunnel to emerge, exhausted and blinking, into the light. Ahead of him was a wasteland, thirty feet of barren ground, empty now but for unoccupied military vehicles. All attention had been drawn to the girl at the gate.

Daniel closed his eyes for a moment, blinking back hot tears, still seeing that last glimpse of Fen swirling through the water, spinning like the wheel that turns the world. He braced himself, then ran for cover across the heart-pounding expanse, into the trees that would hide his passage back into Mississippi and the Outer States of America. In his arms, Fen's baby girl was awake and wriggling against him, waving her small fists at the weeping sky.